Doctor for Christmas

Doctor for Christmas

A Marietta Medical Romance

Patricia W. Fischer

TULE
PUBLISHING

Dedication

The beauty of the world relies in the diversity of its people.
Unknown

To Mary
Thank you for always being such an amazing friend and critique partner.
Now get back to writing!
Hugs

To Mom.
Thanks. Just thanks.
I love you.

Chapter One

"DID YOU JUST kill Santa Claus?"

Dr. Peter Davidson white-knuckled the steering wheel as he stared at the huge structure sandwiched between his car and the tall snowbank on the side of the road.

As the airbag deflated, his mind buzzed from the impact. *What happened?*

Fat flakes stuck to the windshield but were quickly cleared with the rapidly moving wipers he'd yet to register were still running because of the massive structure in front of him.

A sleigh. A Christmas sleigh to be exact.

Shifting the car into park, he replayed the moment when the object appeared in front of his car and... *what happened, again?*

"Peter? Dad?" The frantic voice of his daughter, Polly, filled the car with worry. "Are we going to get put on the naughty list?"

It took a few moments for Peter to register the word "Dad" because he'd only discovered he was a father three weeks ago. Not only a father, but the father of nine-year-old twins. A boy, Digory and a girl, Polly.

He held his hand up. "Give me a second, Pol. Trying to think."

"Okay," she whimpered, which sent Peter's protective instincts in overdrive.

He popped the seat belt and turned around. "Are you two okay? Digory? Polly? Anyone hurt?"

Both children still had on their seat belts and they looked shaken, but no one appeared injured.

Digory pointed, his hand shaking. "You're bleeding."

Touching his forehead, Peter pulled back red soaked fingers. He examined himself in the rearview mirror. "Dammit."

"Dammit is a naughty word, Dad… Peter."

"Sorry, Digory." Out of the corner of his eye, he noticed the fat tears rolling down his sweet daughter's face, her bottom lip trembling. His heart sank to his feet. "Polly, it' a cut. It's fine. I'm sorry. I'll try not to say that again."

"But you're bleeding, Peter… Dad." She sobbed. "You're bleeding really bad."

"Head wounds normally bleed a lot, Polly."

"Okay, Peter." She sniffed. "Dad."

As the Charlie Brown Christmas theme played softly on the XM radio Christmas Station, Peter gathered his thoughts. With all the changes that had gone on for Peter in the last few weeks, he had to remember, his kids were getting used to calling him Dad as much as he was adjusting to hearing it. "All I'll need is a few sutures and some glue, kids. It's going to be fine."

His daughter grimaced. "Glue? Like Elmer's glue? You

can't use Elmer's glue on your face. Lizzie Carlton already tried that at school and when she tried to glue her lips closed and it didn't stick for that long."

"Not Elmer's glue, Polly." He searched for something to soak up the bleeding. The last thing he wanted to do was take off his hoodie to clean himself up. That and the jeans, T-shirt, and light jacket he wore were his only defense against the bitter cold.

"Are you going to be okay?" Digory asked again, his voice laced with concern. "You're not going to die, are you?"

The painful tone in his son's question pinched Peter's stomach with vice-like ferocity. The last thing his kids needed was to suddenly lose the only remaining parent they had.

They'd been through enough, suddenly losing their mother and finally meeting a father who never knew they existed.

Why didn't she tell me?

How am I supposed to do this by myself?

Am I doing the right thing bringing them here?

He hated the sudden uncertainty in his life.

Ever since he'd been a teenager, he'd to take complete control of his world after the death of their father.

Peter had been the steady one.

The one who always had all the answers.

The one everyone turned to for guidance.

Now he sat, crammed between a pile of snow and a sleigh, in the middle of nowhere with two children he had no idea he'd fathered until he'd met them last month.

His usual rational brain had no logical thought.

What the hell?

A round of rapid sniffs brought him back to center.

The kids. Think about your children.

"Polly. Digory. I swear. It's only a cut." He heard the harshness of his voice as soon as the words were out of his mouth. *Calm down! You can't lose it.* "I'm sorry, kids. It's going to be fine. I promise."

"This is the OnStar operator, Carlee. Are you okay?" The voice of a woman with a strong Southern accent stopped the Christmas music before causing Peter's heart to jump to his throat.

He let out a long breath, getting his head around the situation. "Yes. My name is Peter Davidson. I'm with my children outside of, what's the name of this town again?"

"The closest town I see on the map is Marietta, Montana. Is that where you wanted to be?"

"Marietta, right." He spotted the fast-food bag from the stop they made less than an hour ago and grabbed it. "We hit a sleigh."

"I've called the local EMS department and they are on the way." A long pause before… "Sir, did you say you hit a sleigh?"

"Yes." Peter dabbed his forehead with some napkins from the bag.

"Was anyone driving the sleigh, sir?"

His world spun around. Peter swallowed hard before closing his eyes tightly and opening them again as the world slowly came back into focus. "Yes, I believe so."

No, no, no concussion. I can't have a concussion right now.

"Is there someone in the sleigh, now?"

"I'm pretty sure there was someone in the sleigh, ma'am." Polly twirled the tail of a small stuffed unicorn Peter bought her in the airport gift shop during their layover in Chicago.

Sitting up, he placed his head on the headrest as his headlights illuminated the rich wood of the structure. "No idea. I don't see anyone now. It could have been sitting here on the side of the road."

But Peter didn't remember the sleigh being in the road beforehand. In fact, he had no idea where the damn thing had come from.

Tall evergreens stood like toy soldiers on either side of the snowy road and swayed with the gusts of artic wind. They kept a hill of precipitation between themselves and the highway.

Peter anticipated he'd have to get out and inspect the scene, something he wasn't looking forward to because cold weather and he did not mix.

"Sir? Did you say guy in a sleigh?" Carlee's voice quivered as though she were barely holding on to a gut-busting laugh. "And the man is wearing a red suit?"

"No, I didn't say he had a red suit. I don't see anyone right now."

"No reindeer?" The operator snickered.

"Did you send help for us or what? I've got kids in the car." Glancing around, Peter tried to figure out how the sleigh even operated.

No horses or cattle or reindeer. *What the hell?*

Best he could remember he heard what sounded like the roar of a lawn mower and then bam! They stopped where they were right now.

"Yes, sir. EMS has already been contacted. They are getting there as fast as they can. According to their dispatcher, the roads are a mess and they're cleaning up a site south of town. You said you have children in the car."

"Yes." His brain wobbled and he prayed to stay awake until help arrived. *I can't flake out on my kids.*

"Is everyone okay?"

"Operator. Peter's bleeding," Digory yelled, making the ache in Peter's forehead vibrate into his teeth.

"I hit the airbag. I'm okay." Peter let a long breath out. *Stay calm. Stay focused.*

"Is there anyone in town that I can call for you, sir?" Carlee asked as the snow appeared to be coming down heavier and faster than before.

"You can do that?"

"Yes. Who can I call for you?"

So much for surprising them. "My brother, Edmund, and my sister, Lucy, both work at the ER in town. I'd have to look up their numbers to get their cells."

Quick tapping on a keyboard could be heard through the speakers. "I've located the Marietta Regional ER. Is this the hospital, sir?"

The world began to uncomfortably spin. "Yes."

"I'm calling the ER now. Please stay on the line."

"What are we supposed to do?" Polly asked as she

clutched her stuffed animal to her chest. "Can you go check and see if we hit Santa's sleigh?"

"We're supposed to stay here, Polly. It's too cold to go outside." Taking slow deep breaths, he calmed the spinning for a moment.

"For you." Digory rolled his eyes as he held his plush penguin in a white-knuckle grip. "*You* don't have a good coat."

"You're right, Digory. I didn't get a great coat. Been taking care of a few things." Ever since he met his son, they had been oil and water. Peter hoped the animosity of their relationship would calm a bit now that the children's mother's funeral was over and they were out of school for the Christmas holidays.

"I'm worried about you, Peter... Daddy." Polly's sweet voice filled the car with angst. She'd been nothing but helpful and loving since Peter walked into their lives, but he worried her syrupy demeanor served as a defensive act to keep herself from facing the sadness of instantly losing their mother.

To bring the kids to this winter wonderland to meet two of his siblings would be a solid way Peter could get his feet underneath him and his mind on straight. He needed to be grounded by Edmund's level head and Lucy's loving heart since his instant "father" title had thrown him sideways. "It's going to be okay, Polly. I promise."

"They've been notified at the ER." The operator cleared her throat. "Who was driving?"

"I was driving." The bleeding in his forehead slowed, but

he would need some sutures and glue for sure.

"Now, Mr. Davidson—"

"*Dr.* Davidson."

"My apologizes. Dr. Davidson. Who drove the *sleigh?*"

The sleigh? That's right, a sleigh. Thoughts raced through Peter's brain like runners with no sense of direction. His sight temporarily blurred then stung as a warm red drop fell into his line of sight and another on his hand. He pressed the napkins on his forehead again.

Glancing up again, Peter noticed a figure slumped over in the front seat of the sleigh when the wipers cleared the windshield and the snowfall decreased. Reality slammed him to center and his doctor brain took over. "Oh, crap! There is someone out there."

"Peter-Daddy, hit Santa!" Polly screeched.

"Great. Now we're on the naughty list." Digory groaned. "This Christmas stinks."

"Calm down. It's not Santa, but I am going to check on him." Unbuckling his seat belt, Peter struggled to figure out how to unlock the doors of his rental car. "Dammit, how do I get out of this thing?"

"Daddy, dammit is a—"

"I know! I know, Digory!"

Carlee interjected, "Sir, don't get out of the car! It's twenty degrees before wind chill. There's a storm moving in. Sir! Peter! Dr. Davidson! Can you…"

"Kids, stay in the car!" But her voice became a distant whisper as soon as he opened the car door and struggled through the knee-high snowbank to get closer to the other driver.

A hard slam indicated his car door had been closed.

To slow the wound on his forehead, he grabbed a handful of snow and held it against his cut, cringing at the cold bite against his skin. "How the hell does anyone live here?"

Staring at the steel-gray sky of the afternoon, Peter couldn't believe two of his younger siblings impulsively decided to remain in this freezer of a state instead of basking in the endlessly warm climate of the beach town where they all grew up.

"All in the name of love?" The snow fell into his tennis shoes, soaking into his socks. "Bah humbug."

"Be careful, Peter, I mean Dad!" Polly yelled out the window.

"If that's Santa, I'm not with the guy who hit you, sir!" Digory added before they rolled the window up again.

Way to throw me under the bus, kid.

A groan from the driver distracted Peter from his annoyance and steadily growing headache.

Wiping the remaining ice from his face, Peter tapped the man's large black boots. They were a stark contrast to the plush green lining on the floor of the sleigh that sat at Peter's chest level. "Hey! You okay?"

Stumbling back a few steps, Peter took in the massive structure.

There had been no imagining it.

A sleigh with carvings on rich mahogany. Perfectly sculpted flowers alternated with an intricate wooden braid ran along the edge. All along the panel, it appeared to be a village with a large star sitting over the town.

The magnificent craftsmanship took Peter's breath away as did the wicked gust of wind that slapped him in the face. If it had been about forty degrees warmer, he'd go over the structure inch by inch because he could only imagine the time it took for someone to make this beautiful piece.

The driver rested on his right side in the front bench seat and appeared to be sleeping. The slow rise and fall of the man's chest, gave Peter temporary relief that the driver had probably only been temporarily knocked out.

"Sir. You okay?" He tapped the man's shoulder before his own head spun a three-sixty and the winter wind sliced at his skin. The chill easily permeated through Peter's hoodie, T-shirt, and thin jacket as the wet cold seeped into his tennis shoes and jeans.

He cursed himself for not stopping in Bozeman to get a heavy coat, a hat, and gloves, but his sudden decision to board a plane and come to Montana hadn't been well thought out.

Before today, the only time Peter ever needed any sort of jacket had been when the "winter" temperatures of Jupiter, Florida would—rarely—plummet into the forties.

He shivered, knowing full well he'd freeze to death if he didn't get out of this weather soon, but he couldn't leave this man here. Assuming it was a man.

Where the hell is EMS?

The person wore a richly thick red suit that made the wearer resemble a scarlet bear. "Hey! You okay?"

Crawling up the short ladder, he noticed the front of his

rental car had been crushed in, but the sleigh appeared to be no worse for wear.

In fact, it didn't appear to have any damage at all with the exception of a large evergreen wreath that had fallen off and sat on top of the hood of Peter's car.

Merry Christmas to my insurance company.

Still, there had to be damage he couldn't see. Mentally shoving that concern aside, Peter quickly scanned the injured man for obvious signs of broken bones or bleeding.

Nothing. In fact, if Peter didn't know better, he could have sworn the man had fallen asleep.

In the snow? Wearing a red suit while sitting in a sleigh?

Marietta's weird.

Peter shook his head, wondering if he'd hit his face harder than he originally thought. Maybe the overcast sky played tricks with the colors?

Nope. Big person wearing a Santa hat and red suit sitting in a two-bench seat sleigh.

He peeked over the back seat and there sat a large velvet drawstring bag.

This has got to be the concussion. I have to be imagining this.

Digging into his rational brain of why this man would even be here, he recalled his sister Lucy mentioning something about a town holiday event.

Polly rolled her window down again and stuck her head out. "Is it Santa?"

"I don't know, honey. Please, Polly. Stay in out of the cold." The pain in his forehead kicked in again, making him see stars. He plopped down next to the guy on the bench as he shivered uncontrollably. "Way to make an entrance into town, Peter. Kill Santa less than a week before Christmas. Brilliant."

Immediately, the stranger sat up. "Ho-ho-hooo. My goodness. What happened?"

The man's appearance almost sent Peter backward and off the sleigh in shocked amusement.

The thick white beard and rosy cheeks were something straight out of the holiday books he and his siblings would read. The twinkle in the jolly man's eyes sat this side of childishly mischievous or someone who'd sipped a few too many hot toddies at the holiday office party.

Peter could explain the rosy cheeks with the dropping temperatures outside and the wicked winds, but the beard? And the suit? And the sleigh? "Are you Santa Claus?"

As soon as Peter heard how he said the words, he cringed. They almost sounded hopeful, like a child's wish.

What a ridiculous thing to say. I haven't believed in Santa since I was ten years old.

A chuckle arose from the man's round belly as his eyes sparkled before he waved to the car. Cupping his hands and putting them on either side of his mouth, he yelled, "Don't worry, kids, I'm okay. You won't be on the naughty list."

Two honks from the car as the kids had leaned into the front seat and almost had their faces pressed against the windshield.

"Peter, don't worry. Everything's gong to be okay. I'm alright, but you need stitches."

The joyous cadence of his voice immediately erased Peter's frustration and restored his memory with crystal clarity. "You came out of nowhere, sir."

"I'm sorry about that, Peter. I'm trying out a new motor for my sleigh. I did the Christmas stroll in town this year and my sleigh got stuck in a snowbank right in front of Big Z's hardware. I was trying things out with this new contraption. Guess it got away from me."

"Motor?" *Did I tell him my name?*

"Yes. We get some pretty rough weather here in Marietta. It's not always great to take out the horses, so I tricked out a lawn mower motor and installed it underneath and added snow treads in case I need it or get stuck." He pointed to the steering wheel and gearshift in the middle of the front panel. "I can use it this way or stick it in neutral and have it drawn by horses."

"Or reindeer."

A hearty chuckle escaped the man as he turned to produce a large coat from a bag on the back bench seat. "You headed to spend Christmas in Marietta? Nothing like it, you know. Houses all decked out in lights. The town's got all its decorations up. Every storefront has red, green, and white. The air smells of cinnamon and joy."

"Sounds great." In fact, it sounded perfect. Just the hometown type of atmosphere he'd hoped for him and the kids.

My kids. He still had trouble processing those two words.

"And if you don't know, the Palace Theater house plays Christmas movies Tuesday through Thursday. The last one they played was *A Christmas Story*." The man held his hands on his belly. "Love that one. The lamp. Fra-gee-lay. Classic."

"My brother and sister. They aren't expecting me." Peter's teeth chattered and he hugged himself in an attempt to get warm. "Sorry. I didn't plan to get stuck in the snow. Where is EMS anyway?"

"They'll be along soon enough. Weather always slows things down. You need a coat." He handed Peter a jacket and followed with what appeared to be a cup of hot chocolate. "Those will warm you up."

"Thank you. Where did you get that?"

He held up the bag. "I always have supplies with me."

At the first taste of the liquid to his lips, Peter instantly felt the pain leave his body and his spirits lift. "What's in this stuff?"

"Homemade mixture I like to call a holiday harmony."

The buzz of the drink settled deep into Peter's bones lifting the chill off his body. "I am feeling harmonious about now."

"Sage does a great job making some of the best hot chocolate around, but I'd like to think my recipe is special too." He tapped his thick mittens on his knees. "Makes things merry and bright, even in the darkest of times."

"Who's Sage? Your wife?" Peter greedily took another drink, relishing the delicious layers of vanilla, cinnamon, and cream. The air around them warmed and smelled of chocolate.

The man chuckled, making his belly shake like, well, a bowl full of jelly. "I wish, but no. She owns and runs Copper

Mountain Chocolates. It's a shop here in town."

Inhaling, the special hot beverage soaked into Peter's muscles, relaxing him this side of boneless. "I'd agree. This will warm anyone up."

"It's got a wee pinch of a family secret, but no alcohol. I don't hand that out and you don't need any with hitting your head. Hope you don't mind."

"Nope. I don't mind." As he drained the cup, Peter relaxed into the seat and handed the cup back. "Thanks. Helped me stop shivering."

"It's my great-grandmother's recipe. She was from Turkey, you know."

"That's a long way to travel." The buzz of warm spices sat on his tongue and calmed him simultaneously.

"Like you coming here. It's nice you're coming to visit Lucy and Edmund. I'm sure they'll appreciate seeing you." Standing, he held his finger beside his nose before pointing toward Peter's face. "But you probably need to go to the ER, first. You've got a nasty cut on your forehead."

As he threaded his arms through the heavy coat, the heavenly smells of Christmas drifted around him. "Sitting here with you, is this when I tell you what I want for Christmas?"

"Only if you want to." The man's eyes twinkled.

"I want answers. Guidance. A home base." He ran his fingers through his hair, only to get them stuck in the dried blood. "Not to feel so damned lost."

"You're asking for a lot."

"I know." His body melted into the seat and his eyelids became heavy.

"But, I'd bet, you'll find all of that when you least expect it."

"Maybe so." A strong yawn caused him to suck in a lungful of cold air. He coughed to calm his breathing. "I need a nap."

The jolly expression on the man's face waned. "I don't think that's a good idea, Peter. You aren't supposed to sleep after hitting your head, are you?"

"When did I tell you my name?"

"You look just like your siblings Lucy and Edmund. I'd know those kind eyes anywhere. Your sister's treated me a time or two for my asthma and told me all about her family."

"She's a good doctor." Peter began to snuggle down into the warmth of the coat.

"One of the best around."

"What's your name again?"

"Mr. Nicolas." The man sat tall in the seat despite the frigid winds and the constantly falling snow. "Lived in this part of the world most of my life."

"Did you make the sleigh?" Taking a deep inhale of the collar of the coat, Peter's eyelids became too heavy to fight. Snowflakes continued to fall, landing in his hair, on his face, but the warmth of the coat and the magical hot chocolate appeared to be just what he needed after an extremely stressful three weeks.

"Might want to get back in that car of yours. Your kids are worried about you." His hand rested on Peter's shoulder. "You need to get out of this cold, it's sucking the life out of you."

"My kids." A wave of panic washed over him. "My kids.

Yes."

As Peter turned to get down, Mr. Nicolas had already moved to that side of the sleigh. He extended a hand to help Peter keep his balance as he climbed down the short ladder. "How did you do that? How did you get there so fast?"

Did I fall asleep for a minute?

"Your sister, Lucy. She's very patient. I didn't believe her at first when she said I had asthma, but sure enough, she walked me through my medical history and it turns out I do. Stinks for an old guy like me who loves the cold weather." He produced an inhaler from his pocket and held it up for a moment before putting it back. "I always carry it with me. Comes in handy for those long nights on the road and the sawdust I breathe in when I'm working in the woodshop."

They slowly walked back to the car with Peter convinced this entire conversation all played in his head. That he'd hit his head harder than he thought and still sat in his car, with his kids safely in the back seat because when he'd stood near this imagined character, the world around him felt a whole lot lighter and warmer. "Asthma sucks. This coat smells like snickerdoodle cookies."

Opening the driver's side door, his children's heads popped out, their eyes wide with excitement.

"Santa!" they yelled in unison.

"It's Mr. Nicolas, kids." Peter waved them over as he got back into the car. "Mr. Nicolas, these are Polly and Digory."

"Please to meet you, children." The gentleman nodded and handed them each a candy cane. "Now, EMS is almost here. Stay inside. Out of the cold, okay?"

Before any of them could answer, Mr. Nicolas gently closed the door as a massive gust of wind rocked the car and blinding snow surrounded them.

For the next couple of minutes, Peter had plenty more questions running around in his head, but he couldn't figure out which one to grab onto.

"Dr. Davidson, are you back in the car?" Carlee asked, frustration laced her voice. "Your children sure know a lot of knock-knock jokes."

He slouched in the seat, shielding his eyes from the late afternoon gloom that suddenly hurt to look at. "How far out is EMS?"

"They said a few minutes. The roads are difficult right now."

"He met Santa!" Polly spoke about two inches from the dashboard.

The operator asked, "That's nice, darlin'. Where's Santa now?"

"He went back to his sleigh." The back of Peter's head touched the headrest. He reclined his seat slightly while he struggled to keep his eyes open. Inching his fingers on the door controls, he pushed the lock.

"Dr. Davidson, are you okay?"

"My head's killing me. I just need to close my eyes."

"Um, sir, can you keep talking to me? First responders are on the way. Do you think you can stay awake for a few more minutes?"

"I'll do my best." But within seconds, darkness clouded Peter's mind and he drifted off to sleep.

Chapter Two

*H*E DUMPED ME.

Shelly Westbrook mentally hissed to herself as she glanced at her speedometer that hovered at an agonizingly slow forty miles an hour.

In the rearview mirror, she noticed Freddie, her sleeping son, reposition in the back seat. Her niece, Tia Rimes, stared at her computer screen while sitting in the front passenger seat.

Shelly's gut uncomfortably clenched. *He dumped all of us.*

Heat rose on her cheeks as she replayed how easily, Gill, her ex-husband lied to them as they stood there at the altar of the Las Vegas chapel *he* chose, ready to renew their vows just yesterday.

Right as he was about to say his I dos in front of Preacher Elvis, Freddie, Tia, and a few selected guests including her parents, Zora and Frederick Rimes, Gill's aunt and uncle, Louis and Sue Westbrook, Gill's present girlfriend, Serena, arrived. She was heavily pregnant and had two toddlers in tow.

Horrified wouldn't begin to explain her emotional state when Gill sheepishly glanced at Shelly and gave her the mischievous smirk she knew all too well. The one he'd used when he'd been caught in a lie. It would be followed by some practiced response he'd spout off to justify his selfish choices and then his lashing out of her refusal to believe him.

A multitude of profanities threatened to launch out of her mouth, but she decided to simply take off her new engagement ring and hand it to Serena.

Immediately, Shelly noticed how young the woman looked. Not a hint of a wrinkle.

Not a clue of age over thirty.

And her beautiful, round belly.

Damn you, Gill. Holding her tears at bay, Shelly summoned every ounce of strength she could collect, tilted up her chin, and squared her shoulders. "You can have him."

Serena's wide-eyed shock didn't match Gill's, who angrily screamed his disapproval of Shelly "throwing their lives together away so easily."

"I'm done playing this game with you, Gill. You want what you can't have." When she reached the last pew, she turned and pointed. "I deserve a man who wants me, honors and cherishes me, not thinks of me as a prize to dump in the corner when I get... older."

God, how humiliating. Why did I ever say yes when he asked me to marry him again?

A bit of movement from the back seat reminded her of why.

Her son. It had all been for Freddie.

When Gill popped the question at Halloween, begging her to let them be a family again, she hesitated, yet her son's hopeful expression made her swallow her refusal.

They'd all been through so much together over the past seventeen years.

Freddie's premature birth and his subsequent weeks in the neonatal ICU.

The loss of her second and third pregnancies only brought the trio closer together until Gill's wandering eye had him going places he shouldn't.

She tried to keep the family from falling apart, because Shelly didn't want any more losses for them, but when Gill couldn't quit cheating with "younger" versions of Shelly, she kicked him out and divorced him five years ago.

With this year's Halloween proposal appearing to be sincere and heartfelt, Shelly believed him because as realistic as she could be, she still wanted the happily ever after. To be loved by a man who adored everything she was—strong, educated, and close to forty.

A man who loved her body for what it was right now, not for what it was or what it could be after a trip to the plastic surgeon or in a time machine.

Plus, Shelly didn't want to believe Gill would be it when it came to the relationship department for her. That she'd spend her remaining decades getting friendly with battery operated machinery, pining over romantic comedy heroes, and sleeping alone every night.

Ugh, I can't think about that right now. I just want to get home.

She adjusted the never-ending Christmas music playlist a notch higher and tried to happily hum along to Gene Autry's classic version of "Rudolph the Red-Nosed Reindeer," but her mind kept falling back to the disaster of her wedding day.

Within an hour of the "I don'ts," the guests helped pack up the food, cake, flowers to be taken to a local assisted-living facility where the Preacher Elvis's mom resided. After everything had been loaded into Elvis's van, he voiced his appreciation with his signature lip curl and hip shake. "Thank you very much."

An exasperated giggle escaped her remembering the absurdity of it all, but there had been nothing funny about the disaster that brought the end to her marriage.

The very same disaster that would have ended it again had the I dos been completed.

"You okay, Aunt Shell?" Tia asked as she readjusted in her seat, her face now glued to her phone as she still balanced her computer in her lap.

The wipers rocked in rapid tempo to clear the quickly falling snow. Shelly rolled her shoulders and then her neck from side to side, hoping it would shake some of the frustration free. "Yes, I'm fine. Almost there."

"Seems like the drive back is a lot longer." Tia tapped the keyboard.

"We're going slower right now. The weather is kicking in, but we're not far from Marietta." Shelly gripped the steering wheel until her fingers throbbed. As long as she'd lived here, her nerves always got the better of her when she drove these roads during storms.

"Glad we stopped last night though. It had been an insane day. Delete."

"Yes, I agree. Driving thirteen hours may not have been the smartest move." *But it sure would have put some distance between me and that train wreck of a ceremony.* By the time they checked into a hotel in Salt Lake City for the night, relief not anger had taken a solid hold on Shelly's heart.

Relief that she hadn't married him, again.

Relief she hadn't imagined his still wandering eye.

Relief that her eternally optimistic mother finally saw Gill for who he was—a lying, scheming adulterer who valued his wants in life over his family.

Take that back. *His families.*

She blinked back tears.

Really, Gill? She's already had two, soon to be three of your children? What is she, a gumball machine?

For the first time in her life, she promised herself she'd never believe him again and would stick to it.

He'd crushed her trust and tossed it aside like he'd done with everyone else in his life, including their son.

I will never forgive you for this, Gill. Ever.

Sneaking a quick peek of Freddie sleeping, she couldn't remember a day when she didn't love being his mother.

Her smart, kind son who had a solid moral compass, so unlike his father.

Thank goodness for small favors.

"Aunt Shell. You sure you're okay?" Tia's soft voice pulled Shelly out of her introspection. "I mean, really?"

"Yes, yes, I'm gonna be okay." She managed a stressed smile at her niece. "Just thinking about a few things."

"I'm sure there's a lot going through your brain right now. Probably a lot of four letter words. Delete. Delete. Delete." Tia's fingers tapped the keyboard. "Man, that's a great photo."

"There might be a few of those. What are you doing?"

"Editing the pictures I took." She held up her DSLR. "I took a ton of them in Vegas, especially of that Elvis officiant. Going to put them up on Instagram after I edit them on my computer."

"Nice. Glad one of us had fun."

"Well, look at it this way, at least you won't have to smell that cheap knock-off Hugo Boss cologne anymore. Man, did he ever wear that to death." With her fingers sailing across her keyboard, Tia continued, "Daddy said he's sorry he didn't get to come. He's stationed somewhere he can't tell me where. He said it would be impossible for him to leave even before February but he'd be glad to go AWOL to come kick Gill's ass for you. Delete."

A laugh escaped her. "Tell your daddy to stay put. I'm okay."

Tia gave a thumbs-up and continued working on her pictures with laser focus.

Just like her dad.

Shelly's brother, Robert Rimes, had followed in their father's footsteps by becoming a marine officer, but when he became a single father a few years ago, it made his deployments incredibly difficult for Tia.

When Robert called to ask Shelly if Tia could stay with her when he would be sent overseas, Shelly readily agreed.

After Tia had been living with them for the past three years, Shelly considered the girl as close to a daughter as she'd ever have. "He told me a couple of weeks ago he wouldn't be coming. As long as he stays safe, that's all I care about right now. We can celebrate the holidays when he gets back stateside." *And he can kick Gill's ass then.*

"Sounds good, but you didn't really answer my question. *You* doing alright?" Tia closed her computer and tossed her phone in her purse before resting her hand on Shelly's arm.

The innocent question felt like a punch in the chest. Shelly kept it together during the packing up and saying goodbye to her family and friends in Vegas before driving back unmarried. She'd not shed one tear last night as she fell asleep because she didn't want Freddie to know how much his father had hurt her.

Hurt them.

But as she passed the Crawford County line and only a few short miles from Marietta, dread settled having to tell her coworkers and friends about what happened. That only increased the threat of her ending up a blubbering, sobbing mess before she reached her driveway, but that, she would not allow.

Not in front of the kids.

She mentally shook off her angst and let out a long exhale. She'd cry in the quiet of her bedroom later, like she'd done too many times before. "I will be, Tia. Thank you for asking."

"Anything I can do for you?"

"Not unless you have some chocolate in your bag."

Her niece raised an eyebrow. "Chocolate, you say?"

"Yes, I've been craving one of Sage's hot chocolates since we passed through Idaho Falls."

"Now, that I can do." The familiar crinkle of a candy bag filled the car as Pentatonix's latest Christmas song played softly.

Holding up an open bag of Hershey's kisses, Tia smiled. "I bought these at the last gas station. Figured if we get stuck in the storm, we needed supplies."

"You know me too well."

Within seconds, Tia rested an unwrapped chocolate kiss in Shelly's hand and Shelly quickly popped it back, blissing out on the candy as it melted on her tongue. "Mmm, there's nothing like good chocolate."

"You got that right." Freddie's hand extended between them and Tia dropped a handful of candies in his palm. "Thanks, T."

"I figured if we had chocolate, we'd be just fine."

"Smart thinking." A hard gust of wind fought to blow her off the road and Shelly shivered. "It's going to be one cold Christmas."

"In more ways than one," Freddie mumbled as he unwrapped another candy.

The weight of guilt sat on Shelly's shoulders, pushing her to slouch in the driver's seat. For too many years, she'd seen her mother, her aunts, her grandmother speak of their wedded blisses. Shelly wondered how everyone had found true, ever-lasting love with good, faithful men but she had the great knack for choosing the only chronic adulterer in a three-county radius.

Ugh, I sure can pick 'em. I can't believe I bought his BS. As if he could ever change. Jade was right.

But as much as Jade, one of her closest friends, warned her about Gill's inability to keep a promise, Jade would never hold it against her.

Now, her family on the other hand. They were a different story.

Sadly, there would be no avoiding the looks of pity at the next family get-together.

The overexaggerated glances of disappointment.

The whispered conversations that would cease when she entered the room because Shelly would be the only one in her family with a divorce and a failed attempt at reconciliation.

Her stomach uncomfortably clenched at the thought of being the family pity case, but her first concerns would be her son and her niece. "I'm sorry, kids. I really am for taking you all the way there."

"Why are you apologizing, Mom? You're not the one who screwed us over… again." Freddie locked his arms over his chest. "You're not the one who promised he'd changed and lied, about everything. Went off and started another family."

How she hated the vitriol-fueled words in her son's usually calm voice.

How her ex-husband had stolen their son's hope that they would ever be together again as a family.

How setting this crappy example would certainly cause

her son to doubt if true love really did exist or that *he* was even capable of it.

"Yes, he lied. I'm sorry because I should have seen it coming. That I should have known better." Her fingers throbbed from how tightly she gripped the steering wheel. She wiggled them to gain back some blood flow. "That I trusted him after he'd broken his promises so many times before."

"I don't think any of us realized how deep he'd go on the scumbag scale, Aunt Shell. I mean, wanting to get back with your ex-wife while being with some other pregnant woman and them already having little kids is a pretty disturbing thing to do." Tia shook her head, her face back into her phone. "You can't blame yourself, Aunt Shelly. He messed with all of us."

A hard wind temporarily blew the car into the other lane and Shelly quickly guided them back to safety as they crept their way back to Marietta. "Man, that was a big gust. I'll be glad to get off the roads."

"Not many people out." Freddie sighed.

Thankfully, no one was behind her, but then again, the road leading to the idyllic mountain town was usually only populated by locals or those seeking a bit of the mountain holiday spirit.

"Yes, because most are probably already in town or waiting for the storm to blow through." Out of the corner of her eye, Shelly saw a flash of bright color.

"Another chocolate, T." Freddie extended his hand between the front seats.

"Please." Tia dropped several colorfully wrapped candies in his hand.

"Please."

"They aren't Copper Mountain chocolates, but they'll do for now."

"Good enough." He sat back and greedily unwrapped three and popped them back. "What's the plan, Mom?"

"For what exactly?" Shelly loved the way the tall trees lined Highway 89, like a never-ending line of Christmas trees.

"For the holidays."

The holidays. A heavy sadness settled in her stomach. She'd planned their post Christmas joyful events as a family.

Skating at Miracle Lake.

Watching the Charlie Brown Christmas special in front of a roaring fire with their sock-stealing cat, Jingles.

She and Gill dressing up for a fancy New Year's Eve night out then coming home and spending the night in each other's arms.

That last one punched her pride more than she wanted to admit.

He left me for a younger woman.

She mentally shook her head.

No, he cheated on me with a younger woman. He wanted the best of both worlds—the stability and the self-validation.

Even knowing the depths of his betrayal, disappointment settled deep in her gut of not having the feel of his touch on her.

It had been far too long since she'd been with someone,

but it had been her choice not to venture into the world of dating with Freddie still at home.

The dating pool in Marietta lacked a lot of potential, especially being one of the few women of color in town.

Additionally, many of the best guys were either taken or didn't spark her fire.

An online profile was a big, fat no way because she'd gone on her share of blind dates in college and none had ended well.

At least until she went out with Gill.

Now look where she sat.

She'd relied on her never-ending supplies of electronic friends to keep the edge off, but it didn't replace a lover's touch.

The feel of his hands on her body.

The whispers of passion in her ears.

The lust-filled gaze as he made love to her.

The bliss of the afterglow as they lay in each other's arms.

The fantasy of finally spending time with someone who said he cared about her had raised her expectations for the holidays and beyond.

Ugh, Gill, you really screwed up everything.

Turning up the holiday music a notch, Shelly sighed. "I guess we'll make new plans."

"So much for Christmas being memorable this year." Freddie pouted before he popped another piece of chocolate back. "We didn't even get a tree yet."

"We can make it memorable in our own way. I bet Scott's still has a few trees in need of homes."

"It could be like that time on *Friends* when Phoebe wanted all the crappy Christmas trees."

"You remember that one?" Shelly smiled at Tia recalling the series with such accuracy. She and Tia had binged the series on Netflix over the summer. "We haven't watched *Friends* together since before school started."

Tia popped back a chocolate. "The Christmas tree is one of my favorite episodes. We need to get back in that habit of our Friday evening Netflix *Friends* binge. I don't think we finished the series. I still need to know how Ross and Rachel ended up together."

Despite the coldness of Gill's betrayal, Tia's upbeat response warmed Shelly's heart. "I would love that."

Holding her hands up like she was sizing up the perfect photo, Tia closed one eye. "We could have a bunch of those sad little trees in our living room. I can see it now. A few ornaments on this one. Lights on that one."

"Good grief. Sounds like a classic Charlie Brown Christmas." Freddie dramatically rolled his eyes, but immediately let out a gut-busting laugh.

"You two make me smile... what is this?" As Shelly slowly came around a corner, she saw the taillights of a car that looked to be crushed against a tractor.

Tia sat straight up and pointed. "What happened?"

Chapter Three

"LOOKS LIKE SOMEONE went off the road." Shelly's heart went into overdrive as she scanned the area and didn't see anyone waving for help. The steady stream of exhaust came out of the tailpipe. "The car is still running. Must have just happened."

Freddie pointed. "Is… is that Santa's sleigh?"

"Did someone hit Santa Claus?" Tia's eyes went wide with surprise.

Pulling the car to the shoulder, Shelly grabbed her ski cap. "Oh, Lord. I think Mr. Nicolas has been trying out his new sleigh again."

"What? Mr. Nicolas? The old shop teacher?"

Freddie leaned forward. "Didn't he get his sleigh stuck during the Christmas stroll?"

"Yes, and he said he planned to make some adjustments." She checked behind them to verify no one approached before popping her seat belt off. "Tia, call 9-1-1. Stay here, Freddie."

Tia gave a thumbs up and her fingers sailed across her phone screen. "You got it."

"Mom, let me help you," Freddie yelled as Shelly made

her way to the vehicle, peeking inside.

She waved him off. "I said, stay inside, Freddie. Check our supplies. We'll need the first aid kit."

What she didn't need was her son traipsing around in the snow when someone else probably required her nursing skills. Who knew what state they were in if the car still ran. "Hello? Is anyone here?"

The windows were fogged over, but she could see movement inside. "Hello? You okay?"

A steady stream of snow continued to fall, but the winds kicked in, signaling the storm's rapid approach.

Anyone who attempted to go on foot to get help, wouldn't get far without freezing to death. She knocked on the window. "Anyone here?"

The faint sound of a siren echoed between gusts of wind. Shelly pulled her coat tightly around herself as she investigated the impact site.

She'd been so focused on the scene she hadn't heard Freddie's quick footsteps until he was almost beside her.

"Got the kit, Mom. Find anyone?" He panted as the back window slowly came down.

The fresh faces of two extremely cute children appeared.

"Our dad hit Santa Claus," the little girl explained matter-of-factly.

"Your dad? Hit Santa Claus?" Shelly craned her neck to see into the driver's side window, but because of the heat from inside, she couldn't get a clear view.

"He went over to make sure Santa was okay, but then Santa put Dad back in the car and gave us these candy canes.

The car operator, Carlee, told us to stay in the car on account it's snowing outside." The boy added as he dramatically rolled his eyes, "We know not to go out in the snow without a jacket. My dad doesn't have a great coat because he's from Florida."

The little girl held up her candy. "The car operator keeps telling us funny jokes."

"Car operator? Like Siri?" Freddie's forehead creased.

"Probably more like the GPS emergency system." Shelly knocked on the driver's side window. "Sir, are you okay?"

When the figure didn't move, Shelly's mind went into overdrive.

Something was wrong.

Really wrong.

She unsuccessfully tried to open the driver's side door. "It's locked. Sweetie, please open the door."

The children's cuteness waned and they both suddenly appeared unsure of what to do.

"What brings you to Montana?" Freddie casually leaned against the car as he pulled the collar of his jacket closer to his neck. "Can you open the doors?"

"We just met our dad so you'd have to ask him." The boy motioned to the front seat.

Just met your dad? Oh, man, what a situation.

"Stranger danger." The daughter stated and crossed her arms.

"Yes, I appreciate your caution, sweetheart, but I need to talk to your daddy." Shelly's heart rate jumped twenty points. "Right now."

The son motioned to the front seat. "He's sleeping."

"Sleeping?" *Uh-oh.*

The sirens grew closer and Shelly beat on the window. "I need to get in there. Sir, sir, can you open the door? He's not moving."

"Guys, can you unlock the door for my mom? She's a nurse and wants to help." Freddie coaxed, but his eyes were full of angst.

The boy tapped his chin as though he were pondering the secrets of the universe. "I don't know. You're a stranger."

"Can you tell us a joke and we'll let you in?" the girl asked enthusiastically.

Shelly walked around to the look through the windshield. In the driver's seat sat a man who appeared to be unconscious. *Please don't be dead.* "A joke. Okay, how many tickles does it take to tickle an octopus?"

"I don't know. How many?"

"Ten ti-ckles."

The child scrunched up her nose. "I don't get it."

Come on, kids. "Please. If your daddy's hurt, I want to help him."

The little boy shrugged and disappeared into the car. A few seconds later, Shelly heard the familiar thud of a car door being unlocked.

With a flick of her wrist, she opened the door to find a man slumped back in his seat. The airbag had deployed. A laceration and dried blood on his forehead indicated he'd hit something on impact. "Kids, was everyone wearing their seat belts when you hit the sleigh?"

"Yes." The girl nodded, a sudden look of angst in her eyes as if she'd realized the urgency of the situation. "Daddy Peter's going to be okay?"

"This is the OnStar operator, Carlee. Are you one of the first responders?" a voice answered before Shelly could.

"Oh, Jesus!" Shelly's legs almost went out from underneath her suddenly hearing the woman's voice. "Yes, I'm Shelly Westbrook, a nurse at Marietta Regional. EMS has just arrived."

The red and blue lights of the ambulance flashed around the bend a few seconds before the vehicle appeared.

"Freddie, go wave the guys down, would you please?" Shelly quickly checked the father's pulse and breathing. "Okay, okay, strong pulse. Breathing normal."

She grabbed his shirt and lifted it to make sure his chest symmetrically moved and he'd not broken anything on impact.

When she did, she had to swallow her tongue. His toned stomach and chest were certainly results of hard work and before she stared too long, she pulled her hand away as though she'd touched fire.

Goodness, who are you?

Jogging away, her son greeted the first responders.

Tia joined Shelly, her hands shoved in her jacket pockets, her teeth chattering. "Ms. Betty said the roads haven't been cooperating and they've been super busy. Said a call came in on this scene about ten minutes ago from the emergency operator."

"I wondered."

Tia motioned to the sleigh. "That's one big carving."

"Hello!" The kids reached out and touched Tia's arm, making her scream and sending her sideways from the vehicle.

"Oh, man, you two scared me. Don't do that again!" Her niece threw her head back and laughed.

The children collapsed in fits of giggles in the back seat as Shelly continued to talk to the operator.

"We've got him. Thank you for calling it in."

"You're welcome, Mrs. Westbrook. I'll leave Dr. Davidson in your hands."

Hearing the name froze Shelly in midassessment. "Did you say Dr. Davidson?"

"Yes, Dr. *Peter* Davidson. He said he has siblings that work at that same ER. I've already contacted the hospital."

"Yes, he does. Thank you. We'll take it from here."

"You're welcome."

"You're Peter Davidson," Shelly mumbled as she tried not to focus on his beautifully sculpted body.

Clearing her head, she pulled her phone from her pocket and turned on the flashlight, she cupped his face in an attempt not to scare him. "Welcome to Marietta, Dr. Davidson."

Chapter Four

"**A**RE YOU OKAY?" The angelic voice echoed in Peter's ears. He tried to follow her words, but as soon as he figured out from which direction they came, the world became confusing once again. Cold drifted across his body before a warm hand touched his forehead.

"Where am I?"

"You're outside Marietta. I need you to stay calm," she coaxed as a light shone in his face.

He shielded his eyes. "Damn, that's bright."

"Damn is a bad word, Dad," Digory chided.

"I know. I'm sorry."

The voice asked him again after stifling a laugh, "Can you open your eyes? I want to check your pupils."

"Check my pupils? What are you? A doctor? Nurse?" Relief flooded him, hearing her speak to him again. His eyelids were as heavy as lead weights and he couldn't figure out how to open them.

"It's okay, Daddy. She's a nurse," his daughter coaxed, the gentle touch of his daughter's fingers rested on his head.

My daughter. My son. My kids.

"Polly! Digory!" Panic shot through him and he sat up,

but the intense pain in his head made him collapse back into the seat.

"Calm yourself. We'll take care of the kids." The stranger held her hands up in surrender.

"We?"

"My children and I are here."

"Cool, is that an ambulance?" Digory exclaimed as the click of the back door opening caught Peter's attention.

"Kids, where are you going?" Peter attempted to turn his head, but his muscles spasmed.

Shelly patted his arm, her voice low and calming. "It's okay. My teens will watch them."

With parenting being so new, Peter wondered if his zero to sixty response to everything the kids did was within the realm of normal. "They're okay?"

"They're fine, I promise."

He inhaled. The rich scent of roses tickled his nose. "You smell good."

"Thanks. I had a shower. I'm going to open your eyes a little more. Real quick." Her fingers rested on his upper and lower lids and with tender pressure, she examined each side for a few seconds before carefully allowing them to close once again. "My name is Shelly. I work in the ER here in Marietta with Lucy and Edmund."

The blinding light caused him to suck in a hard breath as a sharp pain shot to his temples. "Shit. That hurts."

"Sorry. Sorry. Making sure you don't have an obvious bleed going on." Her hand cupped his face, giving him a momentary distraction to his headache. "You're equal and reactive."

"I don't think anyone's ever called me that before." The corner of his mouth twitched as he leaned into her hand, kissed her palm, resting it against his face. "You're warm. Like a beautiful cup of hot chocolate."

"Beautiful hot chocolate, huh? I'm far from beautiful after driving for two days. You've had a concussion for sure."

As he forced his mind and body to work together, he open his eyes. He'd expected to see a nice smile.

Instead, his heart backflipped as he stared into the gorgeous gaze of a woman wearing a bright pink ski cap, intense hazel eyes, and a look of focused determination. "You tricked me."

Her forehead furrowed as her fingers gently touched his forehead. "What do you mean?"

"You said you weren't beautiful. You are."

She leaned back, an amused smirk on her face. "That's gonna need stitches."

He took in the curve of her full lips. The perfect shape of her eyes. The rich color of her brown skin. "Are you an angel because you sure look like one."

"That's a first."

"What's that?"

"Someone saying I look like an angel."

He kissed her hand again. "You look like one to me."

"Thank you." As professional as she appeared to be, he noticed a split-second wavering in her determined expression at his compliment before she smoothly pulled her hand away.

He might have hit his head and not be making much sense right now, but she'd heard him and it had affected her.

How it had affected her would remain to be seen.

Maybe Marietta has more to offer than weird dudes in sleighs and freezing cold weather.

A long, deep groan came from the woman's right. "You look like an angel? That's the lamest line ever."

"Freddie, please." She turned and stood, talking to someone next to her, out of Peter's line of vision. "You're not helping."

"The kids are in our car, Mom. Tia's feeding them chocolate."

"Thank you, Freddie. Wait." Shelly patted Peter's knee. "Do any of your kids have peanut allergies?"

Do they? Do they? He quickly searched his mental files. "No, not that I know of."

"Okay. Great. Freddie, I'll be there in a moment and then we'll follow EMS into town."

Peter tried to move, but his body protested and his head spun. He pinched the bridge of his nose, hoping to calm his brain.

The lyrics to "Holly Jolly Christmas" played somewhere close by as wisps of the cold weather crept into the car.

Shelly stood but Peter reached out and grabbed her hand. "Thank you."

"For what?"

"Taking care of my children." His hand slid down until he held her fingers with his. Slowly, his thumb grazed the back of her hand. Touching her set his body on fire.

"Oh, of course. Glad to help." Her eyes went wide.

I could get lost in her stare.

What was wrong with him? He'd never been immediately smitten with any woman, ever. Yet, here stood a stunning goddess and he couldn't look away.

Freddie scoffed and reached down, breaking their hand lock. "Okay, Casanova. The paramedics are here. Let's go, Mom."

Mom? Makes sense why he already hates me.

She waved him off. "He's got a head injury. I'll stay here until they get the stretcher."

"But, Mom."

"Freddie, I know we've had a hard couple of days but, please. Do what I ask." Clearing her throat, she turned back to face Peter, kneeling by the car once again. Her gaze rested on his forehead. "What did you hit?"

The fading sound of the steady crunch of snow made Peter believe the son had walked away from the car. By now, he'd been able to keep his eyes open without too much pain. "I guess the airbag. Why has it been a hard couple of days?"

The corner of her mouth curled up. "For someone with a concussion, you have great observation skills."

"I might not remember anything later. Why the bad day?"

She let out a long breath. A look of uncertainty on her face. "My ex-husband said he wanted to get remarried, but then his *twenty-something,* pregnant girlfriend and their two toddlers crashed the ceremony."

"Ouch." Peter cringed. "That sucks."

"Apparently, she can pump babies out faster than I ever could." Her jaw grimaced as though an old wound suddenly opened.

The urge to punch someone in the face made his entire body tense.

"You okay? What just happened there?"

Peter didn't have the heart to admit the sadness he'd seen her express, but he hoped whomever hurt her would never end up in front of his car. "No, I'm good."

"Did you hit anything but your face? Your chest? Does it hurt to breathe?"

"Driving along. My chest is fine. Um… the sleigh's here. Hit my face, got knocked around, but I had my seat belt on." Pushing himself to sit up, he pulled the coat close around him to keep the bitter chill away. Inhaling deeply, he relished how the rich scents of cinnamon and citrus warmed his body, Peter suddenly remembered his host. "Hey, where did Santa go?"

"Santa?" Standing, she moved out of the way as the paramedics arrived at the car. "Keep talking to me. This is Kyle and Chris. Guys. Thanks for coming out."

Whether it was his lack of any sort of social life for the past couple of years or the concussion, Peter couldn't help but stare at her. As best as he could tell, she was tall, athletic, and gorgeous. Her voice settled over him like a warm blanket and her smile lit up the afternoon gray skies like a bolt of lightning right before his brain decided to spin a three-sixty. "Yeah, Santa was here… shit. My head."

"You okay? You got a little green there," the paramedic

with surfer blond hair asked as he checked Peter's eyes. "I'm Kyle. You hit the steering wheel? Airbag?"

"Something." He glanced in the rearview mirror and noticed Digory's penguin sitting in the back seat. "Wait. Where are my kids?"

Shelly put her hands up in surrender. "Like I told you, my teens have them and they are all having a snowball fight right now, off the highway."

He shivered at the cold that pricked at his face "They have on their coats?"

"Yes. Relax, please."

After a series of questions about the accident, Kyle slipped on the C-collar to stabilize Peter's neck.

Never having worn one of these, Peter immediately understood why his trauma patients hated them so much. The hard plastic collar kept his chin up and neck straight, annoying the shoulder and scapular knots that had already formed. "This is uncomfortable as crap."

"I know but we need to clear your neck. Can you walk? Move your legs?"

He wiggled his fingers and lifted his legs without numbness or loss of coordination. "Yes."

Slowly, Peter made his way out of the car. Immediately, the warmth of the heater dissipated. "How do you people live with this weather?"

"The snow? You get used to it." Kyle pointed as he guided Peter toward a stretcher in the road.

Standing next to it was an incredibly tall gentleman who probably played football at one time and might have been in the military.

Peter saluted him as he made it to the stretcher without any limitations. "How's it going?"

"Well. I'm Chris." The deep pitch of his voice matched his towering frame. He locked the stretcher in place and both paramedics helped Peter sit on it before laying down on the hard board. With quick efficiency, they strapped him down, making it impossible for Peter to turn his head. "Is this really necessary? I walked to this thing."

"You know the MVA protocol, Dr. Davidson." Shelly stood over him and walked beside the stretcher.

"This is Edmund?" Chris raised an eyebrow as he guided the stretcher forward.

"No, I'm Peter." Extending his hand, Peter shook Chris's. "Nice to meet you."

"How many Dr. Davidsons are there?" Kyle asked as the click of the ambulance door sounded.

"I'm the last of us. Our sister Susan is a midwife."

Before he could ask, Shelly stood over him and walked beside the stretcher to the ambulance. "Don't worry about your babies. We've got them. We'll follow you into town and I'll call Jade so she can call Edmund."

"Going straight to the ER, Shelly. We'll meet you there." Chris lifted the end of the stretcher.

Peter smiled lazily, appreciating the fact his brain had stopped spinning and he didn't feel like his stomach was about to exit his body. Reaching his hand out, he rested it on her arm, lifted her hand to his mouth and brushed his lips over the tender skin. "Did anyone ever tell you that you're beautiful?"

The corner of her mouth twitched as she sucked in a quick breath. Her eyes darted to Chris and Kyle before coming back to Peter. "Not since the last time you told me."

"Someone should tell you that all the time." He kissed her hand again before, releasing it.

Her nose crinkled. "Have you been drinking?"

"Santa gave me some hot chocolate."

"Yeah, we met Santa down the road." Kyle grabbed another blanket and threw it on Peter's legs after they slid him into the back of the unit.

"Come on guys, don't make fun." Shelly shook her head as she still stood between the open doors.

"No, no. Mr. Nic's down the road. He told us where to go, what to look for."

"The man is quite quick for a man of his age and size," Chris added. "We offered him a ride and he insisted he wanted to walk back to his house and check on something."

Her eyes went wide with understanding. "Oh, Mr. Nicolas. Yes. He comes into the ER when he runs out of his asthma meds."

"That's what he said." Peter gave a thumbs-up. "I'm sure he got knocked out on impact. Someone needs to check on him."

"We'll make sure that happens, Dr. Davidson. That looks like Nick's work." Chris pointed toward the sleigh. "Guess he got it trapped in the snowbank, again."

"No, pulled out in front of me. He said he got a tricked-out lawn mower engine and treads added."

"That explains why it pulled out in front of you."

Peter stared at Shelly. Something about her made his heart happy and had no idea why. He'd known her for all of five minutes and yet, when he looked into her eyes, he felt like he was home.

I've got a concussion. This is all the concussion.

Still, it didn't feel like it could only be his head injury, especially since the idea of settling anywhere but near the warm beaches of Florida had never entered his mind, rational or concussed.

Now he had weird thoughts of cold winter nights cuddling with Shelly in front of the fireplace with a mug of Nick's holiday harmony.

Who would have thought I'd ever find a gorgeous woman at the north pole?

Merry Christmas to me.

Chapter Five

H E HAD TO be the most handsome, confused man she'd ever seen.

When he'd lazily stared at her and told her she looked like an angel, she had to tell herself to breathe again. She couldn't remember the last time Gill had looked at her with such admiration.

Come to think of it, she couldn't be sure if he ever had.

Sorting through her dating memories, Shelly realized that no man had ever looked at her like Peter Davidson did when he first laid eyes on her only an hour ago.

This guy hit his head. He's not thinking straight.

But part of her really wanted *him* to be a man of his words because Shelly, like any woman, wanted to be appreciated for being the strong, intelligent, beautiful woman she knew she was.

Especially by a guy who appeared to be the living, breathing embodiment of sex.

His messy brown hair, his surfer-tanned skin, piercing green eyes and from best she could tell, a body that had seen the inside of a gym many, many times had her brain full of ridiculous possibilities.

A giggle escaped her, remembering how the corner of his full lips twitched as he soaked her in. How his gaze made her insides melt like butter on a hot summer day.

Outside approval from anyone had never been required for her to get through the day, but damned if it didn't look good coming from that gorgeous head injury patient in room four.

Take that, Gill. I'm still sexy. I'm still desirable.

She smirked at her thoughts, knowing full well they would only stay in her head, but getting a better look at Peter Davidson in the lights of the ER, she really, really wanted to believe everything he said, he meant.

As if he'll even remember me tomorrow.

As soon as the words ticker taped through her head, he looked toward her way and motioned her to come into the room.

Cramming her hands in her jacket to appear casual, Shelly channeled every bit of her self-control as her ovaries happily danced while she strolled toward the exam room between the afternoon ER traffic.

As soon as she passed through the doorway, the crinkle of a cellophane rapper caught her attention.

She pulled her hand from her pocket and found a mint.

Score!

She bit it in half before answering. "Good to see you're doing okay."

"Thanks to you."

"I think you give me too much credit. All I did was talk to you." Shelly chewed the mint as casually as she could.

"And made sure my children were okay. Kept me calm."

"You were acting a little loopy." *Good Lord, could he be any more gorgeous?* Even with the bruising around the repaired wound, the sparkle in his eyes and the lopsided smirk filled Shelly with more holiday spirit than a three-second pour of cheap whiskey.

"Where are my kids?" He craned his neck, looking around her.

"They are with your brother and sister."

His playful demeanor faded. "Great. That'll be an interesting conversation."

"Sorry?"

Within seconds, his smile returned. "It's fine. Thanks again. Can I buy you dinner?"

She blinked a few times to process his question. Certainly she'd heard him wrong. "What?"

"Can I take you to dinner, to thank you for your help today?" Sitting up, he rested his forearms on his knees. "If you don't mind going somewhere they serve chicken strips and macaroni and cheese. I have to bring my kids."

The T-shirt he wore wouldn't help him survive in this winter weather, but man, oh man, did he wear it well. Thick cords of muscle on his arms indicated the man liked to work up a sweat. Her imagination ran wild wondering what he'd look like with that stripped from his body. "Oh, I um…"

The playful demeanor disappeared and he held his hands up in surrender. "Sorry, I didn't even ask you if you were married. Engaged. Straight."

"I'm one of those." She raised an eyebrow, realizing he

might not have remembered her confession about her crappy wedding.

He held his fingers up and crossed them. "Straight?"

"Yes."

"Yes!" He gave her a thumbs-up.

"Interesting you presented that particular combination of choices."

"Gotta cover the bases. No one can assume anything anymore."

"That's fair. I appreciate you thinking outside the box." *Because Gill sure as hell never did.* An imaginative romantic gesture from her ex was him taking his plate to the sink and replacing the toilet paper when it ran out.

She casually crossed her arms across her chest as she took Peter in. He was handsome, she'd give him that, but when she studied him again, he was so much more. Something seriously sexy she couldn't quite figure out, but she would be more than happy to try. "Chicken strips and macaroni and cheese, huh? I think I just might know a place."

"Main Street Diner? Damn, my head." Reclining back into the pillow, Peter, closed his eyes. "Lucy and Edmund have both mentioned that place a time or two."

"It's got a variety of things, including an amazing selection of pies and a great cup of coffee. Of course, a kids' menu."

"A good night's sleep, a few parenting books, and a great bottle of wine would work, too." He grimaced. "I'd love some Tylenol."

Parenting books? It sudden occurred to Shelly that no

mention of a mom had been uttered by either of the kids. He didn't wear a ring or have the tan line of one.

Behind her, the door opened and Drs. Lucy and Edmund Davidson entered with Polly and Digory.

"Peter, I mean Daddy!" Polly called out and ran to the bedside. "Look who we found in the hallway."

Peter's face flushed crimson. "Hey, guys."

"What a wonderful surprise." Lucy hugged her brother. "We weren't expecting you. *Any* of you."

"Dad, Aunt Lucy and Uncle Edmund told us all about the Christmas stuff here." Digory held up several stickers. "There's ice skating and snowboarding and a hot chocolate store."

Polly held Peter's hand to her cheek. "And a place where we can see Christmas trees and a sleigh ride. Can we go? Please, can we… Peter, I mean Dad?"

"Yes, *Daddy*. *Uncle* Edmund and *Aunt* Lucy had a great conversation about Christmas stuff." Edmund gave Peter a fist bump as an awkward silence filled the room. "Lots of things to do for *families*."

What's going on? Do they not get along? After working with Lucy and Edmund for the past few months, she'd always known them to speak highly of their siblings Peter and Susan.

With a smirk, Peter agreed. "Thanks for entertaining the kids. The visit was a last-minute thing. Wasn't planned."

"Kind of like you not mentioning you're a father," Edmund mumbled.

"It's a long story." Peter cringed and rubbed his neck.

That's right. The children mentioned they'd just met him. Wow.

Searching her brain, Shelly couldn't remember one story Lucy or Edmund had mentioned about Peter having children and the Drs. Davidson loved to talk about their family.

Did Peter not know either? Oh, geez.

That alone should have sent her running from the room, but something didn't add up. Peter had been incredibly concerned about his children the entire time at the scene. Even now, he'd swept his daughter up onto the bed, helped his son up to join them as he listened with great interest while both children rapidly spoke about the ER and the sticker lady Sue Westbrook, Shelly's aunt by marriage.

No, deadbeat dads, like Gill, didn't give a crap about their kids. They didn't act like they cared one minute and walked away to procreate with another woman the next.

The wound on Peter's forehead had to be killing him and he certainly had a mild concussion, but watching him with his children, no one would suspect he had any pain at all. His smile, his animated conversation with them held no hint of annoyance or frustration.

What is your story, Dr. Peter Davidson?

Peter let out a loud laugh as his daughter told an age-old knock-knock joke and flubbed the punchline.

Lucy and Edmund smiled and joined in, each rattling off a joke of their own.

Without warning, Shelly's heart slammed against her ribs, knocking the breath out of her as her brain raced with thoughts of happily ever afters and beautiful family gatherings.

No, no, no. Don't go there.

As soon as she said it to herself, Peter caught her watching him and smiled. "Thank you for helping us today."

Get out of here before you say something stupid. "Of course. Of course. I'll let all of you visit. I've got to get my kids home anyway."

"Thanks so much, Shelly. We appreciate you." Lucy patted Shelly's shoulder and hugged her, whispering, "If you need anyone to talk to, it's a no judgment zone."

"What do you mean?"

Lucy cringed. "I'm sorry. Sue mentioned… did I overstep?"

"Oh, my didn't happen wedding? Crappy news travels fast I guess. Thanks. I'll keep that in mind." Shelly gave Lucy a quick squeeze and shook Edmund's hand.

Before the door closed, Peter called out, "Remember, chicken strips and macaroni and cheese. My treat."

"It's a date." Never once could Shelly remember looking forward to having chicken tenders and macaroni and cheese as much as she did right now.

Chapter Six

A S MUCH AS Peter hated to see Shelly leave, an explanation was in order to his siblings, especially since his visit had been completely unexpected.

Kind of like when he discovered he was a father.

Lucy, the youngest of the four of them, hugged him carefully.

Edmund and he shook hands before he eyed Peter's forehead. "Tom did some good work. He got the ends approximated, glued, and those Steri-Strips will hold just fine."

"My head's pounding and I look like Frankenstein's monster with this gash in my forehead."

"Too bad it's not a lightning bolt. Then you could be Harry Potter," Digory cocked his head. "Then I might like you some."

"Thanks for being honest, Son." After being under the lights of the ER for the past couple of hours, Peter's headache had leveled off, but it still rattled his teeth. "Does your head injury protocol include Tylenol?"

"Maybe." Lucy nodded. "I'll see if Shelly can grab some before she heads out."

Shelly. The image of her smile sent a wave of warmth over his body and temporarily relieved his bruised head.

Her smile. Her eyes. Her walk. Shelly, the angel nurse who'd taken care of his children as though they were her own. She'd certainly helped the disaster of an entrance into Marietta be far less chaotic.

Lucy peeked her head out of the room and talked to the doctor on duty before returning. Her eyes were wide with expectation as she took a seat next to Peter's bed. "Soooooo, what's new?"

"Apparently, I'm a father." He patted Polly's and Digory's backs as the kids watched YouTube funny cat videos on his phone.

Edmund sighed. "Simone?"

Peter smirked with how quickly his brother always put things together. "Found out three weeks ago."

"Three weeks ago?" Edmund scooted to the edge of his chair. "Why didn't you tell us sooner?"

"I got a phone call about the kids. Wanted to verify things before I told any of you. Didn't seem fair to get us worked up over something I wasn't sure about."

"What, she called you out of the blue to tell say you're a father?" Although Lucy asked the question in her usual joyful tone, Peter knew his sister well enough to know how angry she had to be. Family commitment had always run deep with the Davidson siblings and the same was expected from girlfriends and boyfriends.

"No, she didn't call." A great sadness sat on his chest having to tell the story. "CPS did."

"Child protective services?" Edmund's brow momentarily furrowed before Polly extended her arms and he picked her up. She tucked her head on Edmund's shoulder and wrapped her arms around his neck. "Why? Are they okay?"

"They are okay. Their mom…" The news stuck like peanut butter in his throat. "Car accident."

Lucy gasped. "Oh, no. When?"

"The Monday after Thanksgiving."

"What happened?"

"The only thing I know is someone was on their phone, ran a light, and done." The police officer had explained all this three weeks ago. Even though Peter read the accident report, he'd yet to talk to his family about any of it. The words sliced up his throat like sharp glass, but he swallowed his sorrow.

Now's not the time. "I've spent the last few weeks planning and having the service, and getting the kids through their final weeks of school."

Digory snuggled in next to Peter and played with the hem of the sheet in his lap. "Mommy went to heaven after she dropped us off at school."

Tears welled in his siblings' eyes.

They all knew the pain of losing a parent so suddenly. Lucy had been slightly older than Polly and Digory when a drunk driver slammed head-on into the car their father drove that Sunday morning over twenty years ago.

Their father died instantly. The impact caused multiple life-long injuries for their mother, almost killing Lucy, and shook Peter, Susan, and Edmund to their cores. Being the oldest child, it threw Peter into the instant dad status.

The scar on Lucy's neck reminded Peter of how easily they could have lost her if the first responders and emergency room staff hadn't been so incredible that day. That experience impacted them all so greatly that all four siblings went into the medical field.

With Polly in his arms, Edmund blinked back his tears. "I thought Simone had family in Maine. Parents. Siblings."

Peter shook his head. "She had a grandmother who's gone. Her parents, both passed away before the kids were five and her brother and she haven't talked for years."

"But she was so close to her brother. What happened?"

Peter wondered the same thing. One of the things that had attracted him to the mother of his children was her open and loving relationship with her parents and her brother. That they could discuss anything and be stronger for it. "No idea."

"Then she was raising them by herself?"

"She must have been. She had a strong community of friends. You know Simone could always make anywhere home."

"Except with you," Lucy mumbled.

"Luce. Not now." Peter kissed the top of his son's head, admiring how much Digory's hair looked like Edmund's. Thick, dark, wavy and difficult to control. "Now's not the time."

Pursing her lips, Lucy gave a quick nod. "I guess you made a lasting impact on her. She named the kids aptly."

"From *The Magician's Nephew*. Yes." A dull ache settled

in Peter's chest, the same one that always popped up when his longtime girlfriend's name was brought up in conversation. "One of the many things we talked about when we were together. Naming kids."

"I'm so sorry that didn't work out like you hoped." Lucy motioned for Digory to come to her. He willingly did. "They are beautiful children."

Edmund's forehead furrowed. "Wait, how did CPS know to contact you?"

"She left instructions with a friend and with her work. An open in case of emergency information packet. It had all my most recent contact information, all of your most recent addresses at home and work." A detail he left out was the small envelope that had "For Peter" written on the outside. He'd been instructed by Simone's friend Karen, the contents would explain everything.

As of now, he'd only read the necessary information regarding his kids and hadn't even considered opening that bucket of crazy until this second. Even with all the questions floating around in his head, he had no idea when he'd get to it.

Or if he wanted to know the truth of why she walked away from him so many years ago.

Edmund shook his head as though confused. "Most recent? You mean our addresses in Marietta?"

"Yes. She'd kept up with all of us. Even knew Mom had died."

Lucy clenched her jaw, but continued to hold his son with loving care. "Why didn't she reach out to us? To you?

Just because you didn't end up together, doesn't mean you didn't deserve to know."

He had to give it to his sister, despite her obvious annoyance at the situation, her sweet voice never sounded harsh or bitter when asking such loaded questions.

He knew exactly why.

Because the kids were in the room.

His kids.

My kids.

Even with instant aunt status, Lucy took her role extremely serious. That included not scaring them or showing any hostility toward their mother, but he had no doubt his sister had a lot more to say on this subject.

"Luce, I've been asking myself that question since I got the call." Peter repositioned in the bed. His neck muscles spasmed and he slowly stretched to loosen their vice-like grip hold on his shoulders. He anticipated he'd be post workout sore by this evening and have difficulty sleeping, but he hadn't gotten a decent night's sleep for three weeks. "No idea. I've gone through the information she left about the kids. Their medical histories. Their school information. Their birth certificates. Her will and requests should I ever find out."

"That included what?"

"That I change as little as possible for them."

"Then that means..." Lucy sat forward as Digory appeared to have gone limp in her arms. She turned her body with her nephew in her arms. "Did he fall asleep?"

Peter's heart warmed seeing his son sleeping peacefully in

his younger sister's care. "He's passed out. We got up early to catch the first flight here."

"Poor baby." Lucy stroked Digory's unruly hair and settled back in the chair, propping her feet on the edge of the stretcher. "You were saying?"

"If I can, she requested I move to Maine. Work there. Live in their house."

"Give up your life." Edmund shook his head as Polly played with the zipper on his jacket. "Give up everything you've worked for, sell your place, move away from your family because *she* decided it?"

"Edmund, please. There's nothing set in stone right now. I came here to figure things out." Peter swallowed back the anger of being left out of his children's lives, being deprived of their existence, and now fighting with a ghost's demands. It wasn't the time or place to vent about it. He could take care of that in the gym or vent when his kids weren't around.

Still, he'd asked himself too many times to count why had she kept them a secret? Why hadn't she reached out?

Edmund sat down with Polly still in his arms. "That triggers another question, what brings you to Marietta and can you be *here* with the kids?"

"If you're asking did I abscond with my children, no. The court gave me immediate custody. My name is on their birth certificates and Simone had it all written out in her wishes. There's no one contesting anything. I did let them know where we'd be in case anything comes up or they have any questions."

"That's good. Please give them our information if you

need," Lucy added as she rubbed her nephew's back. "Now, these guys have to be hungry."

Seeing his children in the arms of his siblings gave Peter some much needed comfort and a break. He'd barely had a moment to himself since he arrived in Lewiston, Maine to meet his own children for the first time.

And as angry as he was at Simone for never contacting him, she had put his name on the birth certificate. She had made arrangements if anything happened to her because if she hadn't, where would they be?

With strangers?

Starting over?

Separated by the system because people aren't as likely to adopt sibling groups?

Just the idea of him having children he'd never know about twisted his gut uncomfortably tight, sending the foul taste of frustration on the back of his tongue.

For the past few weeks, his emotions ebbed and flowed between fury, regret, and guilt, but his love for his children only grew exponentially.

Now he simply had to figure out how to be an instant father they needed.

Peter rubbed the bridge of his nose as the pain in his forehead throbbed. "Since this is all new to me, to us, I thought getting the kids around family during the holidays would be a good idea. They're used to snow. Didn't want to shock them too much for our first Christmas together."

"But you hate to celebrate Christmas, Peter," Edmund snarked.

"What? You hate to celebrate Christmas?" Digory's head popped up off Lucy's shoulder.

Lucy laughed. "Oh goodness, Digory. You heard that?"

"Oh no!" Polly wailed. "Does that mean we aren't having Christmas?"

"This sucks." Digory pushed his way off Lucy's lap. "I knew when you showed up, this would never work."

"Thanks, Ed." Peter shook his head as he sat up and hung his legs over the side of the bed. The world spun twice before unsteadily settling on center. "Look kids, Christmas wasn't all that fun for me growing up."

"It used to be, Peter." Lucy rested her hand on his arm.

"I know, Luce, but guys I promise, I have a Christmas plan."

His son stopped ranting and raised his eyebrow. "Yeah?"

Peter couldn't help but smirk at his son's guarded expression. *It's like looking in a mirror.*

Edmund repositioned Polly in his lap. "What is your plan, Pete? To celebrate the holidays then move here?"

"That would be fantastic!" Lucy squealed. "We could use some temporary help during the holidays for sure. It's been crazy here in the ER. Everyone's exhausted already and could use some days off."

Lucy had taken over the directorship of the ER several months ago and knew the ins and outs of running the busy unit. "It's only December and flu season hit early."

"Luce, it takes three to four months to get an MD license. By the time Peter can help, flu season will be over." Edmund pulled out his phone and checked it.

Her shoulders slumped. "Oh, you're right, but if he wanted, he could help during the spring and summer when people request off for vacations."

"I already have it," Peter confessed, appreciating the enthusiasm his siblings had for his presence.

"What?" Lucy's jaw dropped. "You already have it? Why?"

"I didn't think about it until Edmund moved here, but I thought if I took some of my vacation time with you guys, I could pick up a shift or two if you needed help. Like you said, give people some time off if they needed it."

"You'd take a vacation to work on your vacation?" Edmund tilted his head back and forth like he did when he calculated things in his head. "Makes sense. You take your vacation, come visit. Work a couple of shifts a week. Write everything off as a business expense. Still get vacation time and make money."

"Right." Peter chuckled at his brother, the human calculator. "But I'd still have to go through the hospital's vetting process."

"I'll call the administrators tonight and see how fast we can get you approved. Please send me a copy of your license." Lucy pulled out her phone and quickly texted something.

"Are we having Christmas or not?" Digory interrupted.

His son's protests were like a hammer to his brain. "Digory, yes. Please calm down. Your uncle Edmund and aunt Lucy know all about Christmas here in Marietta."

"Is that why you came here? For us to help you with…

Christmas?" The youngest Davidson sibling's eyes sparkled as a mischievous grin spread across her face. "You want *help*? With *Christmas*?"

Her childlike enthusiasm brought a smile to Peter's face. Lucy had always believed in the spirit of Christmas, whether it was a guy in a red suit or simply the joy to the world, good will toward men kind of vibe. "Yes, Lucy. That's exactly why. I need your help with… everything."

"You came to the right place, Polly and Digory."

"Call me Digs." The young man tilted his chin up slightly as he squared his shoulders.

She gave him a quick hug. "Okay, Digs. We are going to have so much fun!"

Polly cupped Edmund's face. "And you can call me Polly."

"Okay, Polly. Call me Uncle Ed or Edmund or Uncle Edmund or hey you or whatever." Edmund smirked as Polly hugged him tightly around the neck. He threw his arms out in a pretend panic. "Can't. Breathe."

Polly let go and cupped his face again. "I'm so excited to have Christmas! We didn't think it would happen, since Peter-Daddy hit Santa."

"His sleigh came out of nowhere!" Peter lay back in the bed, his head pounding like a bass drum during a Sousa symphony.

"That would make me worry about getting Christmas, too." Edmund raised an eyebrow as he chuckled silently.

"I've never been in Marietta for the holidays either, but I know they have a lot of stuff here that's amazing." Lucy tenderly held the children's hands as they both stood in front of her. "They have plenty of snow and snowboarding and ice skating and sleigh rides and hot chocolate and a Christmas tree farm and what else, Ed?"

"A bunch of stuff. Cool stuff." Edmund gave a thumbs-up.

"Thanks for elaborating, Uncle Ed."

"You're welcome."

"The Graff has some children's activities and I believe the movie theater has some holiday classics playing. The Scott's Christmas tree farm has sleigh rides." Lucy gently pulled the children in for a group hug. "Oh, I'm so glad you're here. We are going to have so much fun."

"Not up for a sleigh ride, right now," Peter mumbled.

"Oh, my goodness. This sounds delightful!" Polly excitedly clapped as Digory appeared cautiously optimistic.

Disaster avoided.

Chapter Seven

THROUGH THE OBSERVATION windows, Peter watched the busy ER. It hadn't slowed down since they'd arrived. A town the size of Marietta appeared to have a tremendous amount of patient traffic.

Maybe I underestimated this place.

Staff moved quickly between rooms and each other trying to carry out orders. Holiday décor hung all over the unit with festive stickers on the observation windows of each room and some of the staff wearing Santa hats, jingle bells, or holiday-themed scrubs.

Over the central desk, someone had taken multiple gloves in different colors, inflated them and arranged them in the shape of a small Christmas tree.

String lights of red, green, and white hung over the desk and blinked in lazy patterns.

Along the walls, green, red, silver, and gold garland were pinned in the shape of normal heart tracings as people see on a monitor.

A tall doctor, who resembled Loki from the Thor movies, walked into a room straight across the unit and pointed to the heart monitor before the patient and family began laughing.

Peter recognized him as Dr. Tom Reynolds, the one who sewed then glued his forehead closed.

"Peter. Dad. Can we go?" His son's voice had a hint of a whine.

Before he could answer, a soft knock at the door interrupted his response.

And when Peter saw who entered, he more than welcomed the distraction.

"Hey, guys." Shelly held a pill cup, a glass of water, and an iPad. "They are behind out here so Dr. Reynolds asked me to bring this in to you and go ahead and get you discharged."

"You're an angel." Instantly, Peter's heart rate increased and he became painfully aware he hadn't brushed his teeth since before he drank that third large to-go coffee a couple of hours ago.

"That's what you keep saying." She smelled of mint and crisp air which complemented the healthy pink of her cheeks.

For whatever reason, he loved seeing her blush, but he loved *making* her blush even more. Lustful ideas ran amuck his in mind. What else he could do to pink up her cheeks?

Holy crap. What am I thinking?

He bit his tongue to make sure none of those ideas left his brain much less traveled across his lips. It had been far too long since someone turned his head like she did.

"Here you go." She handed him the medication and water. "Because you're awake, your neuro checks have been stable, and you've got these two to watch you. Dr. Reynolds said you get Tylenol, but nothing else."

"Deal." He downed them in three gulps.

"Where are you staying tonight?"

"You want to know where I'm staying?"

She cleared her throat and tapped the iPad. "You've had a concussion and you need someone to watch you, check on you during the night."

Thank God I didn't say anything lecherous. "We have reservations at the hotel here in town."

"The Graff?"

"I think that's the name."

Lucy nodded. "That place is so pretty for Christmas. Your kids will love it."

"Do they have Christmas trees? Sleigh bells? Snow?" Digory jumped around Lucy's chair.

"All of that and I think they have cookie decorating during the day and a bunch of Christmas trees in the lobby."

"Do you have anyone staying with you other than the kids?" Shelly's playful demeanor shifted slightly serious.

"No, it's just us." *Just us.*

Terror hit Peter straight in the chest. There had been so much chaos surrounding the events of the last three weeks, there hadn't been much time to process anything other than his instant fatherhood. Now, him being a *single* parent with two frustrated kids who out of school for the next couple of weeks, started to sink in.

How am I supposed to do this?

"I can stay with him." Edmund stood and stretched.

"Lucy, you're here tonight, right?"

Lucy tapped her watch. "I'm working seven to seven, so my shift starts shortly. I can come over after I'm done and switch out with you if you need or I can send Thomas if you're too busy, Edmund."

"Nah, I'm good. Jade's gotta be here early tomorrow morning. She'll probably sleep better without me distracting her. Keeping her up too late."

"You stayed up late when you're working?" Polly cocked her head. "Mommy sometimes let us stay up late playing Scrabble, but never on a school night."

Edmund gave a sheepish grin. "Yes, Polly. My girlfriend and I stay up late playing Scrabble."

"How many points for the word sarcasm?" Lucy smirked.

"Eleven." Digory and Edmund answered in unison then gave each other fist bumps.

"Genetics are weird." If Peter ever doubted these children were his, that moment, seeing his brother and son act the exact same way would have erased any questions. "So, Luce. I finally get to meet the man who stole you away from Florida, then?"

The mix of travel fatigue, recent events, and the fact they hadn't eaten in several hours made Peter's brain wobble slightly. He braced himself by placing his hands on either side of him on the stretcher. "Anyone else hungry?"

"Me!" Digory raised his hand. "I vote pizza."

"Thomas didn't steal me, Peter, but he's one of the many reasons I'm staying." Lucy playfully clapped her hands. "Hey, kids, you want to meet more family?"

"We have more family? We didn't have any family in Maine." Polly's eyes went wide.

"Yes, we did. We had Karen," Digory answered, his nose slightly lifted.

Polly scrunched up her nose. "She wasn't family, she was a friend of Mommy's and worked at the same job."

"Karen was the one who helped me with all the paper-work after Simone…" Hearing the woman's words of despair replay in his head made Peter's eye twitch.

Shelly's hand rested on his arm. "I'm sorry for your loss."

"Thank you, Shelly." Her simple gesture of compassion made this entire situation temporarily feel far less over-whelming. His hand rested on hers for a moment before he reluctantly let go.

"Sounds like Karen was a very nice person to look after the two of you." Lucy counted off on her fingers. "Here you have an uncle Thomas."

Edmund smirked. "And my girlfriend, Jade. She always has chocolate at her house and a dog."

"And there's our sister, Susan. Wait. Does Susan know about this? Them?" Lucy quickly corrected herself before her eyes darted from Peter to Shelly and back.

Shaking his head, then immediately regretting tossing his brain around, Peter cringed. "No, because she's finishing a travel nursing assignment in New Mexico. I didn't want to worry her and she'll be done around the first of the year."

"I'd think she'd want to know now, don't you?"

"I'll send her a text to call. This isn't something you send in an email." He pressed his thumb in the center of his forehead, hoping it would encourage his brain to calm down.

By now, Polly unzipped her unicorn backpack and produced a small glittery note pad and matching pen. With great precision, she wrote Lucy, Edmond, Thomas, Jayd, chocolat, and Suzan. "Okay, who's next?"

"There's Charlie, our stepfather."

"Is that with a *Y* or *P*?"

"An *I-E*."

"Did you tell Charlie?" Lucy smiled, her eyes wide with expectation.

Peter nodded as a nurse jogged by with a springy Santa hat that looked like something straight out of a Dr. Seuss book. "Yes, Charlie knows, because he's checking on my house, but I asked him not to say anything until I knew for certain what was going on."

"Cool! The EMS guys are back!" With his back to them, Digory had his face smashed against the observation window, watching the activity race by.

One of the tallest paramedics with a stoic face immediately brightened up when he noticed Digory. The man smiled and waved as they brought a patient into a room in Peter's line of sight.

Waving back, Digory commented, "That guy is tall!"

Edmund turned in his chair. "That's Patrick. He used to be in the air force."

"Cool! Is that a girl?"

"That's Amanda. She's was in the navy," Shelly added.

"They have EMS girls here?" Polly threw her pen and pad at Lucy and joined her brother at the window. "Wow, there's a lot going on out there."

"It's a busy time of day. The evenings are always busier." Lucy placed Polly's things back in her bag. "Lots of things happen in the evening."

Digory tapped the glass. "It sure does. That guy has an icepack on his nads."

"What?" Lucy's head whipped around as Edmund jumped to his feet and stood by the children. "Where did you hear that word?"

"From a kid at school. His older brother says it all the time." Digory shrugged. "Why, is it a bad word?"

"It's not one most people use in polite company." Lucy bit her lip, but her shoulders silently bobbed up and down.

Edmund rested his hands on the kids' backs. "Where?"

"Over there. The guy in the purple underwear." Digory pointed to his left.

"Crap." Peter's head wobbled as he tried to slide off the bed. "What's going on?"

Shelly craned her neck. "A snowboarder who probably didn't wear a cup."

"Purple underwear?"

"Long underwear." Edmund clapped his hands after turning the kids around. "Okay, that's the ER."

"The ER's busy. And there's snowboarding? Anyone of you know how to snowboard?" Digory tilted his head toward the door.

"My son, Freddie, knows how." Shelly tapped the screen and handed it to Peter. "I need your signature here that tells me you understand the discharge instructions for head injury protocol."

Trying to focus on the screen proved to be difficult. Peter motioned to Edmund. "Have him sign it, please."

"You okay?" Her hand rested on his shoulder, giving him much needed calm.

"Yes, still kind of dizzy."

"I think you might want to hang out a little longer."

With you? "No, I need to eat, drink a gallon of water."

"That would certainly help." She grabbed the otoscope from the wall and rested her fingers under his chin. "Let me check your pupils again."

The idea of that bright light in his face didn't amuse him, but Peter didn't want something ugly to get out of hand. Making sure his pupils were equal was an easy check, even if it would temporarily exacerbate his headache. "Fine."

With the flick of her wrist, she turned on the light and flashed it in his eyes, but before she turned to put the equipment away, he caught her gaze and for a brief moment, he soaked in her natural beauty.

The perfect layering of blues and grays in her eyes.

The exquisite arch of her cheekbones.

The lovely curve of her lips.

Her fingers remained under his chin for a few extra seconds and he watched her subtly exhale while she met his stare.

Stare. You're staring. Knock it off! He blinked himself out of his trance and pulled away. "My eyes okay?"

A nervous laugh escaped her. "Yes, your eyes looked great. Pupils are working fine."

What the hell was that? He quick check verified the sheet they'd covered him with before he arrived here still lay wadded in his lap.

Standing, Edmund quickly scribbled his signature on the screen. "Don't worry, Shelly. We'll take good care of him."

"I know you will." She gave them a stressed smile and took the iPad back.

Pulling on her coat sleeve, Digory asked, "Hey, Aunt Shelly! Will your Freddie come snowboarding with us?"

Shelly put a wisp of hair behind her ear a few times, appearing slightly flustered. "I'm sure I could get him to meet you guys. He loves to be outside."

Polly placed her hand on her chest. "Are you okay, Miss Shelly? You look pos-i-tiv-i-lee flushed!"

Lucy bit her lip as her eyes darted between Shelly and Peter. "Where did you hear such an expression, Polly?"

"A girl from my school said it. She's always saying movie lines."

Digory adamantly shook his head. "No, she didn't. You saw it on Netflix."

"As if!"

Without warning, a much needed round of laughter erupted from Peter. The chaos of his children's unpredictable vocabulary and the interactions with his siblings brought back endearing memories of childhood before everything changed.

His mind wandered to possibilities of starting over for all of them, but he mentally shook them off.

Moving them here would be an even bigger shock than

they've already been through. Simone requested I keep them back in Maine.

Peter understood more than most regarding Simone's want to change as little as possible for the children in a situation like this, but what she asked sounded oddly out of character.

I need to read the letter she left me.

Someone clearing their throat disrupted his thoughts.

"You sure you're okay? You looked a little lost there." Shelly's kind eyes shot right into his gut.

Lost. That's exactly what I am.

Digory yanked on Shelly's jacket before Peter could respond. "Hey. When can Freddie help me with snowboarding?"

"Hey? That's how you address a lady? Hey?" Peter shook his head. "Not cool, Son."

Digory stepped back and narrowed his gaze for a moment before trying again. "Hey, Aunt Shelly. When can Freddie help me with my snowboarding, please?"

"I'll ask him. He's in the breakroom." Shelly pointed toward the door.

"Better." Peter had already decided his son would have a far harder adjustment to this sudden shift. As overly welcoming as Polly had been to Peter, Digory had remained distant and quiet, but he couldn't blame the kid for being resentful. Life had thrown him an unfair curve.

"Can you ask him now? Can you?" The child tugged on her coat again.

She pulled out her phone and quickly sent a text. "Sure."

"You don't have to do that." Peter glanced at the clock over the door. "It's past dinnertime. Anyone hungry?"

"Me!" Both kids raised their hands.

Edmund patted his stomach. "Let's get that pizza."

The children squealed happily and Peter tried to focus on keeping the room visually stable. "Pizza would be good."

Polly wrapped her arms around Shelly's waist. "Thank you, Aunt Shelly. Thank you."

Without pause, Shelly hugged Polly back, but her cheeks were full-on crimson now. "You can call me Ms. Shelly if you want."

"Okay, Ms. Shelly." Digs gave her a playful thumbs-up before his eyes met his father's and his happiness waned. "Ready?"

As they all left the ER, Peter couldn't help but look back, wanting to know a whole lot more about the angel who had rescued him from the snow and put smiles on his children's faces.

Chapter Eight

B Y THE TIME Shelly, Freddie, and Tia made it home, it was well past dark and the temperature sat far below freezing.

A steady snow had fallen for most of the day leaving a knee-high thick blanket of white on their lawn.

Walking into the house, she shivered and turned the heat back to seventy-eight.

"I get the bathroom, first!" Tia disappeared down the hall.

"Why do we keep it so cold in here?" Freddie grumbled as he dropped his bag on the coffee table.

A figure from the corner of the couch yawned and stretched, her sparkling blue collar catching the light of the overhead lights.

"Hello, Jingles." Freddie patted the spot next to him on the couch.

Before moving away from her self-made pile of clothes, the silver cat stretched and yawned.

He scratched the feline behind the ears when she got within arm's length. "It's not like we're poor, Mom. Poor Jingles was probably freezing."

Making her way over to Freddie's, Jingles wasted no time curling up on his lap and settling in.

"It was set on sixty-eight and Jingles has on a fur and a fluffy bed." Shelly motioned to the pile of socks at the end of the couch. "I think she's been in your room."

"I thought I closed my door."

She reached down and patted the cat, loving the loud, ragged purr. "I didn't want to keep paying hundreds of dollars to heat the house when your father and I weren't planning on being here until after Christmas and you and Tia were staying with your great-aunt Sue."

Freddie opened his mouth to say something, but bit his lip before answering. "This house doesn't even look like Christmas. Not one decoration."

"I know." Shelly had to admit. The house didn't look festive at all. In fact, it looked downright depressing, but her concern at the moment, sat with her son's refusal to discuss what happened in Vegas.

In fact, Freddie had been almost silent until they crossed the Crawford County line.

Shelly wanted to give him a great holiday regardless of his father's callous behavior, but what she didn't want was her son to be a boiling pot simmering on the stove for the rest of the year and beyond. "Hey, tomorrow, let's get some things put out."

"We getting a tree?" Tia entered, brushing her teeth.

"No, I don't want to mess with it, but I'm fine with all the other inside decorations if y'all want to put them up."

"No thanks." Freddie slouched farther into the couch

and sulked. "It's going to take most of the night to warm this place up."

"Then let Jingles sleep with you."

The cat purred, a look of bliss on her sweet face.

"She hogs the pillow and wants to play at four in the morning." Despite Freddie's complaints, he made no attempt to move the cat off his lap.

She'd cranked the heat down while they were gone to keep utility expenses down. Freddie was right, they weren't poor, but Shelly wasn't fiscally frivolous either. "Would you rather I heat the house while we're gone for a week or spend that money on our book trip?"

Freddie unenthusiastically shrugged. "Good point. When is that again?"

"Probably the day after Christmas. Depends on how many shifts I pick up between now and then."

"You're going right back to work?" Freddie cringed. "I thought you'd still take the time off."

"I'm going in for a few hours the next couple of days, let people get their holiday shopping done, but not entire shifts." *Might as well. It's not like I'll be on my honeymoon.* "Besides, I can tuck that vacation time away for a longer trip in the summer."

"Fine, but our book trip is still on, right?"

"Yep, looking forward to it."

"Book trip 2018, baby!" Tia held her fist in the air as she walked back to the bathroom.

Although the kids were regulars at the local library and their own bookshelves were more than stocked, Shelly always seized opportunities for the kids to gain as much knowledge as possible.

Every year, one day between Christmas and New Year's and the day after the last day of the school year, she'd drive them into Bozeman to Barnes and Noble for their biannual book splurge event. There, she'd wander the aisles for hours and let them loose to buy as many books as they wanted.

Thank goodness she'd passed her love of reading to her son and niece since life in Marietta could certainly get slow, especially during the long winter months and when they ran out of ways to stay busy in the summer.

The high price tag always made her cringe and she'd work several shifts of overtime to cover expenses before they'd leave, but it had always been worth it, especially since it kept them both out of trouble.

Hard to get into mischief when their noses were in a book.

This year, the unused honeymoon money would fuel their brains, build up their bookshelves, and everyone would probably end up happier.

Everyone except, Gill.

Freddie slouched in the chair and put his feet on his bag. "What a day."

Shelly snapped her fingers. "Nope, nope, put your bag in your room. Don't dump your stuff here. And collect your socks."

"I'm hungry."

"I'm Shelly."

"Mom!"

She laughed at her stupid joke as she carried her things to her room but immediately froze in the doorway of her bedroom.

Swallowing hard, she flipped on the light and stared at the room she'd set up before they'd left for Vegas.

The *His* and *Hers* pillows.

The sexy scented candles on the bedside table along with massage oils and creams.

She pulled her suitcase to the very spot Gill's treadmill would have been placed before allowing the case to fall forward as she tossed her coat in her favorite oversized chair.

The script "Get Naked" she'd spent an hour perfectly placing over the doorway so they could see it from their bed.

I was supposed to be married when I came back here.

We were going to be a family again.

Yet, relief flooded her that the entire ceremony fell apart, because no matter how hard she wanted to believe he'd change, she knew in her heart Gill's promises, even ones made in front of God, their family, and Elvis the preacher, would never stick.

At least it fell apart before the I dos.

The comfort of walking away without any legal obliga-tion to him was nothing short of empowering. She held her arms out and did a backward trust fall on her bed, savoring the bittersweet freedom.

Why would I want to share this house, this bed with him? With anyone?

Then a soft voice from the back of her mind whispered, "What about a man like Peter Davidson?"

That made her sit straight up as happy possibilities decided to throw a "what if" dance party with her ovaries.

She wouldn't deny the good doctor sure looked hero-worthy and seeing what his body looked like under that ridiculously thin T-shirt would be worth it, but *should* she even be thinking about him?

All her self-doubt from the past two days bubbled to the surface, angering her. As confident as she'd been walking into that chapel, seeing the beautiful, pregnant woman her ex cheated on her with, shook Shelly's ego until it cracked.

Damn you, Gill, and your constant need for validation.

She buried her face in her hands, her silent tears wet her palms.

I deserve validation as well.

Knowing that wouldn't happen anytime soon only angered her more because Shelly took her job as a strong mom and woman seriously. That meant not screwing around and not dating for the sake of dating.

She'd always been a serial monogamist before she married, but staring into Peter's eyes and thinking about the cords of muscle in his arms, made her want to throw caution to the wind and wrap herself around that chiseled form of his and never let go.

No matter the red flags about him not knowing his children.

That was a mystery she still hadn't figured out.

As best she could tell, his fatherhood had been a recent occurrence, which meant he was a love 'em and leave 'em type or someone kept a massive secret from him and felt justified in doing so.

Yet, when she looked at him, the kindness in his eyes told a different story.

Part of her urged her to look the other way, not to get involved because she'd already been tricked by Gill more times than she cared to admit, but she worked with Peter's siblings, Lucy and Edmund. That same honest compassion reflected in their eyes and both had shown to be quality human beings.

Work with is one thing, but get involved with?

One of her dearest friends, Jade, presently lived with Edmund. She'd been nothing short of happy since they'd been together. Edmund had even helped Jade navigate the insanity of her discovering her brother had been the one driving the car that hit and killed hometown first responder, Harry Monroe.

Would Peter be just as amazing?

The "Get Naked" script over the door didn't help rein in her brain as she pictured peeling the T-shirt off him and running her hands across his muscular chest and lower.

Her body tingled at the image of her hands unzipping his fly—

"Mom! What's for dinner?"

Annnnnd, sexy image is gone. Mom-life is so glamorous.

The pop of the refrigerator door being opened caused her to roll her eyes.

"There's not going to be much in there. Might have to thaw some soup."

An exasperated sigh from the kitchen. "Can't we just order pizza?"

"No. Make a grilled cheese."

"Ugh!" Heavy footsteps made their way toward her room.

So much for savoring the moment. Shaking off her tingles, Shelly moved her bag next to her bed while waiting for Freddie to come in and vent as he always did after dealing with his father's selfishness.

Three. Two. One.

"Mom, why did he do that to us. Again?"

Letting out a long breath, Shelly turned to face her son.

He slid down to the floor, sitting in the doorway, his back to the doorframe. His long legs stretched out into her room.

Shelly was biased, but damn, her son was handsome.

With the exception of him inheriting her creamy cocoa skin, Freddie looked just like his father. Soulful brown eyes, broad shoulders, long, strong legs that helped him easily navigate any hill when skiing, snowboarding, or hiking.

Thankfully, Freddie had also inherited her love for learning and strong work ethic because the last thing the world needed, was another handsome con man.

Freddie sat in silence, as she slowly unpacked her suitcase.

The dull thud softly echoed in the room as the back of his head gently tapping the wood. The profound sadness on his face only reaffirmed Shelly's gut instinct about her ex-husband.

He was and always would be a totally useless piece of shit.

She patted the bed. "Come on. I know you want to un-load."

Within seconds, he stood and launched himself in the middle of her perfectly made bed, sending the His/Hers throw pillows flying in different directions. He kicked off his shoes and lay across the width of the king-sized bed. His head just short to the edge of one side as his feet hung over the other.

"Is this a party?" Tia entered holding a bowl of cereal and curled up in the oversized chair next to Shelly's bookshelf. "What are we talking about?"

"How my dad's an ass," Freddie replied before Shelly had a chance to answer.

Tia nodded and stuffed her mouth full of cereal.

Shelly struggled with what she wanted to say and what she should say since many of her recent thoughts about Gill had included the words murder, euthanize, and castrate. "Honey, I don't know why your father can't figure himself out, but we did our part. We kept our promises, he didn't, but we keep doing the good, right things for our lives and ourselves."

"You're paraphrasing Angie Thomas, Mom. She said something like that in *The Hate U Give*."

Well, that's one parenting thing done well. He loves to read great books. "She's right though. Even when things go down the tubes, the opposite way you hoped, that's not a reason for you to give up. For *you* to do crappy things. You keep doing what you do right."

He curled up with her pillow and shrugged. "You know

what I can't get out of my head?"

"What's that, honey?" As she reached into her bag, the crinkle of the beautifully tissue paper-wrapped lace panties caught her attention. She'd purchased them for her honeymoon, but now they simply jabbed at her pride.

Didn't matter what I did or wore, he'd never see me as desirable enough ever again, would he?

Blinking back the tears that threatened to overflow, she nonchalantly wrapped a T-shirt around the items before moving it out of the suitcase with the rest of her clothes.

Freddie rested his fists under his chin. "The look on those kids... *my* siblings' faces when they stared up at him. Like they thought he was the coolest guy."

"I'm sure they think he's wonderful. You did for a long time." *And I knew it would crush you when you found out the truth.*

Freddie's lip curled up in a snarl. "He's going to hurt them just like he hurts me and you and Tia."

"I say you should let my dad kick his ass." Tia used her spoon for emphasis as she spoke. "I bet my dad knows lots of ways to make it look like an accident."

"I honestly don't know what disturbs me more about that statement, Tia. The fact that you're so adamant when you said it or the fact it's truly tempting." Shelly gave her kids a wink before sweeping up her toiletry bag and pile of clothes into her arms. "Go on, leave me alone for a few. I'll be out and we'll get something ready for dinner."

"Mom, are you sure we can't order pizza?" Freddie asked, a bit of hope in his voice.

"If you want to pay for it, you can."

Immediately, he leapt off the bed, but paused when he got to the doorway and pointed. "Get naked? Gross, Mom."

"I think it's funny," Tia answered as she put her hand to his back and began to push him out the door. "It's her room, Freddie."

Leave it to kids to ignore the fact their parents are sexual creatures. "What? I'm not allowed to be naked? In my own bedroom?"

Freddie's deep voice carried from the hallway. "That was an image I didn't need, Mom."

"You do know how babies are made, right?"

"La-la-la-la-la…"

"What a weirdo." Tia closed the bedroom door behind them, leaving Shelly in the sanctum of her room.

As she began to put her makeup and other toiletries away, the realization that half the counter had nothing on it hit her hard.

Even fifty years from now, she wouldn't regret walking out of that tacky little chapel in Las Vegas, but sometimes being the adult in the relationship really sucked.

And being lonely sucked even more.

She stared at her reflection, appreciating the effort she'd made to keep herself healthy and strong over the years, especially after her pregnancies had wrecked her body of any chance of having any more children after Freddie.

The focus hadn't been a skinny ass, but a strong, healthy physique. A body that would be greatly appreciated by the right man for years, decades.

The kind of man she couldn't wait to see every day and one who made her feel deliciously sexy, even during those times when feeling desirable seemed impossible.

She opened her closet to place her suitcase away and noticed the beautiful off the shoulder Christmas-red dress she'd purchased for their New Year's Eve date.

Even when she tried it on in the bridal store, Married in Marietta, on Front Street, she imagined the zipper being slowly undone as the sheath dress slipped from her body and pooled at her perfectly manicured feet. She'd even purchased sparkly red stilettos. They were completely impractical for the frigid and at times icy parking lot of winters in Montana, but they made her feel sinfully sexy.

Now, like a cold bucket of water, these items would sit in her closet for some extended period of time, never seeing the light of day.

I guess the only time I'm going on a date wearing those will be with my own vibrator.

Her lips thinned as frustration brewed deep in her gut. Even with her hesitation to renew her vows with Gill, she couldn't deny her anticipation at having sex with an actual man again instead of battery operated machinery.

But after what he'd put her through, she decided she liked the machine better. "At least I know where the machine has been."

A soft knock on her door pulled her out of her introspection and made sure her new items were tucked away for another day.

"Aunt Shell. Can I come in?" Tia asked as she peeked her

head around the corner.

"Sure." Placing her bag in the back of her closet, she started to close the door when the fabric of the dress touched her arm. She relished the softness against her skin. "Man, I would have looked so good in this too."

"You would have. I think you should still find a date."

"For New Year's?" She turned off the light and closed the closet door behind her.

"Who?"

Her niece shrugged playfully. "I'm thinking someone new in town. Someone who might need a night out as well. Maybe a single dad."

It took about two seconds before excitement and fear simultaneously slammed into Shelly's brain. "You can't be serious. The man won't even remember me tomorrow."

"Of course he will."

The mere idea being on a date with Peter Davidson had Shelly's ovaries trembling with excitement. "He had a concussion. Patients often have short-term memory loss afterward."

"He's not Dory, Aunt Shell."

"I don't know. What about his kids?" The throbbing in her hands suddenly made Shelly realized she was wringing her hands until her fingers blanched. She wiggled her fingers loose from her grip.

"I'll babysit."

"Why would you do that?"

"Because all these years, I've seen the way Gill looked at you and he never, ever looked at you like Dr. Peter did."

"You've been watching too many romantic comedies." Shelly waved her off, then asked, "When would you have even seen him look at me anyway?"

"I came out to ask Aunt Sue for something and watched the way he looked at you when you two spoke." Tia crossed her arms and leaned against the counter. "I mean, it was so intense, I think I might have gotten pregnant."

"Oh, Lord, please don't tell me this is all a fancy way for you to tell me you're pregnant. Your father is going to kill me."

"Ugh! I'm not pregnant."

"Thank God." *Seriously, your father would have killed me.*

Tia snapped her fingers in Shelly's face. "Listen to me. That guy has a serious thing for you."

She wouldn't lie. The remote possibility that what Tia said was true did spark Shelly's interest. "I don't know. Even if I went out with him, what would Freddie think? You?"

"Please, Aunt Shell. We both want you happy. After that disaster of a wedding day, a disaster of an ex, we both think you deserve a nice guy."

"Freddie's on board with this?" For too many times to count, Shelly had abandoned having any sort of social life because of her son. She didn't want to drag him into any dating dilemmas or have him get attached to anyone that didn't work out, especially when he still hoped Gill would come around.

When Tia came to live with them a few years ago, a dating life simply wasn't in the cards for her at this point of her life.

"No, I haven't said anything to him, but if Dr. Peter is as cool as his brother and sister, I'd say go for it." Giving her aunt a quick hug, Tia added, "Besides, we'll be gone in the next couple of years. You deserve to find someone who makes you happy."

They will be gone and I'll be alone. "He did ask me out to a place that serves chicken tenders and macaroni and cheese."

"See, that's a big step. He wants you to go out with him and his kids."

"And if he forgets he even asked me because of his head injury, what am I supposed to do then?"

Tia fisted her hips and the corner of her mouth slowly curled up. "Are you telling me, that you, one of the fiercest, coolest, strongest women I know, is too scared to ask a man out?"

Even with the compliments, Shelly answered with as much conviction as a boneless chicken. "No."

Tia walked by her, opened the closet door, and flipped on the light. "You're telling me that the amazingly chill woman who wanted to wear this body-hugging dress, is afraid *that* guy will say no?"

Shelly cocked her head, remembering how incredible she looked, even under the harsh lights of the dressing room. "I would look good."

"Yes, you would. Now, I want you to really think about it. Okay?" She began to walk out. "I'm pitching in on the pizza. You want anything special?"

"Nope, I'm good with whatever." As her niece left her room and after the click of her bedroom door closing, Shelly ran her hands down the dress again.

"Could I?" she muttered to herself as she imagined a night out with wine and appetizers and *dessert.*

Remembering the way he brushed his lips on the back of her hand before they loaded him into the ambulance, sent ripples of desire through her. Even now, she shivered, wondering if Peter the Conscious kissed just as well as Peter the Concussed.

And how well he navigated zippers.

Chapter Nine

D UE TO THE time change, Peter had been woken by the kids' upbeat discussions at five in the morning.

Edmund's failed attempts to keep them quiet had only softened by the fresh smell of fresh-brewed coffee.

As Peter sat up, a sudden ache rippled through his back, making him cringe. The hard mattress of the sofa bed had proven to be as uncomfortable as he assumed it would be when he saw the sleeping arrangements, but he couldn't share a bed with either of his children for obvious reasons.

They'd slept in the two double beds of the suite and probably far more comfortably than he or Edmund, who'd taken the oversized chair, did.

As out of whack as his back felt, his head didn't pound or spin, but the repaired forehead laceration ached. He had no doubt he looked like he'd been on the wrong end of a bar fight, but at least he was still in one piece and nothing awful happened to the children.

"I need coffee," Peter mumbled as he noticed the darkness outside the window the two kids and his brother sat in front of. "What are you doing?"

"Morning, Bro." Edmund waved without looking back.

"Telling the kids where things are in town. See that house waaaaay back there with the star on it?"

Both children leaned forward, pressing their faces against the glass. The heat from their breaths fogged it up and they had to wipe it away before both of them insisted they saw what Edmund pointed out.

"That's where I live."

"Wow, Uncle Edmund. How did you get the star up there?" Digory's eyes were wide with surprise.

Taking a drink of his coffee, Edmund shook his head. "It took all day and my dog barked at me through the window the entire time, but it does look nice, doesn't it?"

"Some things never change." The memories of Edmund's insistence that he get to put the star on the top of their family Christmas tree every year flashed through Peter's mind. "Did you say you have a dog?"

"Yes. His name is Fred."

"Oh, I love the name Fred." Polly clapped. "Is he a fun dog?"

"He's really my girlfriend, Jade's, dog. He's great."

The slow drip of coffee into the small pot gave Peter a renewed sense of vigor. As he listened to the banter between his brother and his kids, he slowly stretched the kinks out of his back and neck.

My kids. He still paused when those two words ticker-taped through his mind, wondering what Simone told them about him and his siblings.

Watching the three over in the corner, he didn't observe any hint of angst or concern. In fact, Polly and Digory appeared to be completely happy talking to his younger brother and that gave Peter comfort she'd spoken favorably about them. *But how did you explain why I wasn't there?*

If they'd assumed he'd abandoned them, his transition into their lives would be far more difficult, especially when he had no idea why he'd been unknowingly erased.

So far, the children hadn't said anything one way or the other and they'd had little time to have a true heart-to-heart. He hoped they'd get the time they needed while here.

He glanced at his bag, knowing the answers might be waiting for him in her letter, but he couldn't read it now. He needed to be alone to absorb her words and accept what she'd say, even if he didn't want to hear it.

The coffee drip stopped and he filled the oversized Graff holiday coffee mug, before joining the happy trio. "Where's your house, Ed?"

Pointing, Edmund added, "It's across the street from the park. Two doors down from that big house on the corner there."

Because they were on the top floor of the hotel, they were able to see all the way to the far street where Edmund lived. As best as Peter could see, the top of a large house sat on the right end of the road that ran in front of the court-house and curved around toward Edmund's.

Although most of the lights in the building were dimmed, a streetlight and Christmas lights helped Peter get a general idea of the size of the place. "That something special?"

"It's the Bramble Bed and Breakfast. Descendants of one

of the founding families runs it. Across the street is Bramble Park. We take Fred there all the time." Edmund held his arms out wide. "There's a ton of snow over there. We can build a snowman."

"And ladies," Polly added.

Edmund gave her a thumbs-up. "And snowladies. And a fort and *tons* of snowballs."

"We're pretty good at making snowballs because we've lived in Maine our entire lives." Digory squared his shoulders.

"I bet."

"Does Fred like the park?" Polly took a long sip of her drink. "Will he jump in the snow?"

After a long swig of his coffee, Edmund nodded. "Yes, he loves being outside. I keep him out of trouble when he can play outside."

"Trouble?" Polly held her unicorn as she gently twisted the rainbow-colored tail between her fingers. "What kind of trouble?"

"He likes to chew things. A lot." Edmund's eyebrows arched for effect.

"Where did Aunt Jade find Fred?"

Edmund turned and sat on the windowsill, a wide-eyed look of wonder on his face. The very same look their father had when he would sweep them away with his magnificent storytelling.

The bittersweet memory uncomfortably pinched Peter's heart, making him flinch, but he pushed the pain aside.

He didn't want to grieve right now.

With the twinkling Christmas lights of the buildings along Front Street behind him, Edmund began, "Every year, there's a big party where different businesses in town decorate Christmas trees and people bid on them."

"Oh, trees! I love Christmas trees." Polly nodded enthusiastically.

Edmund continued, "Last year, this physical therapy place decorated their tree with pictures of all the cats and dogs from the shelter on them."

"Smart idea. Raise money for charity. Get animals adopted." Peter relished the coffee creamer cutting the bitter from his java before settling on his tongue. Waking up too early to a non-spinning brain was a welcome feeling, but watching his brother entertain his kids had been worth getting up before the sun. "Where does Fred come into the picture?"

"I'm getting to that, Bro. Jade was inspired to adopt a pet because she lived out on this property waaaaay outside of town and it was kind of lonely out there." As Edmund told his story, Peter's children hung on his brother's every word.

"Did she want an animal because she'd get scared at night? Sometimes I get scared," Polly admitted as she now pet her plush unicorn.

"I don't get scared," Digory interjected, but his sister grimaced.

"Yes, you do. You hate thunderstorms and you're afraid of scary movies."

"No, I'm not!"

"And spiders."

Digory stomped his foot. "So... you're scared of sharks and the giant squid."

"*Diablo Rojo* drags people down to the watery depths! I saw them on *National Geographic Wild*. They eat people's faces."

"You know they can come up from the bathtub pipes." Digory held his hands up like he stalked his sister and made a ghoulish noise.

She grabbed his hands and pushed back. "No, they can't!"

Peter had to stifle a laugh at his children's harassment of each other. It reminded him of many he and his siblings had growing up.

He gently pulled the kids apart and guided his son to sit on the couch near Edmund. "Red devil squid can't come to Marietta, Polly. There's no salt water and it's too cold."

"See!" She stuck her tongue out at Digory who shrugged.

Everyday, he learned something new about his children.

Now he discovered Digory's fear of spiders and Polly's concern about man-eating marine life. "I wanna hear how Jade got Fred, don't you?"

"Yes." His son flopped in the chair.

Edmund continued. "Jade went to the shelter after Christmas, but guess what?"

"What?" the children asked in unison.

"All the animals had been adopted!"

"All of them?" Polly asked, her eyes wide as half-dollars.

"All of them. Even a one-eyed dog, but... as she was driving home, she saw this poor, skinny dog on the side of the road running after a truck. The people had just dumped him in the cold and snow."

Digory clenched his fist and punched his opposite palm. "Grrrrrr, that makes me so mad when people are in-con-siderate."

"But Jade picked him up and brought him home and now he's all happy and fat and hides her keys."

"Hides her keys? Why does he do that?"

"Because Fred's weird."

"We never had a dog with Mommy because she said they were a lot of work." Digs shoved his hands in his pajama pockets. "We asked for a cat and she said no."

"Then we asked for a turtle and she said no." Polly held her unicorn to her chest. "Then we asked for a lizard and she said no way!"

"What about a goldfish? Did you ask for a goldfish?" Edmund gave a smirk he always did when he knew his input would stir the chaos.

"Come to think of it, we didn't ask for a goldfish." Polly held her finger up as though a lightbulb had come on over her head. "What if we—"

"Maybe Uncle Edmund can get a goldfish and keep it at *his* house and you can visit it there," Peter interjected playfully and patted his brother on the shoulder. "How about it Uncle Edmund. You up for a goldfish at your house?"

"*Touché, mon frère.*" Edmund scooped up his coat off the back of the chair.

"What does that mean?" Digory's nose crunched up.

"It means good job my brother," Polly answered as she sipped something from a disposable coffee cup.

"How do you know that?" Peter pointed. "What are you drinking?"

"Mommy told me I was really good at languages so she had our neighbor, Karen, teaching me French." Holding the cup up, she tapped it to Peter's mug. "It's hot chocolate, Daddy. Uncle Edmund made it for me. *Salut!*"

Only knowing the children for a short time, Peter was still learning their routines and moods and what time of day they each loved and thrived, but he hadn't heard his daughter speak one word of French until this very moment.

"Unbelievable." Edmund shook his head. "She's got your brain. Did you know your father speaks French, Italian, and Spanish?"

"*C'est vrai?*" Polly sat up taller.

"It's true." Peter smiled, his heart filled with happiness. "I took classes in high school and college. Lived in Europe for awhile too."

"Wow, Mommy was right. She always said I got that from you."

"She did?" The sharp sting of sadness sliced down Peter's throat at the mention of their mother. "Did she say anything else?"

"Yeah. She said I looked like you, but acted like you." Digory pointed to Peter then Edmund.

The brothers exchanged confused looks and Peter knew exactly what Edmund thought.

Why didn't she contact us?

Staring at his children, he could see the only love of his life. Polly was the spitting image of her mother with her long eyelashes, naturally deep tanned skin, rich dark hair and a smile that would light up a room in complete darkness.

Although Digory looked like a miniature Edmund, he mimicked Peter's expressions. The faint sprinkling of freckles on the bridge of his son's nose reminded Peter of his sister, Susan, but his son's complexion and introspection were exact copies of Simone.

So far, his son had shown to be a thoughtful kid who loved figuring things out. This included everything from recipes to Legos and anything he could take apart as shown by the disassembled robotic vacuum sitting in the middle of the children's living room floor.

"If you're good, I'm gonna take off." Edmund stood and stretched. "Gotta be at the ER at noon."

"Sounds great. Thanks for staying."

"Sure. Glad to have you here." Edmund looked back as he put on his coat. "All of you here."

"Thanks, Ed." Even with all the chaos they'd been through, the Davidson siblings were a tightly knit group and supported each other without question. "I know it's a lot to ask, coming here unannounced."

"They're great kids. Sorry you found out this way." Standing in the hallway, Edmund added, "Why don't we all plan on getting together in a couple of days. I think Lucy said she and Thomas were off on Saturday. I work that night."

"What day is today?"

"Thursday."

"It's December twentieth, Peter-Daddy. Christmas is in five days." Polly danced around her chair while holding her to-go cup of hot chocolate. "The *Timeless* movie is on tonight."

"Yeah! They are gonna save Rufus!" Digory held his fists in the air.

"What?" Peter smirked as his son's enthusiasm.

"It's a time travel show." Edmund playfully punched Peter in the arm. "Ask Lucy about it. She can catch you up."

"Fair enough."

"Maybe we can all get together for an early dinner. The kids can meet everyone at the same time."

"Perfect. Thanks." Peter nodded as his children threw "what if" scenarios back and forth about how the characters would rescue a guy named Rufus.

No sooner had the click of the door echoed into the room, Digory asked, "What's on the plan for today, Peter?"

As much as Peter wished his son would call him Dad, he understood why Digory didn't most of the time. "I thought we'd clean up. Get some breakfast. I didn't think we'd all be up this early and I don't think any place is open yet."

He took over the chair his brother recently vacated as the lights twinkled on the multiple buildings across the street from the Graff. "Tell me, what did Uncle Edmund tell you about the town?"

For the next half hour, the kids reiterated every detail of Edmund's explanation of Marietta. Every building. Every street. Every holiday event. By the time the sun began to rise, Edmund needed a much bigger cup of coffee and a very large plate of food.

Chapter Ten

"MAY WE JOIN you?"

Shelly looked up over her Main Street coffee cup and into the faces of two very bright-eyed kids and one sexy dad. Closing her book, she nodded and motioned to the empty places at her four-seater. "Please."

"You're here by yourself?" Peter unzipped his coat, draping it on the back of the chair as his children did the same.

The song, "Jingle Bell Rock," played in the background as the rich smells of java, fresh baked bread, and cooked meats filled the air.

Shelly tapped her watch. "Yes, I got a call from the ER this morning. They asked if I could come in for a few hours. Give someone time off to finish her Christmas shopping. I need to be there by ten."

"It's barely seven."

"Couldn't sleep. Might as well get up." In fact, between the lingering annoyance of her failed Vegas wedding and then meeting Dr. Sexy, Shelly's mind wouldn't turn off long enough for her to drift into peaceful rest for more than a few minutes at a time.

"My zipper's stuck." Polly turned to Shelly. "Will you

help me?"

"Of course."

"I can get that." Peter stepped forward, but Shelly waved him off.

"I've got it." *Good with zippers, are you, Dr. Sexy?*

With a quick flick of her wrist, Shelly backtracked the zipper and had it on track to unfasten. She helped Polly drape it over the backpack on the chair as Digory refused Peter's assistance.

"I got it." He haphazardly draped his coat over the back of his seat and plopped down.

Peter held his hands up in surrender at his son's rebuttal and approached Shelly after Polly took her seat.

His hand lightly rested on Shelly's back. "Thank you."

"No problem." She paused, her eyes snatched a glimpse of his full lips.

"Once again, you're here to help us."

"Glad to do it." When he kissed her on the cheek, it sent her body ablaze and her mind spinning with endless "what ifs."

Gabby Marcos, the diner's owner, placed a large cup of coffee in front of Peter and filled it just short of the rim. "Good morning."

Shelly blinked a few times before forcing her feet to move so she could sit back down. A wave of heat warmed her cheeks and she had to make a conscious effort not to fan herself with the menu. "Morning, Gabby."

"Morning, Shelly." Biting her lip as though she were preventing herself from saying something cheeky, Gabby's eyes moved back and forth between Shelly and Peter as they sat down. "Now that we have the formalities out of the way, I'm Gabby. What can I get y'all to eat?"

"Pancakes please." Digory held his hands wide. "A big stack."

"Want chocolate chips in those pancakes?"

Digory's eyes went wide but darted to Peter before answering, "Yes, please."

Interesting. He doesn't want his dad's help, but is making sure he can add chocolate to pancakes.

Shelly appreciated the respect Digory gave to his father, even though their relationship was so new.

"That okay, Dr. Davidson?" Gabby walked around the table and filled glasses with water.

The mug stopped halfway to his mouth. "How did you know who I was?"

Shelly smirked while she reined in her emotional fireworks. "News travels fast in this town, Peter. Not much gets by without someone saying something here in the diner."

The corner of Gabby's mouth curled up as a long lock of her rich, dark hair cascaded down the side of her face. "You look a lot like your siblings. Same kindness in your eyes. Plus, one of the guys that came to get you yesterday, is my fiancé. Kyle."

"I see." He scanned the room before his eyes rested on Shelly. "Guess I'd better get used to the small-town gossip train."

Shelly's heart flip-flopped with excitement. "Get used to? You planning to stick around?"

"We're staying here?" Digory's shoulder's slumped. "Ah, man."

Polly pulled out a stuffed unicorn from her backpack and began twisting the tail between her fingers.

Peter sighed as he put his mug down and patted his son's, then his daughter's arms. "I don't know what we're doing long-term yet. I just want to get through the day without a headache. You have any cream or milk, Gabby?"

"Give me a second." Gabby took off behind the counter and refilled every customer's mug until the pot ran dry. With the efficiency of a soldier, she quickly prepared another round on three different coffee machines after placing the half-full pots on the top burners.

"Sorry, I didn't mean to cause a problem." Shelly winced. "It's just that you said get used to and since we just met you all, it would be nice to get to know you, you know, better." *Stop talking. Stop talking.*

Polly smiled and momentarily quit pulling at the plush's tail. "That would be nice."

Peter agreed. "I'd like that. Still figuring things out. Going to take it day by day. Get through the holidays, first."

Shelly nodded as she wrapped her fingers around her coffee mug.

Polly put her toy away. "The people are nice here, but I miss my friends."

"Yes. I bet you do. Sounds like all of you have been through a lot in the past month." Shelly patted Polly's hand.

"Tell me about it." Digory rolled his eyes as Gabby returned to the table and placed a bowl of individual creamers in front of him.

"How is your head, Peter?"

He instinctively touched his forehead. "It's been better, but it's still functional."

"Dr. Reynolds does good work." The innocent kiss had Shelly's body trembling with unexplainable excitement and endless possibilities. With shaking hands, Shelly grabbed a creamer and managed to open it without spilling it all over the table. *Get a grip. It was a gesture of appreciation.*

"Griffin, our cook, cut his hand open last month and Dr. Reynolds sewed him up beautifully. The scar is almost invisible." Gabby pulled a pencil from her pocket and tapped on a notepad with the eraser. "Now, I know just about everyone in this town, who might you two be?"

Peter presented his children. "These are my kids Polly and Digory."

They gave a wave and Polly's eyes lit up as though she remembered something. "You look like Gina Rodriguez."

His forehead furrowed. "Who's that?"

"She's on a TV show Mommy used to watch," Polly answered matter-a-factly. "*Jane the Virgin.*"

"I love that show." Gabby gave Polly a high five.

Digory's eyes went wide as though he remembered something. He pointed at Shelly. "You look like Persephone."

"Persephone? Wife of Hades?" *Great, I'm the wife of the dead. I didn't think I looked that bad.*

"What are you talking about, Son?" Peter's forehead furrowed as he mouthed "Sorry."

"In the movie. *Percy Jackson.* You look like—"

"Rosario Dawson." Gabby put her fist to her hip as she nodded. "Yes, yes I can see that, although I liked the books better. Didn't you?"

"We did." Polly gave an enthusiastic thumbs-up.

"I guess that makes you a goddess." Peter smirked as he put his hand over his mouth as if the word had slipped out.

Heat rose in Shelly's cheeks hearing him refer to her so endearingly. "I appreciate the compliment."

"Anytime."

"Mommy says… said Gina and Rosario are fierce." Polly gave everyone a stressed smile.

Hearing the child use past tense with her mother hurt Shelly's heart. *Damn. What these kids are going through. I can't imagine.*

Shelly's mother, Zora, still called her weekly and the women got together at least once a month. *Losing your mom at the age of nine?*

Shelly fought back tears just considering it. *Ugh, I'd be a horrible wife of the dead if I cried for everyone.*

A momentary look of understanding flashed across Gabby's face. "Your mommy's correct, Polly. Gina Rodriguez and Rosario Dawson are wonderfully fierce. Thank you for sharing that with me. Us."

A look of pride washed across Polly's face. "You're welcome. Do you have cinnamon pancakes?"

"For you, anything you want." Gabby wiped away an escaped tear. "Might I suggest a bit of a twist? I make this amazing orange cinnamon bread that I use for French toast. Would you be willing to try that?"

"Gabby does make an incredible French toast," Shelly agreed before dabbing her nose with the napkin. "I debated between that and the breakfast tacos on my way here."

"*Mais oui!*" Polly applauded. "Orange cinnamon *pain perdu, s'il vous plaît.*"

"Again with the French. *Mon dieu.*" Peter chuckled. "*Bien joué.*"

"Are you two speaking French?" Shelly motioned between Polly and Peter.

"Peter, I mean Dad, and I speak French, but he also speaks Italian and Spanish."

"Good Lord." Without thinking, Shelly fanned herself with her menu, but immediately put it down when it registered what she'd done.

A spontaneous round of laughter burst from the adults.

"*Hablo español.*" Gabby motioned to an empty table to a trio that entered.

"*¿Y usted?* I had to know it working the ERs in Florida. A lot of tourists and citizens from Puerto Rico, Central and South America." He turned toward Gabby. "You?"

"I'm from Texas. Everyone speaks it in my family." Gabby patted Peter's shoulder. "*¿Qué querías desayunar?*"

"What do I want for breakfast?"

"*Sí.*"

His gaze rested on Shelly and for a moment, the world disappeared. His green eyes easily bypassed her defenses and settled deep into her soul. "What are you having?"

"Say it in Italian, Dad." Polly clapped excitedly. "Ask Miss Shelly what she wants."

I want whatever he says in Italian.

A sudden blush of color appeared on his cheeks. "*Cosa desidera mangiare?*"

Oh Lord. Who thought ordering breakfast could sound so invigorating? Nervously, she rearranged her silverware in no particular pattern. "I-I-I'm having breakfast tacos."

With a quick wink, he tapped his menu on the table. "Ms. Gabby, Lucy said you make a great breakfast taco."

Gabby stared at her order pad, her lower lip tucked neatly under her front teeth as a smile spread across her face. "That I do. How many do you want?"

"I'll take three. What do you think, Shelly?"

In the morning light and with the sounds of Christmas all around him, Peter Davidson looked far more awake and dashingly handsome.

Oh, there are so many things I think right now. "I like bean and cheese, bacon, potato, and egg. One with *pico* and one with *tomatillo* sauce."

"You have homemade *pico de gallo* and *tomatillo*? Love that stuff."

"One of each. Wanna try pepper bacon and potato?" Gabby topped off his coffee before heading to another group that just arrived.

"Sounds good."

"Three tacos. Shelly, you're having two?"

"Yes, two." Holding her mug with both hands, she figured she'd have better success getting much needed caffeine to her mouth instead of her nervous hands spilling it all over the table.

"Okay, we'll have that out ASAP." Gabby grabbed three coffee mugs and took them to the newest customers.

"Take out, ready!" Griffin, the cook, called out as he placed a paper lunch bag on the counter. "I got two more coming."

"Thank you, Griffin," Casey called out as she took a customer's order at the counter. Her jingle bell earrings sparkled and chimed when she moved her head.

Pepper Christmas lights twinkled above her.

"Peter. Dad," Polly whispered. "That spiky haired girl has a nose piercing."

"Yes, I see that."

"I sure hope she doesn't get a cold. I don't know how she'd blow her nose with that thing there." Polly shrugged.

"You know, I'd never thought about that before." Shelly laughed out loud. "That's Casey. Her brother, Brett, is a K-9 officer here in town and she's going to school for court reporting."

"What's a K-9 officer?" Digory cocked his head. The inquisitive look on his face reminded Shelly of Peter.

"He has a dog that he works with. Duke."

"Oh! A police dog. Like Uncle Edmund's dog?"

Peter set his mug in front of him. "I don't think Fred's a police dog. For one, Fred steals stuff."

For the next several minutes, the children caught Shelly up on their morning and what they could do in town for the day. Shelly had always loved conversations around the table. Growing up, she'd dreamed of a large family and many discussions over food she lovingly prepared or picked up, depending on which was easier.

It took no time before the subject of Fred the dog's weird thievery habits rolled back into discussion. "You're right! He does steal things. I have to hide my keys when I walk to their house."

"You know, Jade?" Peter leaned forward, his thumb resting inside the handle of his coffee cup.

"Yes, she's one of my good friends." *She's also the one who told me not to remarry Gill.* Shelly sucked in a breath, hoping if she'd let those words escape into the air, she could suck them back in. The last thing she wanted to discuss this morning, was her faithless ex.

"Then you live close to Edmund?"

Relief flooded her, knowing she hadn't said anything about Gill out loud. "Yes, we live down the street from them, across the street from Gabby and Kyle and a few houses away from Lucy and Thomas."

"Here you go, kiddos." Flo, a longtime waitress of Main Street Diner placed a couple of crayons and *National Geographic* coloring pages on the table. "In case they wanted to draw something for our wall."

"Nat Geo!" The children quickly compared pages.

Digory got a panda bear, Polly, a red-eyed tree frog.

Peter held his hand out to shake. "You're the famous Flo."

"That's me." She responded in kind. "And you're the famous Peter, your sister and brother always talk about. Now who are these cuties?"

"These are my kids Polly and Digory."

Her eyebrow cocked. "Like from that book. Oh, what was it?"

"*The Magician's Nephew*," Digory interjected before he went back to work coloring the border.

"From Narnia!" Polly grabbed a blue crayon.

"Yes, of course, but your brother and sister never mentioned they had a niece and nephew."

Peter shifted in his chair, his jaw clenched. "It's a recent development."

"Well, it's sure nice to have you all here." Without a hint of judgmental commentary, Flo patted his shoulder before filling more cups of coffee at neighboring tables.

"That's it?"

"That's what?" Shelly blissed out on the perfect balance of bitter and sweet in her coffee as the chorus of "Grandma Got Run Over by a Reindeer" played over the speakers.

The front door bells chimed when a few other customers left. The cold air rushed in, causing the hanging holiday decorations closest to the door to sway for a few moments before settling back to rest.

"She's not going to ask about them?" Peter took the yellow crayon Polly offered.

Out of the corner of her eye, she watched Digory glance up and see Peter helping Polly. Reaching out, Digory picked up a red crayon and cautiously offered it to Shelly, who accepted and started to fill in a flower.

"Flo's not one to gossip. She'll eventually find out what's going on because people talk in here, but she's never one to spread gossip. Now, Carol Bingley at the pharmacy and

Betty, she works at the police department, those two *love* to gossip."

And I'm sure they are having a wonderful time talking about my chaos.

With purposeful strokes, Peter filled in several leaves on a tree. "At the pharmacy, huh? Guess she keeps track of people's *personal* purchases."

"And that's why people buy their condoms in Bozeman." Shelly nodded.

"What's a condom?" Polly inquired as she switched colors with her father.

"You can fill them with water and drop them off the tops of the house," Shelly answered without missing a beat.

"Kind of like water balloons." Digory stuck his tongue out as he colored the background.

"Yes. Exactly." Shelly learned long ago if parents got weird about words, it only stirred curiosity and more questions. Confident answers always shortened awkward conversations.

"You're good." Peter raised an eyebrow.

"I try." Tingles danced across her body at his appreciative stare.

The intoxicatingly rich smells of vanilla and fresh baked bread drifted around them as the kitchen continued to place order after order on the pass-through window.

Booths lined two main walls and all along the front windows. Tables big enough to seat four to eight people filled in the rest of the room. The retro chairs had steel frames and chrome finishes. The solid sparkly vinyl covers were different colors at each table.

Their table had a green, a blue, a yellow, and a pink one. Polly claimed the yellow chair, Digory the green.

Every red leather-covered, short back stool at the long counter had a customer either reading the paper or working on their phones.

The seats were solidly grounded into the wooden floor, but appeared to swivel with ease.

The large kitchen pass-through window was big enough to get a quick view of how far back the kitchen stretched and to the left, a set of three-quarter, wooden swinging doors, decorated with gold garland, led to the back.

On the far wall, a large mural appeared to be the town as though someone were looking at it from the mountains.

The extraordinary detail indicated it had taken hours to painstakingly present every commercial building and street labeled perfectly.

"Peter-Dad, she has a Christmas tree." Polly motioned to the corner of the counter where a small tree had been decorated with miniature kitchen utensils.

"She sure does." Peter nodded as he handed the crayon back.

"When are we going to get our tree, Dad?" Digory asked as he hung his coat on the back of the chair after it had fallen to the floor.

"A tree?" A look of panic filled his eyes. "You want a tree?"

Oh, gosh. What's that about?

"Of course, silly." Polly giggled. "Everyone who celebrates Christmas gets a tree. How do you get the Christmas sprit without it?"

Clearing his throat, Peter slowly shook his head. "Um, we're staying in the hotel, not really a place to have a tree there."

The sparkle in his daughter's eyes dimmed. "No tree? Not even a little one? A pretend one?"

Shelly's heart broke witnessing Polly's bottom lip quiver. "Sweetie, there are going to be a bunch of trees all around town for the charity auction and in the lobby of the hotel."

Nodding, Peter added, "Didn't Lucy and Edmund say something about hot chocolate?"

"Hot chocolate isn't a tree." Digory crossed his arms over his chest and slouched in his seat. "It's enough you tried to kill Santa, now you won't get us a tree."

Oh, man. This got complicated really quick. Shelly wasn't sure if she needed to help or step back. Looking at Peter, she cringed at the stress on his face.

He clenched his jaw before exhaling a long breath. "Look, kids. I'm trying here. I'm really trying, but we're all learning about each other right now. It's a lot to process."

"I want a tree," Digory huffed.

"I want a tree, too." Polly sniffled. "Is it because you hit Santa? Santa's okay, right? Are we on the naughty list?"

"Santa's fine and no we're not on the naughty list." Peter rubbed the bridge of his nose.

"*We* aren't Polly, because *we* weren't driving." Digory glared at his father.

"Great. I have an accident with one mythical character

and I'm Satan." Peter clenched his jaw.

Biting her tongue to keep from laughing, Shelly realized the good doctor needed a bit of help. Grabbing the children's hands, she tugged them toward her. "Did you know the Graff, the hotel you're staying in, has a Christmas tree auction?"

"It does? What's an auction?" Digory's eyes narrowed.

"A contest. A Christmas tree contest."

Digory's eyes lit up. "Uncle Edmund said something about that. Last year, a therapy place won and all the animals got adopted."

Excitement quickly replaced Polly's sadness. "At our hotel?"

"Yes, and I believe they have activities during the day like cookie decorating and Santa comes to visit on the weekends. That's on Saturday. Day after tomorrow."

The kids leaned in closer to her. Before she could continue, she noticed the grateful nod of their father and that had Shelly feeling warmer than a shot of cinnamon Fireball. "We can take you all to Miracle Lake for ice skating and maybe some snowball fights in Bramble Park."

Digory snapped his stubby fingers. "That's where Fred goes."

"Jade's dog? Yes, Fred goes there."

"And you have Freddie. Fred. Freddie." Polly laughed. "What else? What else?"

The idea sat in her head for about two seconds before it fell out of her mouth without hesitation. "Since you're staying in a hotel and don't have any place to put a tree, what if you went with me and my kids to pick one out at Scott's Christmas tree farm?"

"I've always wanted to go to a Christmas tree farm. We always went to the local guy down the street for a tree." Polly grabbed her backpack and pulled out her journal and flipped to the calendar. "What day do you want to go?"

Drumming his fingers on the counter, Peter gave a stressed smile. "Polly, why don't we let Ms. Shelly decide?"

"Tomorrow?" blurted out before any thought came to her.

Good grief. Could you sound any more desperate? "I mean, if you're free."

Peter looked over Polly's shoulder. "What do you think, Polly? What's on our schedule?"

"I have us down to watch *Timeless* tonight, but we don't have anything scheduled for tomorrow." She tapped the pen to the paper. "We are totally free on Friday."

"Tomorrow it is. I'll pick you up around ten." Elation washed over her, followed by a pinch of panic.

"It's a date." Digory held out his hand to shake and Shelly accepted his gesture.

"Yes, I guess it is." *A date?*

Excitement and terror simultaneously lodged in her throat. She hadn't been on a date for almost twenty years.

Oh, Lord. What have I done?

"Yay, a date." Polly jumped from her chair and threw her arms around Shelly's neck. "You're the best, Ms. Shelly."

"Thank you, Polly." Holding the sweet child in her arms brought a sudden onset of tears. The stressors of the last two days and lack of sleep had finally caught up with her. Shelly couldn't fight them off, no matter how hard she tried.

Great job. He'll think you're a blubbering mess.

By the time Polly sat back down, Flo set a bottle of syrup and more napkins on the table, letting them know their food was on the way.

Shelly couldn't be more grateful for the distraction. She dried her eyes with her napkin as Peter reached across the table and laid his hand flat in front of her.

"You okay?"

She smiled through her tears. "Yes, I'm completely fine."

"Here we go." Gabby arrived with two plates and Casey came up right behind her with the rest.

Flo refilled coffees and waters while verifying everyone's orders before helping other customers.

As they ate and continued upbeat conversation, Shelly couldn't help but look around the table and wonder what it would be like if Tia and Freddie were here.

And they could all enjoy this meal like a big family.

A family?

Shelly mentally shook her head as she blissed out on breakfast. Somewhere between the bite of the cerrano mixed with tomatillos, she attempted to devour her amotions away from crazy ideas like blended families and happily ever afters.

No, Shelly, don't even go there.

But her heart had no intention of listening.

Chapter Eleven

WITH FULL BELLIES, Peter and the kids said their good-byes to Shelly and headed down Main Street.

He glanced back to watch her walk across the street before disappearing around the ice cream store.

Her compassionate nature and ability to immediately bond with his children had him wanting to know her a whole lot better.

Woman warms my soul in more ways than one.

When a strong gust of wind blew by, Peter decided a hat and gloves were in order to keep him warm when she wasn't close by.

They stopped in the western wear store down from the diner and met Joanie Monroe, the owner. She gave them a quick overview of the layout and offered a few thoughtful suggestions about which gloves might work for Peter before returning to customers at the counter.

Polly requested a few scarves and one beautiful embroidered coat for Christmas.

"For Christmas?" Peter's mouth went dry.

Oh, shit. First no tree. Second, no presents.

Frustration threatened to ruin the fantastic breakfast he'd

consumed an hour ago.

Way to go, Pops. You'd better get your ass on Amazon Prime.

He'd barely had time to think, much less shop for gifts in the past month. "Polly, can you write those things down in your journal so I don't forget?"

"I can help her." Joanie held her arm out to Polly, who quickly accepted. "Come on, sweetie. Show me what you like."

"Thank you, Ms. Monroe."

"It's Joanie." She winked.

The more people he met in town, the more Peter understood why his siblings liked it here. People cared.

They looked out for each other and they were quick to offer a helping hand to anyone who needed one. Everyone had been thoughtful and positive, something that would be hard pressed, but not impossible, to find in the chaos of a big city.

Peter wondered if they'd lived in a community like this after his father's death, how differently the Davidson siblings' lives would have been. Would they have struggled as much?

Would more people have stepped up to help?

Would Susan and he have been given the chance to stay teens instead of becoming instant parents to their younger siblings?

"Hey, Peter." Digory held up a pair of gloves with a red bear paw on them. "Can I get these?"

Pulling himself back to center, Peter inspected the thick

material. "They look warm, but don't you have a pair already?"

Digory pulled out his black gloves from his coat pocket. "Yeah, but I like the colors on these."

The striped gloves had a maroon five-fingered bear paw embroidered on them.

"That's the University of Montana logo, by the way," Joanie called out before walking behind the counter and helping the line of customers that had formed. "If you get two more, it's thirty percent off the least priced pair."

"Dad! Can I have these?" Through clenched fingers, Digory impatiently shook the gloves. "Please."

"Why? I just got you some gloves two days ago when we were in the Chicago airport."

"But these have a bear paw on them."

Polly shook her finger. "Bears don't have five fingers. Don't you remember that from Scooby-Doo? That's how Velma knew it wasn't a real ghost bear because real bears only have four claws."

Giving his sister a stay-out-of-this face, Digory moved around her and shoved the gloves in Peter's face. "Can I have them anyway? They look like Gryffindor colors."

Gently pushing the items away from his nose, Peter shook his head before grabbing a blue ski cap and a pair of matching gloves. "Add them to your Christmas list, Son. You've got a nice pair of gloves already."

"Yeah, but these are cool and there's only two pairs left."

"Yes, they are, but that's not what we're doing right now."

"Why do you get gloves and I don't?" Digory snapped, making several Christmas shoppers' heads turn in the store.

Peter stopped in his tracks and slowly turned as multiple women watched, eyes wide with anticipation of Peter's next move.

Is this what parenting's like? Everyone judging you anyplace you go? "Son, I get you like them, but you have a nice pair of gloves right now. Put them on your Christmas list."

"But—"

"Christmas is less than a week away. Put the gloves back."

Digory's jaw set as fire burned in his eyes.

Peter knew that look all too well. The fury of being in a situation he had no control over. Would his son be more like himself or Edmund because if Digory chose the latter, all hell was about to break loose.

"Fine." His son chunked the gloves back in the bin and locked his arms across his chest.

Peter exhaled a breath and scanned the room of the on-lookers, who gave him approving nods.

As Polly got her journal put back into her bag and thanked Joanie in French—of course—for her help, Peter paid for his purchases.

Polly tried to make lighthearted conversation with her pouting brother while Peter leaned forward and whispered, "Can you hold those gloves and whatever she picked out for me to come get later?"

An all-knowing smirk spread across Joanie's face. "I figured you'd say that. I'll have it all behind the counter."

"Feel free to go ahead and ring it up in case I need to send Edmund or Lucy in here."

"We appreciate your business, Dr. Davidson." She handed his card back.

"Can we go?" Digory stewed by the front door.

"Being a dad is fun." Peter sighed.

Joanie nodded. "It's got good days and bad days, that's for sure. Just keep breathing and always have a couple of beers chilled in the fridge ready to go."

"That's good advice." With his new gloves and hat on, Peter didn't cringe when they stepped out into the frigid temperatures again. Walking from the Graff to the Main Street Diner for breakfast almost did him in for the day, but the new clothes gave him renewed hope he wouldn't give up before lunchtime.

"It's so beautiful. Let's look around, Pe… Daddy." Polly took his hand and pointed to the decorations along the sidewalk. "Daddy."

Daddy. Tears of joy at hearing her say that simple word, threatened to choke him, but he swallowed them back and extended his hands. "Sounds great, Polly. Digory?"

With his arms still crossed, Digory emphatically shook his head refusing Peter's offer, but walked alongside them.

The sun peeked out between the overcast sky as they soaked in the sights and sounds of Christmas.

Main Street had been decked out with twinkling lights, rich green garland on every light pole, and wreaths on doors.

Storefront displays captured the colors of the season. Beautiful reds, greens, silvers, and golds flashed on trees, around windows, and on merchandise.

In the Java Café, small tea and coffee cups with reindeer on them surrounded the bottom of a stack of red and green books in the shape of a tree. Blue and white stringed lights were draped over the stacks.

The nail salon had a huge Christmas tree display made of nail polish arranged in tiers with decorative colors as photos of holiday themed nail art hung over it.

Once they reached the boutique at Main and Third Streets, they crossed over and headed back toward the Copper Mountain Chocolate Shop.

"Can we at least have hot chocolate?" Digory snarked as they approached the travel agency next to the chocolate shop. "You *owe us* that much."

Peter stopped in his tracks. A surge of frustration hit the front of his brain as he turned to his son. Anger flashed through Digory's eyes and Peter remembered that same fury when life so cruelly changed for the Davidson children, but he wouldn't allow his son to be disrespectful.

Searching for the right words, Peter eyed the pictures of the beaches in Hawaii in the travel agency's display window and wished they were there right now. "I owe you?"

Digory's eyes went wide as dinner plates as though the words had finally registered. "Um…"

"Look, I get you're mad. I understand it more than you know, but you don't get to act like an entitled brat every time you don't get what you want."

Mentally, Peter cringed at the irony of his statement. He remembered his father saying the same thing to him and each of his siblings when they'd acted like idiots.

Digory's bottom lip quivered.

The sight stabbed at Peter's heart, but he wouldn't raise a jerk of a kid. *I've been a father for three weeks and this already sucks.*

So far, he and Digory had butted heads, but it hadn't gone farther than that. Peter had a feeling with the impending holiday and being away from their home, the kids would soon give up decent manners and go full-on meltdown.

"Wow." Polly's eyes were as wide as half-dollars.

"What is it, Polly?" Peter knelt down, the knee of his jeans immediately wet and cold as soon as it touched the sidewalk.

"Mommy would say the same exact thing to us when we were bad." Fat tears rolled down her cheeks before she threw herself into his arms. "I miss her."

Without warning, Digory wrapped his arms around his father and smashed his face into Peter's coat collar. "I want my mom."

Great sobs erupted from his son and all Peter could do was hug them both tightly right there on the cold wet sidewalk.

With the constant bombardment of legal paperwork, funeral arrangements, and the kids still being in school, the last few weeks had been a blur and had given none of them true time to grieve or even talk.

Peter had shed a few tears at the funeral, but he'd not allowed himself to face his sadness of Simone's death because he'd already lost her ten years before.

Now, here they all were, huddled together on the slushy sidewalk in the freezing cold, crying.

"We're going to be okay, buddy. I promise," Peter coaxed, but he didn't know exactly whom he was trying to convince.

His kids or himself.

"I miss her so much," Digory croaked. "I miss my mom."

"I bet you do, Son. She was a good woman."

"The best mom ever."

"The best mom ever." Yet, as much as Peter wanted to believe that, he wanted answers more. *Why didn't you tell me, Simone? What did I do to make you keep all of you out of my life?*

"Peter. Dad?" Digory lifted his head, his face stained with tears.

"Yes, son?" Drying his son's face with his glove, Peter held Digory close.

"Can we get out of the cold, now?"

"I think that's a good idea." With his knees freezing and soaked, he gave his children another hug before getting to his feet. As soon as he stood, Polly gasped and pointed.

Peter turned to see Mr. Nicolas sauntering up the street, wearing a heavy dark green coat, black boots, and a broad smile.

"Santa!" Polly jumped up and down.

"Well, hello Polly, Digory, and Dr. Davidson." Huffing and puffing, he extended a hand to shake as one rested on Peter's shoulder. "How are you today, sir?"

"Better. Thank you for asking. You okay?" Peter nodded and once again, a wave of calm washed over him. "You look like you're having a little trouble breathing."

"Got my inhaler." He patted his front pocket and took a labored breath. "What's this? Have all of you been crying?"

"Yes." Polly rubbed her eyes, but held onto Peter's hand.

"It's supposed to be the most wonderful time of year. What could cause such tears?" He held his hands out in grandiose fashion before succumbing to several tight coughs. The shiny buckle of his thick black belt sparkled from the sunshine.

"That's kind of a loaded question, Mr. Nicolas. You sure you're okay?" *He looks like he's working too hard to breathe.*

Digory wiped his nose with the back of his gloved hand. "Yes, sir. I'll tell you. My mom died, sir."

With such news, most would crumble and walk way, but the man's joy shifted to compassion as he knelt in front of Digory. Mr. Nicolas took the child's non-snotted hand. "I'm so sorry to hear that, Digory. Moms are special people."

"Yes. I miss her so much. Every day."

"Of course you do, son. Of course you do." Cocking his head, the man pointed to Peter. "Digory, did you know your father understands what it's like to lose someone?"

Peter almost asked how Santa... Mr. Nicolas would know that, but with Lucy in town for the last several months and him being a frequent ER visitor, Peter's guess was Lucy had told him their story.

Digory sniffed and shook his head. "No."

Despite the gentle wording, the sadness of the day that

changed everything in the lives of the Davidson siblings sat forefront. "I do, Digory. I lost my dad to a car accident."

"You did?"

"Yes, I did."

"I didn't know that," he replied through sniffs. "What did you do?"

Moving backward, Mr. Nicolas encouraged Peter to take his place and for the first time in a long time, Peter felt the possibility of hope in this chaotic situation.

With his arm around his daughter, Peter brought the three to face each other. "My brother and sisters and mom and I, we worked together. We helped each other every day."

"How long did it take?"

"For what, Digory?"

"Not to be sad anymore." Polly dried her eyes with her unicorn, leaving a faint line of glitter on her cheek.

"There are days when I'm still sad, but it doesn't hurt as much." Peter rested a hand on each of his children's faces. "I want you to always love and remember your mom. When you need to talk about it, I'll be here. So will your aunts and uncles."

"And Miss Shelly?"

Without even trying, the woman had become an integral part of their lives. "Yes, even Miss Shelly, but let's work together to help each other because I really want to be your dad."

"You do?" Leaning forward, Digory touched his forehead to Peter's. "Really? You're not just saying that because you're here now?"

The question cut Peter deeply. *What had Simone told them about me?* "Son, I can't imagine anything I want to be more right now."

"Anything?" Polly joined them, touching her face to theirs.

A quick gust of wind whipped around the corner and plowed into them, sending them slightly sideways.

"Except maybe warm. I'd like to be warm, right now." Peter stood and tilted his chin toward Copper Mountain Chocolate Shop. "How about it?"

"Yes, please." Digory nodded and took his father's hand.

"Polly?"

"*Oui.*" She grabbed his other hand.

"What about you, Mr. Nic—" The man had vanished. Peter craned his neck but in the holiday foot traffic, there wasn't a hint of the jolly old elf anywhere.

As they walked toward the chocolate shop, Peter caught a glimpse of the eccentric gentleman turning the corner a block away. Before he was out of sight, he turned to Peter and touched his finger beside his nose and nodded.

Peter responded in kind as Digory yanked on his father's hand.

"Dad!" Digory tugged. "Dad, come on. They have a big cauldron of chocolate in there. Like Harry Potter. Dad!"

Dad? "What?"

"Dad. Look!" Digory pointed at the colorful display in the window, but the only thing Peter could focus on was the word.

That simple three-letter word he never thought he'd hear

his son say with such joyous enthusiasm.

Glancing back where Mr. Nicolas stood, the man gave a quick wink and disappeared around the corner.

Peter said a silent thank-you because for first time in far too long, he began to believe in the magic of Christmas.

Chapter Twelve

"PATIENT IN ROOM four is sleeping now. Respirations are twenty-six. Less labored, no retractions. Oxygen level is ninety-eight." As her fingers flew over the keyboard, Shelly updated Dr. Tom Reynolds on the patients that still remained in the ER after their morning rush. "Room six hasn't vomited since that second dose of Zofran. In room twelve, Mr. Nicolas said he's feeling better after his third breathing treatment and would like to go home because he has things do get done before Tuesday."

"What's Tuesday?"

"Christmas." *And I am not ready for it at all.* Especially since she'd impulsively invited Peter and his children over to decorate their nonexistent tree tomorrow.

"Right." Tom flicked one of the flashing lights that decorated the central desk. "Don't want to keep one of Santa's helpers out of commission."

Sue Westbrook turned and asked, "Did you ever get an answer about how he got that sleigh out on Highway 87?"

"The one Peter crashed into? Mr. Nicolas tricked it out with a lawn mower motor and added treads, but he lost control." Shelly entered in room six's last set of vital signs.

Mr. Nicolas had come in for months to get his asthma treated as he would wait until his symptoms got bad enough he needed more help than his rescue inhalers could provide.

Shelly smiled at the jolly man's sweet nature, but had a bit of frustration against him for driving a tricked-out sleigh on icy roads. "Room three is new. Has a two week history of headache, tooth pain, and green snot."

"That's disgustingly accurate. What's Edmund doing?" Tom yawned, stretching as he stood.

"Dr. Davidson was called upstairs to help with a delivery. They're really busy up there. Apparently, there was a big winter storm about nine months ago and the ob-gyns and midwives are maxed."

"Better him working maternity than me. That was my least favorite rotation in medical school and ER residency."

"Not my favorite either." *Liar.*

Early in nursing school, Shelly considered becoming a midwife because she'd loved her OB-GYN rotation, but that was before having Freddie.

Before Gill stopped looking at her as his wife when she couldn't carry another baby to term and he started venturing to younger pastures.

She shook off the melancholy that threatened to take hold every time she thought about it too long.

I have Freddie. I have Tia. I'm blessed to have those beautiful children in my life.

Sue chuckled, making her jingle-bell earrings shake. "Happens every time with a natural disaster or when the cable goes out. Babies. Babies. Babies. You'd think people would pick up a book every once in a while."

"That's the solution to over population, Mrs. West-brook? Literacy?"

"Can't hurt."

"True." Drumming his fingers on the counter next to the bobblehead Buddy the Elf, Tom picked up an iPad. "Let me know when room six uses the bathroom. After he urinates and finishes this bag of fluids, let's redo vitals."

"Right, his tilt test was pretty positive."

"Sixty-eight beats a minute laying down to one forty standing is significant enough I'm concerned about him hydrating well enough to go home." He turned to Sue. "How are we on hospital beds? Any open?"

"Yes, the doctors sent a bunch of patients home today since Christmas is in a few days. A lot of people were *suddenly* well enough to take their medication and complete their physical therapy." Sue tapped her computer screen. "Yes, there are three open beds on the med/surg floor so if you need to admit, let me know. I'll give the charge nurse a call."

"Thanks, Sue. When was the last recimic epi treatment on the kid in four?"

Shelly scanned the respiratory therapist's last entry. "About an hour ago and steroids were given two hours ago."

"Okay, keep watching him. Give him another hour. He drinking okay?"

"I just weighed a very wet diaper." *Man, I have such a glamorous life.*

"Doesn't sound like she'll need an IV, then. I'll go see green snot person."

"Good luck." Before Shelly finished her charting, she asked, "Hey, Sue. Can I get you any coffee?"

"No, sweetie." She held up a large to-go mug. "I'm all set. How late you staying?"

"Lucy asked me to come in until about two so I'll head home when Dave and Jade get back from their lunch breaks. Pepper said she needed a few hours to finish her Christmas shopping." Shelly took the chair next to one of the few members of Gill's family she got along with.

"Nice of you to come in and help out."

"Might as well. It's not like I need to use my vacation time for my honeymoon right now." *Since Gill's off with his young, baby-making girlfriend.*

Sue pursed her lips before taking a quick drink of her coffee. "You know how I felt about my nephew."

"Yeah, I do." More than once, Sue had made it clear to anyone within earshot that Gill would never fall on her favorite list. "And that alone should have discouraged me from ever believing anything the man had to say."

"I love you as if you were my own daughter. You're a good woman, like your mother and a good woman deserves a good man." Sue squeezed Shelly's hand. "Zora fell in love with your dad as soon as she saw him. Said she knew a good man and snatched him up before someone else did. She thinks everyone has the capability to fall in love like that, but they don't."

"No, they don't." She tapped her pen on the counter. "At least it's not the kind of love that lasts."

"I hope she finally sees what a slime Gill is. She has to."

"Not everyone can be my dad or your husband." Shelly shrugged.

"Sadly, no. They can't. A lot don't want to be, including my nephew but lucky for me and your mom, we did snag two perfect men."

"Do you believe in love at first sight?" Why she asked the question, Shelly couldn't be sure. She'd never been a believer, even when she did love Gill.

"Yes, absolutely. Why?" Sue pulled a patient's billing sheet off the printer.

"Gill told me he loved me on the first date, but people don't really fall in love like that, do they?"

Sue shrugged. "I don't know. Your father and mother, me and my Louis. We're all doing pretty good and I loved Louis the moment I saw him."

Unconvinced, Shelly crossed her arms across her chest. "Don' t you think that was lust?"

"For certain, but lust isn't what kept us together for this long. No, honey, when it's love, it lasts."

The numerous conversations Shelly had with her mother over the years about her marriage and then divorce had given Shelly more than her share of headaches.

Zora Rimes had always been a woman of her word and a strict rule follower. Divorce would have never been anything she would have chosen or even considered but then again, Shelly's father, Frederick, and Sue's husband, Louis, were best friends in the military.

Her mother's kind heart assumed every man aspired to be like her husband or his best friend and couldn't understand why they wouldn't want to.

Of course, Gary, Gill's father, had gotten the short end of the stick when it came to family responsibility. He didn't serve in the military like his brother, Louis, and he'd yet to hold a steady job.

"Why did I think Gill would make better life choices than his father did?"

"Because you're a positive person, like your mama, but you're not clueless."

"I remember when I told her Gill cheated on me that first time. Her expression went completely flat and she actually told me she didn't believe me." The pain of reliving the conversation still hurt.

Sue's eyes went wide with surprise. "No, she did not."

Mortified didn't begin to explain Shelly's reaction when her own mother accused her of lying about Gill's infidelity. "She didn't want to believe anyone related to your husband could do something so betraying."

"Well, you can pick your friends, but you get stuck with family."

"When I told her I actually caught Gill with the other woman, she simply wouldn't even consider the idea he would betray his family like that ever again. Even then, she was one of the strongest supporters of us getting remarried."

"She better see what he is now because he's more than given her reasons to. His baby mama waddling in there, all big and pregnant." Sue scoffed. "I love Zora, but man she can be blind sometimes. That was sure nice of you to give your parents the honeymoon suite."

"They weren't going to give us our deposit back, might as well give it to someone who would actually enjoy it." Although now that Shelly thought about it, the idea of her parents using the honeymoon suite did send a shudder through her.

Freddie's reaction to her wall art came to mind and she had to laugh at herself.

"You back tomorrow?" Sue took the unused iPads the staff used for charting and plugged them in behind the counter.

"No, we're going to pick out a Christmas tree and have a decorating party."

"Oh, who's going to be there?"

Shelly moved the pens around her pocket. "My kids, Peter and his kids."

"Peter? Now who's this Peter person?"

Oh, man. I didn't mean to let that slip. "Lucy and Edmund's brother."

"The one who you came to town. Ran into Mr. Nicolas?"

"Sorry about that!" The man called out. "The dang thing got away from me."

"Everything's good, Mr. Nicolas." Shelly held her hand in front of her mouth to muffle a giggle. "That man has the hearing of a hawk."

Sue's earrings jingled as she moved around the desk. "Someone needs to get a handle on Mr. Nicolas and his runaway machinery. Mr. Nicolas needs a wife to keep track of him."

"Had a wife. God rest her soul."

Sue jumped to her feet. "Now, Mr. Nicolas, that's the first time you've ever mentioned a wife."

"I know. She was the love of my life. Died a while back."

"I'm sorry to hear that, sir."

He thinned his lips for a moment before he shrugged. "But if you've got someone in mind, Mrs. Sue, please send her my way. I may not be as spry as I once was, but I do make a great pot roast and I always put the lid down," the man called out again.

"A woman would be lucky to have you." Sue chuckled and playfully waved him off. "I'll keep my ears open."

"Thank you, Sue." He coughed a few more times, this time the effort sounded more productive.

"Now tell me, why is Peter coming to *your* house to decorate a tree?" Settling back into her chair, Sue gave her niece a sideways glance as she appeared to be organizing another pile of forms. "Is that why you're asking about love at first sight?"

Shelly coughed. "No, no of course not!"

Liar. Yeah, maybe if you say it loud enough you'll convince almost nobody.

"Uh-huh."

"I invited him over. He and the kids won't have a tree this year because they are staying at the Graff." As much as she loved her, Shelly already knew what Sue thought. "And don't get weird. It's a nice thing to do. I'm being nice."

"Uh-huh. Did you already have a tree?"

With a quick shrug, Shelly tried to avoid eye contact as

she became fascinated with stacking the Post-it pads in front of her. "No, but I called out to Scott's farm and they have trees left. Thought it would be nice to show him and the kids the farm, take a sleigh ride."

"Their sleighs are only horse drawn," Mr. Nicolas called out, his voice not his usual deep luster. "Do you have enough Christmas ornaments? I've got several in my workshop."

"Thank you, Mr. Nicolas. That would be very nice of you." Shelly walked in his room and glanced at the monitor. "Your oxygen level's improved and your heart rate came down. You're up to ninety-three percent. Can you cough for me?"

He inhaled a wheezy breath then ended up in a coughing fit.

She handed him some water and encouraged him to take a few sips. "Might help with the dryness in the back of the throat."

The patient did as he was asked as his breathing calmed. "I guess I shouldn't have run out of my inhaler. Lucy always tells me not to, but I've been so busy. So many people need things this time of year, handmade ornaments for one."

"Maybe you should wear a mask in your workshop. Might help cut down on the sawdust you inhale. At least that coughing fit you just had popped a mucus plug loose. You're up to ninety-five percent oxygen." Shelly appreciated Mr. Nicolas's dedication to his craft. For years, he'd created works of art and beautiful wood furniture, but best she knew, he worked alone and apparently, in an open workshop full of dust and cold air.

Shelly couldn't help but notice the sparkle in Mr. Nicolas's eyes had returned from when he walked in the back doors winded and tired. "You look a little more perky than when you arrived. I guess the steroids kicked in."

"They sure did. I could eat an entire reindeer right now." He chuckled until that sent him into another round of him trying to catch his breath.

She patted his back and glanced at the monitor again. "Well, the good news is all that effort loosened those mucus pockets up. You just jumped another point on the monitor. Ninety-six percent."

"Much obliged. You know, Shelly, on the way here, I saw Peter and his children. They were crying."

That got Shelly's immediate attention. "Crying. Why?"

"Digory told me their mother died. Horrible thing to lose a parent and being so young." Mr. Nicolas shook his head. "But Peter would know about that. Losing their father when he was a teen."

"Yes, Lucy's mentioned that before." *And I can't believe any of them survived it.* Months ago, curiosity had gotten the better of her one late, restless night and she'd looked up the accident online. The front of their parents' car had been crushed in. All the windows were blown out. The accident had been no less than brutal and she could better understand how their mother suffered long-term pain from her injuries. "They'd been through a lot."

"I'd say that might have been the first time they all cried together about it."

"They *all* cried?"

"Yes, right there in front of the chocolate shop." His lips went thin as he appeared to be deep in thought. "I think we get our frustrations and barriers out of the way with a good cry. It's healthy to let out that pain and anger, to free up that sense of loss."

Shelly gave him a stressed smile, but not understanding why his words bothered her. "Are they okay? Do they need anything? What can I do to help?"

Reaching his hand out, he grabbed hers. "Child, settle down. After I left them, they were all drying their faces and going into Sage's for a much needed treat."

"Well, if they were going into Sage's, she'll have them feeling right as rain in no time." Sue entered, bringing a cup of ice and a bottle of apple juice. "This will help cut some of the dryness in your throat and get rid of some of that post-nasal drip."

"I appreciate that, Ms. Sue. You sure you don't have any sisters or cousins that I can call?" He gave her a wink.

"You're a wonderful flirt, Mr. Nicolas. I'll keep my ears open."

He toasted her before draining every drop of juice.

"Better?"

"Much. When can I get going?" Like a light switch, his breathing relaxed, his heart rate decreased to the eighties and his oxygen level popped to ninety-nine percent.

Sue returned to the desk as Shelly took another set of vitals and entered the man's information into the chart. "Goodness, something worked."

"Always happens that way. When things look bad, they

can better sometimes when you least expect it." He gave her a curious look. "You know what I mean?"

"Yes." But Shelly had no idea what he meant as Mr. Nicolas oftentimes spoke in riddles and pearls of unsolicited wisdom. "I'll give all this to Dr. Reynolds when he comes out of the other room, but I know he's going to want you to keep those oxygen levels above ninety-five for a bit longer."

"Fair enough. Glad my kids are coming in today. They can help me finish my orders." He rested back in the bed and closed his eyes.

"You've been in here how many times and finally tell us you were married and have children?"

"I like to keep people guessing, like Carol Bingley."

"Well, she does like to know everyone's business, that's for sure."

He rolled his eyes. "Carol Bingley better stop butting into everyone else's lives or she'll never be off the naughty list."

"Her keeping her nose out of everyone else's business. That would be a Christmas miracle. How many children do you have, Mr. Nicolas?" Shelly slapped on the automatic blood pressure cuff and pushed the button. The low hum of the machine filled the room.

He yawned. "Twelve. Six boys. Six girls."

"Twelve. That's wonderful. I always wanted a big family. Lots of children." Four to be exact. Even growing up, every time she played dolls or imagined her grown-up life, she always had four children.

A good husband and four children had always been her

happily ever after.

The sadness of only being able to have one baby laced Shelly's voice. She hated how such a thing held to her pride for years afterward. "But I have Freddie and I'm always grateful for him."

Glancing up, a compassionate smile set on the old man's face. "You deserve so much more than you think you do, dear, but don't worry. Wonderful things are going to happen for you, very, very soon. Your happily ever after is soon to come."

She removed the cuff and tucked it back on the hook. "What a curiously lovely thing to say, sir."

"Not so curious if you believe it and you should. You're a good person. Freddie and Tia are good kids." He slapped his hands together. "When I get home, I will make all of you some ornaments for that tree you're decorating tomorrow."

"That's sweet of you, sir, but I want you to focus on getting better."

He tapped his iWatch. "I'll do as you ask. My son should be here in about an hour. I'll try and rest for a bit."

"Good idea. You don't look as winded." She raised the bedrails, gave him a blanket, and dimmed the lights. As she walked away, she glanced back and smiled. "What an interesting man."

"Just the fact people know so little about him makes him interesting." Sue chuckled. "I know it makes Betty and Carol nuts that they can't find out anything. Betty complained to me in the middle of Monroe's grocery that Mr. Nicolas's never forthcoming about himself when he's at the pharmacy picking up his medications."

Sitting at the desk, Shelly looked in the room again. "I think he might have fallen asleep. He looks tired."

"He's sick and he needs to be more compliant with his medications."

"He just told me he has twelve children."

"Well, that'll make you tired." Turning toward her, Sue raised an eyebrow. "Speaking of kids. Do Freddie and Tia know?"

"About what?" Shelly scanned over the latest labs for another patient as David Bowie and Bing Crosby sang about peace on earth over the hospital PA.

"About your Christmas tree farm visit tomorrow."

"Not yet. I just came up with it." Her hands began to shake at the excitement of it all. "But you should have seen the looks on the kids' faces when I told them about it. Polly and Digory were so happy."

Sue stated in her most inquisitive voice, "I haven't seen your eyes sparkle like that in a long time."

Thinning her lips, Shelly shifted in her seat. "I'm not sparkling."

"Oh, honey. You might as well have covered yourself in glitter and stuck a disco ball in your mouth."

"That's pretty sparkly."

"That Peter Davidson, he's a good-looking guy."

Good-looking? He's absolutely gorgeous. "Yes, he's nice to look at."

Her aunt scoffed. "Nice looking. Stop it. I watched him when they were in here. All banged up and he made sure those kids were okay the entire time. That's a good man."

"Yes. He does appear so."

"But…"

"I'm not gonna lie, I like talking to him. Being around him. He makes me feel noticed and appreciated, but Auntie, I don't know if I can be with someone this soon after Gill."

The entire time she dated and then married Gill, Sue always had the perfect thing to say. This moment would be no exception. "Sweetheart. Gill's been out of your heart ever since the first time he cheated on you. You stayed because you didn't want to upset Freddie, upset your family, because Lord knows, you'd all been through enough."

"Yes, I wanted it to work in the worst way." Unexpected tears ran down her face and she quickly grabbed a tissue, drying her cheeks. She refused to cry over Gill anymore. He didn't deserve her tears.

"You didn't want Freddie to know the truth about his father. Well, now he does. You need to admit to yourself you fell out of love with that man long ago. The only reason he still has any contact with you is because of your son."

Her words, although brutally honest at times, had always been comforting and validating. "Yeah, I did. The second I caught him with another woman, I promised myself I wouldn't let him hurt me again, but Freddie. Ugh, Freddie, I tried to save him the heartache."

"You can't and you shouldn't, not anymore. He needs to know what kind of man Gill is so he will know how not to be such a worthless human being."

"You know, when Gill asked me to marry him again, he

did it in front of Freddie." Shelly tossed the tissue in the trash.

"He didn't." Sue's bright red lip curled into a snarl. "What a crappy thing to do. Set you up like that. Freddie isn't stupid. He knows why you divorced Gill, right?"

"Oh, yes, I told him. I've always been extremely honest about this, but Gill has been doing this pity party crap every time Freddie goes to visit. 'I'm so lonely without your mom.' 'I really screwed up.' 'I need to make things right.' Those types of things. My son is smart, but he's also hopeful and, like any kid, he wants his parents together. He sees his father is sad and thinks I can fix it by being there for him. It's all manipulation. Gill counted on that; used it like only he can."

Wearing a red Santa hat with Spiderman on the cuff, Dave Fletcher walked back in and tossed a wadded napkin in the trash before washing his hands. "What'd I miss?"

Shelly pointed to the patient board. "Not much. Everyone is resting and recovering. Where's Jade?"

"She went upstairs to see if she needed to help Edmund. So far, he's helped deliver two babies." A machine beeped from one of the rooms and Shelly stood. Dave waved her to sit. "I've got it. Get on out of here."

"Thanks, Dave. They need a recheck on their tilt test."

"Got it."

The back doors of the unit opened and within seconds the newest nurse to the ER, Pepper Henderson came flying around the corner, her cheeks were pink from being in the cold.

"Thank you so much, Shelly."

"How did your first time shopping in Montana go?"

Running her fingers through her hair as she held a hair tie between her teeth, Pepper sighed. "Thank goodness for online ordering. I walked in, paid, walked out and got some really cute stuff for my brother and sisters."

The triage bell sounded and Pepper motioned for Shelly to sit before she even began to stand. "I've got it. I'll be back to get report so you can go."

She headed straight for the front of the unit as Sue pulled out a large roll of Snoopy Christmas stickers and began to tear them into individual squares. "You were saying?"

"I wanted to say no to Gill's proposal, but that hope in my son's eyes, I couldn't do it. I couldn't tell him I wouldn't give our family another chance and I worried the entire drive back from Vegas that Freddie would give up on love. Think it was a waste of time, but then he told me he worried more about Gill's new kids and how they would be heartbroken when he screwed them over."

"Freddie said that?" Sue beamed and joyfully clapped her hands. "Oh, my goodness. You have raised a solid, good-hearted young man right there."

"He's a good kid."

"And taking in Tia while your brother is deployed, basically being her mother and that girl is going places."

"Have you seen her photos? She's got a great eye."

"And a big heart. That's you doing that because we all know that's not her mother's natural nature. Honey, I know you wanted a big family, but take pride in what you've done. It means something."

"I do, but after being dragged through this insane wedding crap with Gill, I... ugh... I hate being alone."

Scooting forward on the rolling chair, Sue cupped her niece's face and kissed her forehead. "Sweetie, you deserve someone who believes that as much or more than I do. As we all do."

You deserve. She smirked at the two words after hearing it from two people in the past few minutes. "I appreciate that, Sue. I do."

Unexpected tears escaped, hearing her aunt's praise.

Her aunt wiped them away with her thumbs before kissing her forehead again. "I want you to remember something."

"What's that?"

"It's not that your heart isn't ready to be loved. It's more than ready to be loved by someone who *deserves* you."

Chapter Thirteen

B RIGHT AND EARLY Friday morning, Shelly pulled into the parking lot of the Graff hotel, her nerves buzzed as though she'd been tazed. Turning to Tia and Freddie, she asked, "How do I look?"

"What do you mean, how do you look? You look fine." Freddie yawned before taking a swig of his his large Java Café tumbler. "It's too early. Why are we here again?"

"Ugh, Son, you're no help." She checked her eyeliner again, glad it hadn't run or smudge since this last time she looked, which was all of five minutes ago.

"You look beautiful, Aunt Shell." Tia unbuckled her seat belt, grabbed her camera, and zipped up her coat. "I'll come with you. I want to see the trees in the lobby. Take some pictures."

"Are we seriously going to entertain little kids all day?" Freddie's voice held just the hint of a whine.

"Yes, because we want to get a tree and they can't put one up in their room so I invited them to come with us." Popping the lock, she tried not to run inside as though she'd appear anxious and far too excited.

"Two days ago, you said you didn't want to mess with a

tree, Mom." Freddie followed them.

"I changed my mind." She wrung her hands nervously, then shook them out.

"They have trees all over the place in here. Can't they use one of those?"

"Would you have been happy with that answer when you were nine?"

He grunted and stuffed his hands in his coat pockets as the automatic doors opened.

Entering the Graff, they were immediately greeted with the smells of evergreen and sugar cookies. Thick green garland wrapped around rails of the grand staircase that curved toward the second floor as ribbons of red were perfectly positioned at each base of the staircase lights.

Several large trees sat in the curve of the staircase, across from the front desk, where the attendant waved them over.

His colorful snowman-themed sweater vest matched his deep green button-down shirt. "Good morning. How can I help you today?"

"It's beautiful in here."

"Thank you. It's my favorite time of year." As they approached the desk, he tapped a bowl in front of him full of brightly wrapped treats. "Raspberry candies if you want one."

Shelly eyed his nametag as Freddie and Tia both grabbed a sweet. "Thank you, Bob. We're looking for Peter Davidson's room."

His fingers sailed across the keyboard as the lights overhead shone off his partially bald head. "Your name?"

"Shelly Westbrook. These are my kids. Freddie and Tia."

"Pleased to meet you." His eyes settled on Tia's camera for a moment. "Look around. Take all the pictures you like."

"Thanks, Mr. Bob." Tia took the lens cap off and tucked it in her pocket before snapping a photo of him. "Smile, sir."

He grinned, even blushed a bit as Tia took several shots in a row.

"Check it out, Mom." Freddie's excited voice boomed across the lobby. "This tree has a bunch of book ideas."

It always amazed her how labile teenage emotions were. Her son went from pouting about being out of bed before ten to excitement and awe of a literary Christmas tree before she could say Rudolph. "Take pictures. We always need good book suggestions."

Freddie pulled out his phone.

"That's one of my favorite trees. The library does that one every year. It's not flashy, but it's a great tree." Bob tilted his chin up as he continued to type. "There's also one over there from a dentist out of Bozeman. I think she also does lip fillers or something in the office because she has a bunch of lipsticks and candy lips hanging from the branches."

"That's clever." Shelly realized she had no particular theme to their tree. Year after year, they simply put on the same ornaments they always had. "A themed tree sounds like fun."

Bob motioned toward decorations in the lobby. "I think so. I do love a tree with a message. I've let Dr. Davison know you're here."

"Oh, you can do that?"

"Computers are fabulous things. Please feel free to look around." He handed her a flyer. "There's going to be a cookie decorating event tomorrow and we'll have Santa if your kids want to join or even volunteer."

"Thank you, Bob." Shelly absorbed the old hotel's charm and holiday cheer.

To her right, a large set of double doors sat open to the grand ballroom.

As her kids showed each other multiple ornaments on the different displays and Tia moved about the room to photograph, Shelly stood in the doorway and watched the multiple staff members organize.

Windows lined the entire right side of the space, allowing a tremendous amount of natural light in. The large wooden floors shone like glass as the tables had been neatly arranged to the sides of the room for the Mistletoe Ball and Christmas tree auction that would happen this weekend.

The cleverly themed trees would be auctioned off, bring in money for local charities and raise awareness for community projects. People with deep pockets would descend on Marietta for an evening of never-ending champagne, dancing, and great music.

It had been one of many social events Shelly had never attended because of work schedule, no babysitter, or simply having no one to go with.

This year, she'd miss it and any sort of New Years frivolity. *Too bad because I look so good in that red dress.*

Turning back, she watched her son and niece laugh about a book they'd found on the library tree.

154

A calm descended watching them interact.

She might want a few more things in life, but she had all she needed at this moment.

Healthy kids. A good job. A family who loved her, flaws and all.

Still, it would be wonderful to fall in love again and find that happily ever after.

The rapid speech of a happy child pulled Shelly from her pity party. She looked up to see Polly and Digory coming down the stairs with Peter a few steps behind them.

Peter wore a dark blue shirt, jeans, boots, and a heavy coat. As soon as his eyes met hers, Shelly had to remind herself to breathe.

Oh, my. Staying at home alone with a man who looks at me like that would be worth giving up every fancy night out for the rest of my life.

Tia stood next to her and whispered before she snapped a few photos. "You gonna ask him out or y'all just gonna go ahead and get married?"

"Put that camera away." Shelly gave a nervous laugh as butterflies slammed against her stomach. "I love your faith in me, Tia, but right now, I just want to get through the Christmas tree afternoon."

"Okay, but I'm telling you, he's gonna say yes."

"To what?"

"Looking at you like he does, to anything you ask him." She gave her aunt a wink and jogged to the bottom of the stairs.

Shelly's body buzzed with excitement and she checked

her breath again.

"Happy Christmas tree day, guys!" Polly squealed as she waved frantically. Her unicorn backpack draped over her shoulder.

"Merry Christmas, Miss Shelly!" Digory threw his scarf over his shoulder as he jumped down two stairs and landed with a loud boom on the lobby tile.

Tia gave him a fist bump. "Hey, kid. What's up?"

"Nothing. Is that your camera?" Polly tapped on the top of the flash.

"Yep. Smile."

Polly threw her head back and posed as though she were walking the red carpet before grabbing Tia's hand and pulling her along. "Did you see this lip tree over here? It's so amazing."

Freddie sauntered over to Digory and the boys gave each other a nod as they each stuffed their hands in their coat pockets.

"You like books?"

Digory gave a thumbs-up.

"Follow me." Freddie walked back over to the library display with Digory right beside him.

"Morning." Peter kissed Shelly on the cheek as his hand rested on the small of her back.

The subtle scent of mint tickled her nose as the warmth of his breath caressed her cheek.

She shivered. "Morning. You look rested."

"I'm not sleeping on the pull-out couch anymore. The room next door opened up."

"The kids are by themselves?"

He put on his jacket. "Nope, the rooms adjoin. I have a king-sized bed to stretch out in."

She imagined them stretching out on a king-sized bed. It flashed through her mind and she tried to shake it off, but it stuck like peanut butter.

Good grief, Shelly. It's Christmas tree shopping day. Get your mind out of his pants.

"Thank you for taking us today. The kids haven't stopped talking about it since we saw you yesterday."

Out of the corner of her eye, she saw quick movement. She turned and watched Digory, Freddie, Tia, and Polly point to different bookplates on the tree.

Suddenly, seeing the kids together, tears welled in her eyes. She fanned herself, cursing the makeup job she'd certainly ruin. "Sorry, it's nice to see."

"You okay?" Taking her hand, Peter kissed the back of it. "Anything I can do?"

Biting her lip, Shelly snuggled next to him and took a mental picture of the children. "No, everything is perfect."

The corner of his mouth twitched. "Glad you think so."

The touch of Peter's hand against hers felt like the most natural thing in the world, like this was where she, they, were supposed to be.

I need to calm down with the Christmas spirit.

It's just hand holding. Get over yourself.

But when he touched her, Shelly felt empowered, appreciated, sexy.

If this is how I feel with hand holding, I'm gonna die if we go farther, but it would be so worth it.

"Come here. Come here, Daddy. Miss Shelly." Polly beckoned them over to the dentist's tree as Tia had just lowered her camera.

"Shall we?" He tucked their hands against his chest and walked with her to the Christmas tree displays.

Shelly marveled at the detail of decorations and the perfectly placed ornaments.

Winter-themed toothbrushes and hand-painted ornaments with the information of the dentist's office were alternately layered with information cards with small samples of the lip plumpers in various colors. Strings of bright pink lip blinking lights wrapped around the tree.

"I'm never this good with crafty things. I'm always grateful for those who are." Shelly flipped a tooth light that hung upside down. "The lip plumpers are a good side gig for the dentist. Very smart marketing, but I've never needed help with that."

"Your lips are perfect." Peter's eyes rested on them for a moment before giving her a stressed smile. "Sorry, it's been a long time since I've been on a date. Not sure how to flirt anymore."

"A date." The word alone caused her blood pressure to rise. "Yes, that's what the kids said. It's a date."

"Then your lips are perfect comment was okay?"

Shelly always appreciated smart men who were honest when they had no clue about dating, sort of the classic nerd. Although Peter Davidson didn't physically appear to be someone they'd cast on the *Big Bang Theory*, she could tell from the worry in his eyes and the rapid beat of his heart at the pulse point on his neck, a *date* just might be his undoing. "You're flirting just fine, Peter."

He let out a long breath. "Good. Okay. Good."

His desire to impress her only made him all that more appealing. *Oh, my gosh. Could you be any sexier right now?*

A giggle came from behind them.

Peter turned. "What are you up to, Polly?"

Without saying a word, Polly motioned upward.

Shelly's heart slammed into her ribs when she saw the branch of mistletoe hanging over them from the dental tree. She wanted to grab the small mouthwash she saw dangling from the branches for good measure.

"You know the rules." Tia shrugged as Polly agreed.

"It's true. It's the Christmas rules."

"Polly, I don't think—" Peter protested as his daughter jumped up and down like a rabbit that had too much coffee.

"Daddy. It's tradition."

"Well, if it's tradition, how can we say no?" Shelly had no idea how she had the strength to say that and quite honestly didn't care. Her eyebrow cocked, hoping he'd bite. Or kiss. "Right?"

After almost constantly thinking about him since they'd met, she'd take either.

"Right. Tradition's important." Leaning forward, he held their hands against his chest. "Shall we?"

How many times had she dreamed of kissing him? Now that the chance arrived, Shelly's stomach felt like it was full of caffeine filled hummingbirds. "Yes."

Inching toward him, she met him in the middle, expecting a quick, non-sexy peck, but when Peter brushed his lips against hers, Shelly's body came alive like a light switch.

He followed with a slow, soft-mouthed bone-melting kiss that almost had Shelly grabbing handfuls of his shirt and pulling him flush.

O. M. G!

A throat clearing made her reluctantly pull away.

"Mom?" Freddie's arms were locked across his chest, the corners of his mouth turned down "We doing this tree thing or what?"

Her eyes remained locked with Peter's, her mind raced with endless possibilities. *Good Lord, I could love you so hard.*

"Should I come back? Get you two a room instead of making out in front of all of us."

Digory's look of disgust almost made her laugh. "Is this a kissing date?"

"Give it a rest, guys." Tia's hand pressed against her chest as her eyes welled with tears and her camera resting in her other hand. She gave Shelly a thumbs-up.

Shelly would probably have to sit in the snow before she could get a good night's rest this evening but experiencing those kind of fireworks was worth it. "Yes, yes, Freddie. We're heading to the tree farm."

"Yes, it's a kissing date, Son." Peter gave her another quick peck.

Polly giggled as she turned, pointing over the adults' heads. "It's misty-toe, Freddie. It's tradition. They have to kiss."

Digory scoffed. "Tradition, huh? Well, sometimes traditions are gross."

"Or they suck," Freddie mumbled.

"No, Freddie." Without a hint of sarcasm, Tia answered, "Sometimes, they just change."

Chapter Fourteen

THE WORLD SMELLED of crisp evergreen and clean air. Growing up in Florida, Peter remembered picking out a tree at the local hardware store with his father in the thick humidity or the seasonally warm temperatures of December. There, the hot aromas of pinesap and car exhaust mixed with sea air that would blow in from the Atlantic.

Flavors far different from what he experienced today.

This had been what he'd always imagined a Charlie Brown Christmas to be.

Blankets of snow, sleigh rides, clean air, and freshly cut trees lined up, waiting for their homes.

Snowball fights with the kids.

The sweet steam of hot chocolate rising off the rich sugary liquid as they walked the rows of potential candidates that would perfectly fit Shelly's living room.

All that they needed was a beagle who had a knack for decorating his doghouse and his yellow bird friend and they'd be all set.

Peter closed his eyes and inhaled again, relishing the crisp cold mixed with the rich layers of a classic Christmastime morning.

The laughter of his children and Shelly's two playing a game of snow dodgeball relaxed him for the first time in weeks.

"What are you doing?" Shelly slid her glove-covered fingers between his as they walked a row of extremely tall firs.

"Taking it all in. I've never been to a Christmas tree farm in the snow before." He wandered the remaining trees with her by his side as his children ran from tree to tree, throwing snowballs. "It's straight out of a holiday card. Thanks for inviting us, Shelly. Especially this close to Christmas Day."

"Our pleasure." She pointed to a Douglas fir about six feet tall. "That might work. Not too big. It'll fit in my car."

"Is that part of the Christmas tree requirements?"

"I need to be able to get it home and we only have a couple of days to get it ready for Santa." She thinned her lips as they stood in front of the tree. "I honestly don't want a big project and I didn't plan on even having a tree this year either."

"Because you planned to be out of town, right?"

"Right." Her jaw clenched.

As much as Peter appreciated Shelly mentioning little about her ex-husband or the disaster of her nonwedding, he had to admit, his curiosity had grown. After getting to know her and her son and niece, he had to wonder how much of a dumbass this Gill had to be for throwing away an opportunity to spend the rest of his life with such a fantastic woman and her kids.

After tossing his empty drink cup in the trash, his arm slid around her waist. "You could do what my parents did."

"What's that?" She gave him a stressed smile.

"Open a bottle of wine and let the kids decorate the tree. By the time you're done with the wine, you don't care what the tree looks like as long as the boxes are put away." He kissed her forehead. "I'll bring the wine and two kids."

"I've got two kids I can add to the mix and plenty of wine." Her eyes sparkled as she gazed into his. "You really do have amazingly green eyes."

"And you're beautiful." Beautiful. The word seemed too ordinary when describing her, but he couldn't grasp any other word that fit because everything about Shelly West-brook radiated exquisite perfection.

Her compassion.

Her empathy.

Her intelligence.

Those along with the fact the woman got him hot and bothered just walking into a room and it had been entirely too long since he'd felt this kind of overwhelming, all-consuming passion for a woman. "You're the most beautiful woman I've ever met."

"You know, for a guy who said he's not good at flirting, you're sure doing a good job." She stepped closer as the gentle breeze momentarily kicked in.

The distant laughter of their children helped him know they were safe and occupied. He pulled her between a couple of very tall and full trees and cupped her face. "I can do better. A lot better."

"Show me," she whispered, her eyes set on his mouth.

He brushed his lips against hers, before he slid his tongue

along the seam.

The simplest of touches and already, Peter never thought he'd get enough of her. Her mouth opened and his tongue swept in. The sweet of chocolate mixed with her delicious touch, all sending a thrill straight to his jeans.

He couldn't help but moan when she grabbed handfuls of his jacket and pulled him flush right before a slam of cold hit him in the back of the head.

Immediately, he stepped backward and shook out what he could, but several nuggets melted under the collar of his coat and ran down his back. He shivered and fanned out his coat, getting rid of any remaining ice.

"What happened?" Shelly craned her neck around the tree and her eyes narrowed. "Freddie."

"Freddie. Nice aim." Peter chuckled. *Serves me right for kissing his mom in such a public place.* Not that Peter regretted it one bit.

"Thanks. I've had a lot of practice living here." Her son tossed a snowball between his hands, a look of *there's-plenty-more-where-that-came-from* challenge in his eyes. "Hey, Mom, I found a great tree."

Shelly brushed snow out of Peter's hair. "That's great, honey."

"Mr. Scott has it at the front. I wondered—" Snow exploded off the back of Freddie's coat, sending fine pieces of ice in his hair.

Peter stepped back to see his Digory standing behind a small Christmas tree. The impish smirk resembled his brother and Peter had no doubt Digory could stir the pot as well as Edmund could. "Did you just throw that?"

"Yes." Digory made another snowball as he spoke.

"You've got a good arm."

His son beamed.

"Digs, you keep this up, I'm gonna get you back." Freddie kept his back to Digory, but the corners of his mouth curled up while he appeared to be waiting for another snowball to fly.

A loud snap and explosion off Freddie's coat as Digory jumped out from his hiding place. "You gotta catch me first, Freddie."

"Are you having... fun?" Shelly voice held a hint of sarcasm. "With *little* kids?"

"Yeah, yeah, I know. Don't rub it in." Freddie leaned over and grabbed a handful of snow, patting it into a large ball and packing it tight. "I'll meet you at the front."

She grabbed Peter's hand. "Guess our tree shopping is done. Where are the girls?"

"I think they're hanging out around the horses. Tia's getting pictures." In a loud voice, he announced, "I think I'm done. I'm ready to go."

Digory peeked out from behind the pile, a look of annoyance on his face. "Freddie! You can't quit now—"

Spinning around, Freddie launched a snowball that hit Digs square in the chest, sending snow in multiple directions on impact and Digory on his butt.

The young one's jaw hit the ground and at first Peter thought he might have gotten the wind knocked out of him. He began to lean forward to check on him, but a broad smile spread across the child's face. "That was so cool! Did you see all that snow, Dad?"

He called me Dad. "Yep, I did."

"It hit me so hard, I fell backward." Without standing, Digory chucked a snowball at Freddie, hitting his arm.

Freddie's head fell back as a lusty laughter escaped him. "Man, I almost got you right in the face."

Scrambling to his feet, Digory took off with Freddie in hot pursuit.

"You okay there?" Shelly stood in front of him, her hair resting about her face as the pink snowcap held the locks down.

"What do you mean?"

"I felt you tense up when Digory got hit with that snowball. You know that's what boys do, right? Beat the crap out of each other." She tugged his arm, walking them to the front of the lot.

"Guess I'd forgotten all that. Keep remembering about taking care of Lucy and Edmund after our father died. Before then, it's kind of a blur." Peter let out a long breath. The chill of the air tickled his face. "Still don't have a handle on this parenting thing. I think the protecting them from everything button is on ten."

"Is that what you did after your father died? Had your protective button cranked to ten?"

Her words made him stop in his tracks. "You're perceptive, you know that?"

"Lucy's told me about how you and Susan would care for them and your mom after the accident." She pointed to a bench. "That you'd work one sports season and she the opposite so you could have income coming in and the other would watch the kids and get to do their extracurricular."

"We did what we had to do. Mom was too beat up and the settlement only carried us so far. We had to be mindful. Careful."

"Admirable."

The heat of embarrassment warmed his face. "We did what we had to."

"See, that's where you underestimate yourselves. You did far beyond that, you and Susan became their parents, even for your mom and you gave up a huge amount of your childhood to have to grow up far too soon."

"I appreciate the analysis, but I'm wondering where you're going with it."

"Maybe having your own children is a way for you to recapture some of that. To experience the unexpected joys of life."

His children's laughter echoed in the air around them and Peter soaked in the bliss of the moment. "Maybe so."

She threaded her arm through his as they sat down. "How's your visit going so far?"

"Decent." *More than decent.* He got a whiff of pepper-mint as the wind waved her hair about her face. The length of his coat covered his physical reaction to her standing so close for most of the morning. His thoughts had been far from sugar plum fairies dancing in his head.

In fact, his thoughts would put him on the naughty list.

The very naughty list, especially after that kiss.

She shivered and scooted closer. "The kids adjusting okay to the time change?"

"And everything else."

"I have no doubt it's a lot to go through."

Peter's cheeks puffed out and he let out a long exhale. "Polly's a gem, but sometimes I worry she might be avoiding what she's really thinking. Feeling."

"She might. I worked with foster children during nursing school. The social worker mentioned a lot of the time there's about a three- to six-month honeymoon period where kids are on their best behavior, afraid of what will happen if they aren't."

"Great, then our summer should be a blast." Even though he tired to make light of the situation, Peter worried about his ability to help his kids where and when they needed it.

"What about Digory?" She leaned closer as a gust of winter wind sailed by them.

"Since day one, he's been guarded. He's not afraid to tell me I don't meet his approval most of the time."

"Did you expect anything else? You both know so little about each other. I'm sure you're not going into this without reservations or frustrations."

"Right. I think what he's doing is normal. Sometimes his anger is easier to deal with than Polly's constant demand for attention. I know exactly how he feels about this entire situation. About me. But then yesterday"—Peter nodded as he watched the boys chase each other in the snow—"after we left you, we had a good day."

"Is that why you all were crying yesterday?"

He leaned away from her without unlocking their arms. "Crying? Does news travel that fast in town?"

Her shoulders slumped. "No and this is a HIPPA violation, but Mr. Nicolas was in the ER yesterday midday. He had an asthma attack because he'd run out of his inhaler."

"I wondered. He looked like he was having trouble... oh, I see. And he told you he saw us."

"He said all of you were crying, but he also said sometimes, that's a good thing."

His heart warmed at her concern. "He's right. It was a good thing. You know, until yesterday, Polly was the only one who'd called me Daddy. Only Daddy. Not Peter or Peter Dad." He exhaled a long breath, watching the steam escaped his mouth. "Digory had a fit over these gloves at the western wear store that I refused to buy him."

"Ah, the you-won't-buy-me-what-I-want trigger. It's a pretty powerful one. Freddie had one massive tantrum over a stuffed animal once. I'm sure he's still traumatized that I didn't get it for him." She rested her chin on his shoulder. "What did you do?"

Even though her story had meant to be funny, it gave Peter great comfort to know she'd been through similar parenting events. "I told him he had a pair of gloves. That Christmas was only a few days away and he got upset because I got gloves and a hat. Pretty much yelled that in the middle of the store." Sandwiching her hands between his, he adjusted on the cold wooden bench. "We got out of the store without him screaming any more, but when we got in front of Sage's, he demanded hot chocolate and I told him I wouldn't buy it for him if he kept being a jerk."

"Sounds like you played that well."

Her words wiped away a layer of angst that had weighed heavy on his conscious since the meltdown. "You think so?"

"You don't reward a kid for bad behavior. If you decide to bribe or negotiate, it never sticks. If you give in, they know at some point you'll crack and give them what they want anyway. It's just a matter of when you'll crack, not if."

"Well, he cracked. Began crying over what I said because it was what his mother would say." Even now, Peter couldn't believe he and Simone had been so in sync regarding parenting, which again begged the question… *Why did she keep me out of their lives*? "He stared crying. Polly started crying. I started crying."

A tear ran down Shelly's face.

"Now you're crying." He gently brushed it away. "Lots of tears and since then, both kids are calling me Dad more."

"Sounds like an emotionally cathartic event you all needed." She rested her head on his shoulder. "That's beautiful."

"I have to believe their mom, Simone, told them something good about me."

"There was probably a lot to tell."

"Now who's flirting?" He joked and tucked his hand deeper into his pocket in an attempt to stay warm and pull her closer.

Sitting up, Shelly sat sideways on the bench and faced him. "No, I'm serious. Your siblings talk volumes about you and now, having met you, I can see why."

Her honest compliment made him suck in a breath.

Ever since he'd received the phone call about Simone's death and about his children, he'd been asking himself what he'd done that made her decide to erase him from their world.

Hearing Shelly speak his praises had him wondering if he deserved them. "I appreciate that Shelly, but if I'm so great, why did Simone leave me after I proposed to her?"

Shelly's forehead creased. "What?"

"We'd been dating five years. I planned this whole seductive and incredible evening. Proposed the next morning. She turned me down flat." Other than his siblings and stepfather, Peter hadn't talked to anyone about the last time he'd seen Simone.

"Did she ever say why?"

"Not really. Just that she planned to go back to Maine. Open a nurse practitioner clinic with a few classmates. That she loved me, but she didn't want to marry me."

"After five years?" Her thumb tenderly rubbed back and forth on his arm.

Even after a decade, the rejection still stung. "Yep. She said no, walked away, and never talked to me again. I guess that night, we got pregnant. Now here we are."

"Did you ever try to reach out to her after that? Maybe time softened her reasons and you could get some better answers?"

Peter appreciated Shelly's compassionate way of speaking about the mother of his children. A lot of women he'd met in the past would have called his ex multiple names by now, but Shelly appeared to have a positive spin on pretty much everything. He loved that about her.

Wait. Loved? Uh-oh.

Immediately, he stood to get some sensation in his backside and put a little bit of distance between himself and his obviously confused brain. "Shelly, I did everything short of being a stalker. Simone wouldn't return my calls, emails, messages sent through friends. Nothing."

Shelly pulled her long legs in front of her and hugged them to her chest. "That's tough. Did she leave you any insight with the children?"

"She gave me copies of their medical records. Their school information, grades, teachers, friends, neighbors, pictures."

"Any letters or messages about why she did what she did?"

"Funny you should say that. There is a letter for only me."

"I see. What did it… I'm sorry." Shelly put her hands up, stood and walked to the other side of the bench. "It's not my business to ask you about it."

Again, her unassuming nature only made him love her more.

Love? Dammit. "I haven't opened it. I have no idea why."

She pursed her lips. "You don't want to know, do you?"

Locking his arms across his chest like a defiant child he said, "Not sure, but does it matter what she wrote anyway? Doesn't change anything."

The cold wind blew a lock of her hair across her face.

"It's like ripping off the Band-Aid. It's got to be done."

"I get that it's what needs to be done, but that doesn't make me want to read it." In fact, Peter had already wondered if it even mattered.

The corner of her mouth twitched and she approached him, placing her hands on his arms.

"What?"

Resting her hand on his face, she smiled. "You're gonna have to rip the Band-Aid off and know what happened. Otherwise, you'll never move on."

Move on. At that moment, it dawned on him that every part of him had moved on except his heart.

That had been left back on the night Simone turned him down and until now, he didn't have a reason to move on.

But that was before he found out he had children and that was before he'd met one very beautiful nurse.

Chapter Fifteen

THE UPBEAT TEMPO of the Charlie Brown theme filled the house as Tia and Polly danced, bouncing their heads from side to side before falling on the floor in a pile of giggles.

Freddie and Digory opened boxes of ornaments and laid them out on the coffee table as the lights twinkled on the large tree they'd brought home from Scott's farm.

It hadn't been what she'd anticipated she'd buy today, but then again, she hadn't anticipated being so passionately kissed by Peter Davidson between two very itchy evergreens. But it had been worth getting ice down the front of her shirt because of her son's snowball interruption.

That was a jerk move, Freddie.

Still, she'd give her son a pass on this one. Him seeing her kiss anyone but his father had to be a bit of a shock, especially after recent events.

She decided if the worst resistance she got from her son was a perfectly placed snowball to the back of her boyfriend's head, she'd call herself lucky.

Boyfriend? Potential Lover? Casual Acquaintance?

What to call Peter Davidson other than drop-dead sexy?

The morning visit had to be the most fun she had in a very long time.

The pop of the cork caught her attention. Peter walked in with a bottle of red and two glasses. "Hope you don't mind. Figured we could because they appear to have the tree covered."

"Well played." She soaked in the scene of the four children discussing tree decorating strategy.

Four children. She choked back an unexpected sob as her heart pounded against her ribs. *Four. Just like I always wanted.*

"You okay?" A glass appeared in her line of sight.

"Yes. I'm fine." *And freaking out a little.* She gently took the glass from his hand and he kissed her cheek.

"Sit with me?" He held out a chair for her at the dining room table and they settled in.

Taking some large gulps of wine, she hoped the red liquid would work its magic and calm her nerves. She glanced back at the children again.

Four.

"You've got good kids." He tapped his glass to hers and gave her a wink.

Her insides melted like butter. "Thank you."

"How long has Tia been with you?"

"A few years."

"She's your niece, right?"

"Yes, Robert, my brother and his wife Brenda, were together for several years. They had Tia, but divorced a few years afterward." She rolled the stem of the wineglass between her fingers. "When her mother decided she wanted to start her own family with her new boyfriend, she sent Tia to live with Robert."

Shaking his head, Peter growled. "I really don't get people sometimes. Kids aren't disposable."

"No, it was better for Tia not to be with her and her boyfriend of the day."

"I see. How long ago was that?"

"About five years ago and don't get me started on that woman." Shelly sipped her wine, loving the layers of berries and pepper.

"Your brother? Where is he?"

"He's with the marines and, at the time, was stationed in San Diego. When he was deployed again, he asked me if he could send Tia here to give her some stability with friends, school." Shelly thought of her brother doing God knew what in who knew where. Everyday, she prayed for his safety. "After she'd been here six months, Tia asked to stay instead of being sent back and forth between us."

"How did your brother take it?" Peter added an inch of wine to his glass as he listened intently.

"He was a little heartbroken, but he understood it. He'd gotten a promotion that sent him overseas in a non-family friendly area of the world. Her staying here would have eventually happened." A flash of green caught Shelly's attention.

Tia and Freddie hooked it above the living room doorway as Polly and Digory secured at the lower levels.

His gaze wandered toward the other room. "Then she

was old enough to know both of them. Not like my two. Man, I have no idea what they think of all this."

"Anything you care to vent about? Sometimes getting it out of your head helps." She realized their fingertips were inches apart. Shelly leaned back, hoping not to overwhelm him.

"No. Yes. Maybe. Hell, I missed nine years of their lives. Nine years. It's not as though I can waltz in and expect them to welcome me unconditionally."

"Of course not, but you're trying." *Like a father should.* She mentally shook her head, thinking about Gill and his inability to consider anyone else but himself.

"Like I mentioned. Our breakthrough yesterday. I'm sure there will be plenty more to discuss. To learn. Understand."

"You don't think she told them anything about you?"

He ran his fingers through his hair before resting his chin in his palm. "No idea. We haven't talked about too much yet, but from what I can understand, she talked about me favorably. They've mentioned a few things she's said."

"Maybe you could start the conversation with telling them about her."

"What?"

"Well, they know her as Mom, right? They don't know about who she was before then and you have no idea what she told them. Maybe start with something fun. Like how you met."

Instrumental Christmas songs softly played from the other room as the children debated how best to arrange the solid colored ornaments.

The wind moaned outside and the sun began its quick descent for the day.

"Maybe." His fingers drummed on the table as he appeared to be deep in thought. "Where would I start?"

"Wherever you think would inspire the most conversation." But, Shelly had to wonder why a woman would walk away from a man like Peter Davidson.

He had a loving family and a great job.

He was kind, intelligent, and gorgeous.

He spoke four languages.

He'd wholeheartedly accepted his sudden role as father.

After working with his siblings, Shelly couldn't believe he had some weird, dark side of him that would have a woman keep his children away.

Maybe he had some weird fetish?

Drank out of the milk carton?

Hated puppies?

Didn't recycle?

Peter shifted in his seat. "Simone was the smartest girl I'd ever met. There wasn't a trivia question she couldn't answer on almost any subject. I made the mistake *one* time of being up against her in a trivia drinking game and lost miserably. Had the worst hangover of my life."

"Ha. All good college stories start out with bad hangovers, but maybe skip the hangover part when you tell the story. Where did you meet?"

His mouth curled up as the memories appeared to give him moments of happiness. "Last year of college. Colleen, her roommate was a friend of mine from high school.

179

Simone had transferred down from Maine her junior year. Their families had been friends since the women were kids."

"And you were where?"

"University of Florida."

"Gill and I met at the University of Montana. Sophomore year and no hangover was involved in that meeting."

"Fair. How did you meet?" He licked a drop of wine off his lip.

"Blind date. His uncle was, is best friends with my dad. They served in the military together. Their wives, my mom and Sue, the sticker lady, suggested Gill and I go out."

"Guess the date went well?"

"It went great. We stayed up until late into the night. By the second week, he said he was in love with me and wanted to spend the rest of his life with me." She rolled her eyes and took a long drink of wine. "But people don't fall in love that fast."

His forehead furrowed. "You don't think they can? Love at first sight?"

"No. I think it's more lust than anything, but love like that, love that lasts, it doesn't just happen." The corner of her mouth twitched as she tucked her frustration about her ex away. She wouldn't let him steal any more time from her, especially when she sat across from a man who made her feel more than beautiful. "We got married two years later. A year after that, we had Freddie."

"How old is Freddie again?" He pointed.

"Seventeen. He'll be eighteen next year." *Great. Now he'll for sure head out the door.* When Shelly turned thirty was when she first suspected Gill began cheating on her. That only escalated the closer to forty she got.

"Then you're…"

"White-knuckling on to thirty-nine." She took another sip of wine.

"Then I'm younger than you by a few years." A wicked smirk replaced his charming smile. "I always wanted to date an older woman."

"Careful how you use the word *older*." She half-heartedly joked.

He leaned forward and pressed his lips to hers for a moment before whispering in her ear, "Should I use the word better? Exceptional? Superior?"

"Better, um, works, but I won't lie. I'm kind of liking superior." The warmth of his breath on her skin sent shockwaves through her as her body ached for his touch. Then she decided to torture herself. "Say it in Italian. French. Spanish."

Smiling against her skin, he kissed her check. "You're beautiful. *Sei Bellissima. Tu es belle. Estas bella.*"

"Oh, that's amazing."

"So are you." He kissed her cheek again and sat down. "I'll save superior for when you're really pissed at me."

"I can't wait to hear that one." Shelly adjusted in her chair as she repeatedly rearranged a lock of hair behind her ear. Her body simmered with lust and her imagination ran wild. "You really are good at flirting."

"I'm glad you approve."

"You were saying about the children's mom?" She cleared

her throat and took a large gulp of wine.

Good pivot. A discussion about ex-girlfriends will be like sitting in a bucket of cold water.

He began to answer, but finished the wine in his glass and refilled. "Simone planned to go to nurse practitioner school there. I thought great, I'm going to med school."

"Having common interests. Seems like a natural fit."

His fingers tapped his glass before he took a long drag. "I thought we would work together when we were done with school. It made sense. We made sense."

"Love at first sight, huh?" *As if that actually exists.* But watching him tell the story, Shelly wanted to believe it could.

He chuckled, "Something like that. After that night where she kicked my ass in the trivia drinking game, I asked her out. Figured I'd better say something quick before someone else did."

"She sounds amazing." Shelly couldn't help but feel slightly jealous of this Simone person, knowing Peter so long ago. If she had, she might not have been dragged on the emotional roller coaster by Gill, but then she wouldn't have Freddie.

"She is. Was." The corner of his mouth curled down for a moment before he continued. "We dated that year and my four years of medical school. She finished her masters in nursing. By then we'd dated almost five years, I was about to start my emergency room residency and I thought it was time for a major change in our relationship."

A great sadness replaced the joy in his eyes. He rested his forearms on his knees, his gaze in the direction of the children. "I planned this elaborate evening. I took her to dinner, her favorite place to watch the sunset. I wanted everything to be perfect."

Shelly realized she'd leaned forward, anticipating his next sentence. She straightened up and settled back into the chair.

"She spent the night and it was an *incredible* night." His eyebrow cocked as he gave her a quick sideways glace. "The next morning when she got up, I had breakfast made, my speech prepared, the ring ready, and she told me she wanted out."

"I'm having a hard time understanding why she broke up with *you*." *What, was she crazy?*

"Yep, just like that." He snapped his fingers. "I never saw it coming."

"Why do you think she would she change things like that?"

"She said she never anticipated we'd last as long as we had, but she had big plans, none of which included settling down in her twenties." Peter slouched back into the chair. "When push came to shove, she didn't want to say yes and then resent me later. Said she had to get something out of her system first."

"And what did she want?"

"She told me she'd taken a job back in Maine. Karen, a friend of hers from high school had started a private practice and had already hired her. It was closer to her family. My residency wouldn't allow much time to travel, nor would I have much flexibility immediately following. She said she didn't want to spend the next three years waiting for me to come home and having no time off."

Shelly shook her head because none of it made sense. "She knew you were in medical school. She had to know what your residency would be like years before this point in your relationship."

"I didn't hold anything back from her. Explained to her many times about the stress of it all, the time commitment. But, in my mind, it would lead to freedom later. Put in the work now for a good, solid life that would could be built on."

"Then you had talked about your future together."

He hung his head as his finger tapped the stem of his barely touched wineglass. "Many times. I'd talk about stability; she'd talk about making her mark in the world. I talked long-term plans and she'd talk short-term goals. I told her everything I wanted out of life and she said she still hadn't figured certain things out."

"Certain things? Like what?"

"She never elaborated. I should have seen it, but I guess I thought I could love her enough, promise her she would get every single thing checked off her mental list and she'd stay."

A giggle from the other room caused them to look up. Polly held up a carrot ornament with a Santa hat. "This is funny."

Tia nodded and the girls continued to decorate the tree as the boys debated on which Marvel and DC superheroes ranked for the higher branches.

"Were children in your life plans?" The question slipped out before she had a chance to catch the words. Shelly slapped her hand over her mouth as if she could scoop them out of the air and shove them back in. "I'm so sorry. That didn't come out right."

Peter gave her a sad smile. "Absolutely. I'd talked with Simone many times about having a family, but she said she didn't want to think about it until her thirties. Guess these two changed that."

"They are beautiful children." Shelly moved closer. "And you're doing a good job."

"I'm on a hard learning curve right now."

"Yes, you are."

"Learning something each day. Nothing like they say in the books, I can tell you that."

"It never is. What's possible in a vacuum or on the pages never exactly translates to real life." She sipped another bit of her wine.

Digory reached for a tall branch to put on an ornament. Freddie lifted him up so he could place the piece exactly where he wanted the bauble to go.

The scene warmed her heart. "Did you ever suspect about the kids?"

"Nope. After that morning, Simone took everything of hers out of my place and I didn't hear from her again. Her forwarding address was her classmate from college's. She walked away and, best I can tell, never looked back."

"You mentioned you reached out to her. I'm surprised she never replied."

"I called. I emailed. I talked to mutual friends. Tried to get her to talk to me, but nothing." He cleared his throat. "I understood from our mutual friend, Colleen, as soon as they threw their caps at graduation, Simone packed up and moved back to Maine. She didn't stay in contact with her either."

"Wow. I wonder why the shift?"

"I don't know. I've dissected it over and over again for an answer. Nothing comes up, but I can tell you this. I certainly wouldn't have been MIA for those two in there. I can't believe she didn't tell me."

"Anything?"

"Anything. Until I got that call a few weeks ago from her friend, Karen, I didn't know they existed."

Shelly didn't think she'd seen someone as fierce about being a father as Peter. Considering he'd only known his parental status such a short time, his commitment to his children was nothing short of impressive. "That must have been a shock."

"It was. You know, you've got a good son there." Peter pointed as Freddie and Digory settled on the floor, figuring out an ornament that appeared to have fallen apart before they'd pulled it from the box.

She swallowed back her sudden onset of tears. She couldn't be sure exactly why the urge to sob had hit her without warning. Could it be his trust in her to tell his story? Or his compliment of her parenting skills? Or the fact he'd surprised her with his immediate commitment to his children?

Maybe because this looks like happily ever after?

She dried her eyes with the back of her hand, refusing to

let her heart get away from her. "Thank you. Some days I don't think I'm doing all that great as the mom and dad." She shrugged. "Of course, there are others where I know I'm the most brilliant mom on the planet. At least for my kids I am."

"I'm still learning what kind of father I need to be."

"What kind of father do you want to be?"

"A damned good one. A dad who's there for you when you need it, even on the days when it's tough to be the parent. A dad who's there because he wants to be, not because he has to be."

After dealing with her ex-husband's excuses and empty attempts to better himself, hearing a man honestly embrace fatherhood set Shelly wonderfully off-center. If the kids hadn't been in the house, she would have crawled into his lap and made his Christmas present come early... several times. "Sounds like you had a great example on how to be a father."

"I did. Do."

"That's an interesting answer." Shelly took a sip of her wine, savoring the way the liquid lingered on her tongue.

He scooted closer then, resting his arm on the table. "After my father died, it was just the four of us and our mom for years."

The familiar Whoville song from *The Grinch Who Stole Christmas* started up in the next room.

Polly and Digs grabbed Freddie's and Tia's hands and pulled them to the couch to watch before standing in the doorway and motioning to the adults.

"Miss Shelly. Daddy. Come on. We're watching *The Grinch*," Polly said excitedly.

"Give us five minutes, sweetie," Peter replied without taking his eyes off Shelly.

Peter flipped his hand over so their palms rested on one another. "A few years after the accident, this local reporter, Charlie, wanted to do a follow-up piece on us, see how we were doing."

"Why?"

"The guy who hit us was up for parole. Charlie had a brother who had been killed by a drunk driver and he wanted to make sure this guy stayed in jail. He asked if he could interview us on it."

"Seems like it's a bit of rubbing salt in your wounds." She grimaced and finished off her wine.

Peter nodded. "My mother agreed to talk with him, but after spending the day with us, he didn't run the piece. Said we shouldn't have to relive it, but instead ran a segment about drunk drivers getting out early from their sentences and used our cases as one of many."

"Sounds like a good guy." Shelly's finger traced the lines of his palm. "Looking out for all of you."

"Charlie's a good man. He fell in love with my mother and took care of her until the day she died. Him being there gave me part of my life back. He helped us each get scholarships for college. He helped Lucy and Edmund when Susan and I were living on the different campuses."

"He sounds amazing." She tried to focus on his words, but touching him sent tingles all through her body. "That's a lot to process. I can't imagine what it was like for you, going through all that."

"It's what had to be done. That tickles." He closed his hand on her fingers that had apparently been brushing the tender skin of his hand.

"Sorry. I didn't realize…" Heat spread to Shelly's cheeks and she chewed her bottom lip.

"I love seeing you flustered," he whispered, the delightful curl to the corner of his full mouth as he slightly leaned forward. "It looks good on you."

"Oh," was the only word Shelly could enunciate because Peter's honest compliment had her flustered in ways she didn't know she could still feel. "I think you've graduated to master flirter."

Leaning in, he whispered, "What qualifies me as expert?"

"I think that might require a kid-free zone," she replied.

"I think you're right." He stood and offered his hand after they were requested by their children for a second time. "Think one of yours would watch mine so we could make that happen?"

"Absolutely." She slid her hand into his as they walked the short distance to the living room where they all snuggled in on the couch until the roast beast got served.

Chapter Sixteen

"ARE YOU SURE you want to do this?"

"No." Peter laced up his skates for the third time, hoping it would help support his ankles better. He stood and realized that ice skating was probably the dumbest sport ever invented. "But the kids wanted to come, so here we are."

After an incredible day with Shelly, Tia, Freddie, Digory and Polly asked if they could all go ice-skating on Miracle Lake the very next day to which the older two kids gave an enthusiastic thumbs-up.

Since they didn't have any place to be until the afternoon, Peter agreed as he started to run out of ways to keep the kids busy.

What he didn't anticipate was his complete inability to stay upright while standing on blades while on an extremely smooth and slick surface.

What could possibly go wrong?

"Peter, you don't have to skate," Shelly coaxed as he attempted to stand upright without looking like a complete idiot. "It's perfectly fine to stand off to the side—"

"No, my kids asked me to skate and I'm gonna skate. Because that's what dads do." He held his hands out wide as his butt tilted behind him. He tried to push off, but he only ended up inching along.

Snails moved faster than this.

Glancing up, he noticed Shelly biting her lip, her shoulders bobbing up and down.

"Are you laughing at me?"

"Only because you're so adorable trying this hard."

"I look like an idiot."

She kissed him on the cheek. "I think it's sexy."

"Really?" He lost his footing and fell on his ass.

"Oh, my gosh. Did I make you fall?" She tried to help him up, but she couldn't get him to his feet.

He sat with his legs in front of him, his butt cold and wet. "Go ahead, Shelly. I'll catch up."

"You sure?"

"Yes, I'm fine. Go, go check on the kids for me." He joked but he couldn't be more frustrated. Peter had always been good at whatever sports he tried, but this, this proved to be the great equalizer and potentially the demolisher of his ego.

He turned to the right and tried to push himself to his feet.

No luck.

He fared no better on the left.

A three-year-old skated by without effort.

Shit. This sucks.

Digory went around him without pause as Polly followed, motioning him to catch up. "Come on!"

Peter somehow managed to get to his feet and walked his

hands up his legs to stand. "Watch out, kids. Don't fall. Watch out for other skaters."

But they were already well out of earshot. He inched along about a yard before he lost his balance and ended up on the ice once again.

Who invented this ridiculous idea?

Slamming his hand on the ice, he muttered a few four letter words before strong hands helped him to his feet.

"Tuck your butt, man. You can't skate in a squat like that." A large kid helped Peter stand and it took two seconds to realize who it was.

"Freddie?"

"Yeah, come on. You can do this," he said with about as much enthusiasm as a sullen teen finds acceptable. "I'll help you."

"Where's your mom?"

"She's with Polly and Digs."

Peter's arms flew out to his sides as he attempted to stand upright.

"You look like you're having a seizure. Calm down. Focus on holding your core strong. It'll help you keep your balance." Freddie skated at a turtle's pace while Peter slowly got the groove of simply standing upright.

"That better?"

"Well, you haven't fallen on your ass for the past five minutes. I'd say it's an improvement."

"Thanks, man." Holding his body upright, Peter's confidence grew stronger for every minute he didn't wipe out. "Now what?"

"Push off with your skate. Like this." Freddie got in front of him and gently pushed with his right skate. The morning sun shimmered off the frozen lake, highlighting the scratches and scrapes of the skates. "Did you see what I did?"

"Yeah, I think so."

Several elementary school kids drifted by and one high-school-aged girl waved at Freddie.

He unenthusiastically waved back. "Try it, but don't shove. Glide."

"Glide." Peter cringed but pushed off and didn't fall on his face.

"I think that girl wanted to get your attention."

"Who?"

"The brunette in the purple sweatshirt." Peter motioned and almost ended up at square one again.

"Tighten your core." Freddie pulled Peter up by his shoulders, helping him find his center. "Okay. Glide."

A few gentle pushes later, Peter hadn't come close to wiping out. "Check me out."

"Way to go. Try it with the other foot, otherwise you're gonna skate in a circle all damned day."

"Damned is a naughty word." Polly playfully shook her finger at Freddie as she skated right past him.

"Sorry. My bad," the teen called out.

The brunette in the purple sweatshirt sauntered by again, this time she said hello.

Pushing off again, Peter made it about five feet before he had to push off with his right. After several successful attempts, Peter began to get more confident, but Freddie still remained at his side. "I appreciate you helping me."

"Sure."

"And for being so great with my kids."

For half a circle around the lake, Freddie didn't say anything. "I heard about your story. About how you didn't know you had kids."

That unexpected comment almost made Peter fall, but he tightened his stomach and managed to stand upright to regain his flow. "I won't lie. It was a shock, still is sometimes."

"How so?"

"I missed nine years of their lives. Nine years I won't get back and that's nine years of them not knowing me either."

"That's tough." Freddie turned and skated backward as he spoke.

"See, now you're just showing off. Skating backward."

Freddie smirked. "What are you going to do?"

"About you skating backward?"

"No, about bonding with your kids. Getting that time back."

With his ankles shooting pains up his legs, Peter motioned to a bench where they both sat down. "I can't. I can't get that time back so I take the time I have and do things like take my kids to Christmas tree farms and make an idiot of myself ice-skating. We'll probably get a goldfish when we get back. Maybe a lizard. Or a dog."

"Get back?" His eyes narrowed. "You're not staying?"

A round of laughter caught Peter's attention. Polly, Digory, and Shelly were in the middle of the lake, skating. Tia stood close by taking pictures.

The scene warmed his heart and the pull to stay grew stronger. "I don't know what I'm doing yet, Freddie."

"Okay." He rested his hands on either side of himself and began to stand but sat back down. "Can you do something for me?"

"Sure. What?"

"Don't hurt my mom."

"What? I would never do that."

He shook his head. "She likes you. I can tell she really likes you and I get it. My dad he… he's screwed up a bunch. Dragged her through some ridiculous shit."

Dragged you through it too. "That's what she's told me."

"But you make her smile. You make her happy and she needs that. Deserves that, but I don't want her hurt."

"You're a good kid, Freddie. I appreciate you being honest with me." Peter decided he'd do anything in his power not to hurt Shelly. Even something as stupid as more ice-skating.

"Just… if you're not gonna stay. Don't string her along, okay?"

Peter nodded and extended his hand. "That's fair."

He responded in kind. "And the brunette? She's not my type. Too self-absorbed."

"You've got plenty of time to worry about that."

Giving Peter a nod, Freddie skated away and joined a group of teens at the far side of the lake.

Within moments, Shelly came over and sat next to Peter.

She gave him a quick kiss on the cheek. "Having fun?"

"I've fallen half a dozen times, I'm gonna feel beat-up tomorrow, and I look like an idiot, so yes, I'm having a blast."

"You're funny."

The giggles of his children caught his attention once again and he tilted his chin toward them. "If that's what I get to hear doing all this crap, then yeah, I'm having fun."

Shelly helped him stand. "Well, then, let's get you out there so you can fall another half dozen times. Isn't parenting wonderful?"

"It's a blast."

AFTER A COUPLE of hours of skating, then lunch at the Pizza Parlor across from the Graff, they got ready to head over to Lucy and Thomas's house for an early dinner and a proper introduction.

Upon arrival, Peter and the kids walked into the house that smelled of lemon chicken and chocolate pie.

Lucy gave a quick round of hugs before introducing them all to her fiancé, Thomas and Edmund introduced them to his girlfriend, Jade.

Within thirty minutes, they were all sitting at the round table passing plates and catching up.

Digory, Lucy, and Thomas. Polly between Jade and Edmund. Peter sat between Jade and Lucy.

"How's your visit been so far?" Thomas nudged Peter with his elbow, making Peter cringe. "Sorry, you okay?"

"We went ice-skating this morning."

Edmund laughed and jumped from his chair. "Then you need a beer, because I know you're beat-up from falling."

"It was so cool. There's this group of kids who play hockey out there," Digory explained as he put a large piece of bread over his broccoli. "And Freddie can skate backward."

"Freddie? You mean Freddie Westbrook?" Lucy smiled as she placed some chicken on his plate.

"Yeah, and Tia, she took all these pictures. So cool." Polly reached for the green beans, but had trouble picking up the bowl. Before Peter could help her, Edmund already had it well in hand.

"Freddie and Tia are great kids." Jade held up the salad dressing, the international sign of *who wants this one*. "I still want to punch Gill in the face, though."

Edmund, Thomas, and Lucy agreed.

Peter raised his hand, but the muscles in his shoulder spasmed. *Good grief. I need to work out more.* "We've had a lot of fun with them lately."

"Them?" Lucy cocked her head, a mischievous smirk on her face.

"Miss Shelly, Freddie, and Tia took us to the Christmas tree farm yesterday." Polly shoved a large spoonful of mashed potatoes in her mouth.

Biting back a smile, Lucy nodded. "That sounds wonderful. Did you get to decorate their tree?"

"Yep, and we stayed and all watched *The Grinch*."

Thomas raised an eyebrow. "Wow, you work fast, Peter.

In town three days and you've already helped decorate a Christmas tree and watched a holiday classic."

"Better be careful. You might not want to leave," Edmund added.

"Yeah. Maybe not." Panic twisted his gut uncomfortably tight.

Lucy leaned over. "Hey, if you're going to bounce your knee the entire meal, could you move it over a little? You're going to rub a hole in my boot."

"Sorry. Sorry." Peter took a deep breath and readjusted his leg.

Once they'd gluttoned themselves and the kids were given the assignment of decorating Lucy and Thomas's tree, Lucy and Edmund pulled Peter aside.

"Hey, how are you holding up?" Lucy patted his shoulder.

"I'm exhausted, Luce."

"I bet you are, but you've done this before." Edmund took a long swig of his beer.

Peter leaned back, his brow furrowed. "What are you talking about?"

Lucy raised an eyebrow. "You raised Edmund and me. Helped out Mom by getting a part-time job."

"Only half the year. Susan gave up one season, worked the opposite."

"But you organized that. *You* did that. You made sure Edmund and I did our homework, got our lunches made, got us to school until we could do it on our own." She wrapped her arms around his shoulders. "Peter, you've got all the skills to do this."

As much as he appreciated his sister's praise, he couldn't quite believe her. "Yeah, but this is different, Lucy. These are my kids. Mine. The entire weight of responsibility falls to me."

Edmund leaned against the wall. "It did last time too. Mom couldn't do anything and who else did we have until Charlie came around? Just us."

His siblings were right, of course, but this time was different. This time these children were his and his alone.

All alone.

Rubbing his shoulder, Peter cringed at the soreness that had already started. "I'm going over this in my head every time someone asks me if I'm staying. How am I going to do this on my own? How did she do this on her own?"

"My guess is she had help. A lot of help." Lucy crossed her arms. "Did she give you any information on who she hired or better yet, why she never contacted you?"

"Hey, Peter… Dad." Digory walked into the hallway.

"Yes, Son?"

"Uncle Thomas said you can string popcorn and put it on a tree. Can you really do that?"

"Yes, people used to do it all the time."

He turned, announcing, "It's a go, Uncle Thomas."

Edmund tipped up his chin. "Peter, what can we do to help?"

"I don't know. Her friend, Karen, gave me an envelope with a bunch of information in it. Told me to open it when I had time. Said it answered my questions."

"So have you?" Lucy leaned forward.

"No, not yet." He leaned against the wall next to Edmund.

"Why not?"

"What if I did something that I can't forgive myself for? What if I drove her away and had no idea? Maybe I don't want to know why."

The children giggled in the other room, making his throat go dry. "Maybe, I just want to start right here. Right now with my kids and not think about why I've missed nine years with them." *Because I'll never get it back.*

"Peter, I can't tell you what to do, but you're exhausted." Lucy grabbed his hand.

"You do look wiped out." Edmund playfully punched him in the arm.

"Why don't you let the kids stay here tonight?"

"You'd do that?" The idea of sleep without listening for every little sound from their room did sound appealing.

"Of course. I'm off tomorrow. Why don't you let us take them to the movies or skating again and we'll bring them back to the hotel after lunchtime?"

"Can we go back before then? They are having a cookie decorating in the lobby." Standing in the doorway, Polly held up a Christmas ornament that looked like a superhero. "Mr. Bob said it's at eleven. Is this Black Widow?"

"Yes, I think it is." Lucy nodded. "We can have you back for the cookie decorating."

Polly gave a thumbs-up and returned to ornament arranging.

Edmund motioned for Peter to follow him back into Christmas-tree central. "Give you time to breathe. Come on, let's get this tree decorated and I'll get you back to the hotel before I go to work."

The children and all the adults spent the next couple of hours perfectly decorating the tree, just like they'd done when they were children.

Edmund allowed Digory to take over the tree-topping and lifted his nephew to place the start on the top.

Stringing the popcorn proved to be more of a challenge than Digory anticipated, but Polly's nimble fingers handled it well.

When Digory tried, most of the popped kernels fell off the string and he ate the other half.

By the time they were done, Peter hurt all over and the kids were ready for their sleepover with their aunt and uncle.

Edmund dropped them back to the hotel to grab a quick bag and went to work. Lucy arrived not long afterward.

As much as Peter wanted sleep, his anxiety kicked in seeing the children leaving. "You sure it's not too much trouble, Luce?"

"It's fine, Peter. We've got this."

Digory and Polly threw a few things in their suitcases, each gave Peter a quick hug and ran out, both declaring it was their turn to push the elevator button.

"Get some sleep."

"Hey, Lucy. Thomas seems like a nice guy. I'm glad you're happy."

"And I want you to be, too," she replied. "Because after all you've given us, you should be."

Chapter Seventeen

C HRISTMAS EVE MORNING arrived and the ground hadn't lost its beautiful carpet of white. Peter stared out the window of their room at the Graff, watching the town come alive and the twinkling lights dim with the morning sun.

It would be Peter's first Christmas without the beach.

Without wearing flip-flops and shorts and without working.

Because all of them were older and without children, the Davidson siblings always worked on Christmas Day so families with little ones could be at home to play Santa and open presents with loved ones who had limited time off.

Charlie, their stepfather, would offer to work as well at the news station Christmas morning. For the past fifteen years, he'd become the local Christmas-caster where he'd show a video montage of his visits from the previous month to local pediatric hospitals, homeless shelters, foster homes, and hospice patients.

He'd bring food, gifts, supplies, and award scholarships to those trying to go back to school and better their lives and then they'd all get together on December twenty-sixth for their holiday celebration.

"I'm gonna miss seeing that." Peter began to turn away from the window until a bit of movement caught his attention.

Edmund jogged down the length of Front Street before turning down Court.

"It's gotta be freezing ass cold out there. No thanks."

$$\sim\!\!\!\sqrt{\heartsuit 2}\!\!\!\sim$$

HE TOSSED ON some workout clothes and hit the gym hard. Afterward, he returned to the room and soaked his aching muscles in a hot shower before ordering room service.

A little before eleven, he met Lucy and the kids in the lobby.

Mr. Bob set up several tables in front of the gift shop. Other children from town were already present, donning aprons and picking out the shape of cookie they wanted.

Lucy reported she had some last-minute Christmas shopping to do and headed out.

The air smelled of sugar cookies, cinnamon, and evergreen.

Polly and Digory quickly grabbed spots across from each other and a young woman named Trinity helped them put on their aprons.

Polly narrowed her eyes. "You look familiar. You smile like the lady at the diner."

"Well, that's good because that's my mom," Trinity replied enthusiastically. "She helped me make the cookies you're about to decorate,"

Offering the kids choices of a snowman, a house, a reindeer head, or a snowflake to decorate, Trinity added, "You might get to do two if we have enough."

"Do you know Freddie and Tia?" Digory asked as he picked out the perfect canvas. "Because Freddie hit me in the face with a snowball the other day."

"That was you? He said you hit him with a snowball too." Trinity's eyes went wide with mock surprise. "Said you have a good arm."

Digory threw his head back and laughed. "I did and snow went everywhere in his hair."

"Yes, Freddie and Tia are some of my best friends. They'll be here anytime to help."

"Yay!" his children cheered and Peter inched closer to the table, awaiting instructions to help out.

Trinity patted his shoulder. "Go take a break, Dr. Davidson. Go get a cup of coffee or take a nap. We've got it covered."

The idea of a little more downtime certainly appealed to him, but he didn't want to leave his kids if it would cause them any stress. They'd handled their sleepover at his sister's perfectly well.

If he hadn't been so exhausted that night, he would have spent the entire time worrying about them. As soon as Lucy closed the door to his hotel room, he'd wandered over to the bed and laid down, only planning to sleep for a few minutes, but ended up waking up with the sun shining on his face and every muscle in his body on fire.

When he checked his phone, he had two missed calls from Shelly and one from the kids' neighbor, Karen.

And he'd missed them terribly the entire time they were gone and couldn't wait to hear about what they'd done.

This moment would be no exception. "You sure you want me to go? I could stay and help?"

"We're fine, Dad." Polly waved him off as she stared at her cookie choices.

Relief and guilt simultaneously slammed into him. *Is it like this for every parent?* "I'll have my phone, if you need me."

Trinity pointed to the door. "Go. We've got a bunch of stuff planned. Santa's, well, Mr. Nicolas is going to be here in an hour. Then we'll have one more project to do before they're ready to be picked up."

"How long again?"

She rocked her hands back and forth. "Let's say two hours."

Panic set in, but he pushed it aside "Two hours. Okay."

"Bye, Dad," Polly called.

"You sure you don't need me to stay?" *Please say no. I mean yes. I mean… shit, I don't know.*

"Dr. Davidson. It's okay. Go do something fun." Trinity laughed. "The kids are in good hands."

"See you later." Digory gave Peter a high five before he returned to picking the perfect color hat for his snowman right as the front doors opened.

Half a dozen more children walked in along with Tia and Freddie.

The joy on his children's faces almost sent Peter to his knees when his children ran to meet the older two, who immediately hugged them as though they were longtime friends.

As soon as his two were back at the table, they met other children including siblings Pippa, William, and their cousins Zachary, Matthew, Madeline, and Luke.

The children all began speaking at once and, somehow, understood what each other were saying as the teens worked around the table preparing bags of icing, passing out plates, and helping the kids make their choice of cookie.

Mr. Bob, the front desk guy, smiled while helping a family with check-in. His Christmas-lights sweater intermittently blinked from small lights sewn into the garment spelling a script Ho-Ho-Ho.

The Christmas trees behind the entire cookie decorating activity made the moment holiday-card worthy.

Comfort settled around him like a warm hug and he couldn't help but wonder if Marietta, Montana, might be where he and his kids could start their lives together.

The idea of settling here, took a firm hold on his future plans.

He could now easily understand why his siblings fell in love with this world.

Why they fell in love with the people.

How they fell in love with that one special person in this idyllic town.

Love?

The mere thought of Shelly put his life back into focus

and a smile on his face.

He loved that about her.

Loved? No way.

A rich round of laughter pulled his attention from his introspection.

Freddie, Tia, Digory, and Polly stood together, helping one another complete their crafts. Digory said something that had all of them smiling.

Tia snapped several pictures of the children working and more kids arrived to participate, including a girl from Denver named, Phoebe, who talked about being in Marietta for Christmas, with her father.

The moment hit his heart as he recalled so many times he and his siblings found joy in the simplest of things like making cookies.

Even in the darkest of times, they'd found ways to keep each other sane. Happy. Entertained.

The bond between his brother and sisters only strengthened after the loss of their father and later their mother.

He couldn't imagine the world without them.

He couldn't imagine *his* world without them and, at that instant, Peter wanted the same for his children.

A life full of love and laughter.

Yeah, he loved it here. He loved everything about it.

Damn. How did that happen so quickly?

If he'd been asked a month ago what his Christmas plans were, he would never have predicted he'd be standing in a small Montana town trying to make the first Christmas with his children as memorable as possible.

PATRICIA W. FISCHER

Or that he'd fallen in total love with and lusted after a dark-haired beauty who he couldn't stop having erotic dreams about.

The very same beauty that he swore stood under the mistletoe of the dental tree right now.

He blinked to verify she actually stood there.

Crooking her finger, she raised an eyebrow.

Looking around, he made sure she hadn't motioned to anyone else. When he looked back, he pointed to himself. "Me?"

"Yes, you," she mouthed.

He swallowed hard and like Molly Ringwald did in *Sixteen Candles*, he walked straight to the object of his affections with great anticipation.

"Merry Christmas Eve to you." She cocked her head. "Fancy meeting you here."

"Yes. Fancy that." He anticipated kissing her. "That was quite a Jake Ryan-Samantha Baker moment."

"I wondered if you'd get that."

"I did. I missed you." Her lips were the perfect shade of pink.

"I missed you. Sorry I didn't get back to you yesterday. I crashed."

"What?" Her forehead furrowed.

"Lucy took the kids Saturday night after you and I went ice-skating. I passed out until Sunday morning." He rolled his head from side to side. "Still sore from falling on my ass so much."

"Well, it's a great ass if you ask me."

Her comment made his pants began to feel a bit snugger. "What brings you to the Graff today?"

"Since the kids were busy if you'd like to go do something, just us? Unless you have some Christmas shopping to do."

"Just us?" His heart beat double-time as his pants became uncomfortably tight. "Shopping's done. Lucy picked up my stuff from the western wear store and the rest I ordered through Amazon Prime."

"Need help wrapping anything?" Shelly chewed on her bottom lip.

"Nope. Ordered it all already wrapped. Thanks, Jeff Bezos."

She gave a knowing nod. "He's kept many, many parents sane during the holidays."

The delighted voices of the multiple children discussing their decoration decisions filled the lobby.

Shelly smirked as she ran her hands down the front of his shirt. "Well, sounds like you've got all that taken care of."

"Would you like to go get a cup of coffee?" Which wasn't really what Peter wanted to do, but he didn't want to push this any faster than she wanted to go.

"Coffee sounds nice. Or…" She leaned in brushing her lips against his. "We could go upstairs and you could practice your master flirting skills."

The warmth of her breath tickled his ear and he couldn't think of any place else in the world he'd like to be at that moment. "I do love practicing."

"Okay, then. Lead the way."

Chapter Eighteen

WITHIN MINUTES THEY were back in his room. He put up the do not disturb signs on his and the kids' rooms and halfway closed the door joining them.

She tilted her chin up, looking deep into his eyes. "Peter, if you don't kiss me soon, I'm gonna—"

He brushed his lips against hers, before sliding his tongue along the seam.

The simplest of touches and already, Peter never thought he'd get enough of her.

Her mouth opened and his tongue swept in. The sweet flavor of peppermint mixed with her delicious touch.

He couldn't help but moan, which only appeared to encourage her.

He pulled her flush as he nibbled her lower lip.

Sliding her hands around his body, she deepened their kiss, her tongue sliding along his.

It had been too long since he'd been engulfed with this kind of passion. All consuming. Wild. Hungry.

He restrained from ripping the buttons on her shirt off and getting his hands on her bare skin sooner.

"Shelly." He nibbled on the pulse point of her neck, inhaling the lavender scent of her hair.

She gasped, grabbing handfuls of his shirt. "Yes, Peter."

His mouth covered hers again. "You taste good."

Even with previous women, Peter didn't experience this kind of chemistry and certainly not this quickly.

He ran his hands inside her coat, pushing it off her shoulders and letting it drop to the floor. His thumbs tenderly brushed the sides of her body, her breasts as he moved his hands back up.

He gasped as he came up for air. "Shelly."

"Yes?" she panted, her hands running down his chest.

"Any chance you'd like to move this closer to the bed?"

"Yes." The corner of her mouth curled up. "But I haven't been to Bozeman."

"What does that mean, again?"

With quick fingers, she unfastened the top button and moved on to the next. "That means I don't want Carol Bingley in my business so I don't have any condoms."

"I don't have any either." *Dammit.*

"You do know"—she panted as she kept loosening his buttons—"that you not having anything tells me you didn't expect anything and that's a big turn on."

"Seems kind of counterproductive. Wanting something, but not preparing for it." He exhaled when her hands ran across his bare chest and slid his shirt from his body.

"One of the great paradoxes of life I guess. Do you know how long I've wanted to see you without your shirt?"

"No."

Placing her hands on his skin, she fanned out her fingers

and let her fingertips trace along the lines of muscle. "Just like I remembered."

"What?" His forehead furrowed as she placed featherlight kisses across his skin.

"I had to see if you had chest trauma after the accident. I assure you my observation was specifically clinical." She ran her tongue over his nipple, sending shockwaves of desire through him.

"Clinical, huh? As long as it was for a good reason, I can't complain." With his hands on her wait, he moved backward and sat on the bed, guiding her to stand in front of him.

She moved closer, the delicious smell of lavender drifted around them as she cupped his face. "I never thought we'd get time alone."

"Me neither." His fingers traced the gentle slope of her neck, making her shudder. "I'm not gonna lie, I've been thinking about you a lot."

"Yeah, how much?"

"Every waking minute." He nibbled the pulse point of her neck and his hand cupped her breast over her perfectly fitting sweater.

"Take this off me." She held her arms over her head and he made quick work of releasing her of that extra layer, leaving her in her tank top and bra.

"Perfect." Greedily, he placed kisses along the swell of her breasts.

She sighed and ran her fingers through his hair. "Oh, my, that's, that's—"

"Yes, it is." He brushed his lips along the curve of her shoulder to her ear. "What can I do for you?"

She swallowed hard. "For me?"

"Yes. For you. *To* you." Her shocked look made him wonder what raced through her brain. "Do you have any idea how long I've waited for a woman like you?"

"Tell me."

"A long damn time."

"Damn is a *naughty* word, you know."

"And I can do naughty things."

She playfully answered, "What kind of things?"

"If you let me take that top off you, I'll show you."

"Can you do some of those things while you say them in another language?"

"*Sí. Oui.* Yes."

"That's an offer I won't refuse." She pushed him down to the bed before straddling him.

His slid his hands up her back and expertly relieved her of her top before laying a path of kisses from her cleavage to her collarbone. As his fingers gently pulled straps off her shoulders. "Can I take this off you... real slow?"

"Don't go slow," she panted, "I want your hands on me right now."

"*Ti desidero.* I want you." With nimble fingers, he popped the clasps and her bra ended up somewhere near the bedroom door. His hands slowly inched up her body, his thumbs grazing over her nipples before sliding over her waist, her hips, and up again.

When he brushed the sides of her breasts, he watched her

anticipation of his thumbs tracing her sensitive flesh once again.

"You're flirting extremely well." She gasped. "More."

"*Mas?*"

"Are you asking if I want more?"

"*Oui.*"

"Yes. Please, *mas.*"

He more than complied, cupping her and slowly brushing her nipples with each finger as he fanned them over her. "You like that?"

"Yes."

"You make me crazy. *Mi fai impazzire,*" he whispered, loving how she reacted to his words. "*Bellissima.*"

"Is this still part of the naughtiness you've promised?"

"You're damned right it is." His voice rasped low and lusty. His pants uncomfortably tight, but his body buzzed from her touch. "How far do you want this to go?"

She raised an eyebrow. "We can't have sex."

"Right, because neither of us have been to Bozeman." His hands moved up and down her back. "Clothes stay on then."

Shelly bit her lip. "I want to see all of you."

"I thought you said no sex." Although seeing all of her would certainly make his holiday wishes come true.

"Okay, most of you."

"Most?" His hands cupped her butt and pulled her flush to him. "You'll have to tell me what stays and what goes."

"That's fair." He sucked her bottom lip.

Running her fingers through his hair, she moaned and

pulled him closer.

Inch by torturous inch, he slid his hands up her body until he brushed across her nipples. His tongue teased the tender tips. "You like that? What about this?"

Her fingers dug into his shoulders. "Don't stop touching me."

"*Oui, madame.*" His tongue danced against her nipple before sucking one as his fingers tenderly brushed against the other. The sweet smell of lavender on her skin, the feel of her in his mouth only made him crave more.

When sucked her harder, her hips ground against him.

Any reservation he had of getting involved with her dissolved. Without even trying, she'd stolen his heart and now he wanted nothing more than to get as much of Shelly Westbrook as possible.

Running one hand along her back and then along the waist of her pants, he cupped her butt. "You've got a great ass."

A nervous giggle escaped her. "Thank you."

Sweeping his fingers beneath her breasts, he brushed her peaked, sensitive flesh again.

"More. *Mas.*"

He smiled against her skin. "What's more?"

"I want yours and my pants off."

"What about under that?"

She swallowed hard, hesitation in her eyes. "Did you go commando?"

"No. Not today."

"Underwear stays on."

"*Claro*," Peter whispered against the area between her neck and shoulder. "Wrap your legs around me."

Holding her in his arms, he stood, turned around and set her back on the bed.

"Oh, you're good." Shelly giggled.

"Now, stay there," he coaxed. Peter moved his hands down the slope of her belly, her hips. When he reached the seam of her pants, he raised an eyebrow as though waiting for to her to give him a nod.

Sitting up, she grabbed him by the shoulders and kissed him. "Stop being so gallant. I'll let you know when it's time to stop."

"Deal." Making quick work of the button and zipper, he slipped his thumbs through the side belt loops and slid off her pants.

The more of her legs he exposed, the more her breathing quickened. She grabbed handfuls of the bedspread when he rested his hands on either side of her.

Without a word, he marveled at the perfect curves of her body. They were like a gently winding road and he decided he hadn't traveled quite enough.

His hands itched to wander across the smoothness of her skin, the fullness of her breasts, the muscles of her thighs.

"Touch me."

He growled as his hand fanned out over her belly before inching them down between her legs and under her panties.

She sucked in a breath when he took one nipple in his mouth and tenderly sucked. His finger ran along the seam of her outer lips and back up again.

Her pink-laced panties were beyond wet with anticipation as she moaned while he intimately touched her.

Her response to his touch sent him spiraling to an early climax and he popped the button on his pants, hoping to give him extra time.

With his tongue on her breasts, his fingers stroking the most intimate part of her, she arched her back.

Her fingers dug into his shoulders. "Please, don't stop."

Her hips began to move with his hand when his thumb pressed on her hard swollen nub and his fingers slipped inside her.

"Peter." She moaned rocking with the tempo he set. "Yes!" she gasped as she leaned her entire body into him. "Yes, Peter, yes."

As he increased the suction on her nipple, her hips moved faster. "Yes. Oh, yes."

"*C'est bon. It's good.*" And when his thumb stroked the hard knot of her sex, he wiggled against it. Her muscles gripped his fingers like a vice and bathed them in her liquid heat.

Her hips thrust and her thighs squeezed around his wrist. The ripple of her orgasm massaged his hand.

"And that's how you reach expert status," she sighed blissfully.

He slipped his hand out of her panties, but before he could back away, she sat up and grabbed him by the belt loop.

"Where the hell do you think you're going?" Without taking her eyes off him, she unzipped his pants and pushed them off his body.

"Not sure." He honestly wasn't since her hands were wandering his body, his mind had gone completely blank. "Isn't hell a naughty word?"

"Well, you aren't the only one who wants to work on their flirting skills."

When her fingers ran along the edge of his underwear, he grimaced, hoping to keep control for as long as possible. "Whatever I can do to help you perfect your craft."

"And to answer your question, yes, it can be naughty." She pushed his underwear halfway off his hips before taking him in her hand. "Very, very naughty."

Chapter Nineteen

SHELLY DIDN'T THINK there could be anything that would bring her off her glorious high after spending some very much desired alone time with Peter Davidson.

Even during the short drive home, her body continued to tingle from his masterful hands and attention to detail.

He'd excited her so intently her concerns about her age, her physical failures, her flaws disappeared.

Instead, she soaked in every erotic moment, relishing his touch and how he'd exuberantly responded when she returned the favor.

He'd done it tenderly, masterfully, exquisitely.

And in multiple languages.

A satisfied sigh escaped her thinking of him, barely dressed, hovering over her, bringing her to climax.

With tomorrow being Christmas and everything being closed, she wondered if a quick trip to the local pharmacy would be worth it because she'd never make it to Bozeman before the stores closed.

It would certainly give Carol Bingley something to discuss over her holiday dinner.

She glanced at the clock.

Four.

Shoot, missed the Christmas Eve hours.

"No worries, I'll just make our Bozeman book trip the day after Christmas." She laughed at her need for prophylactics at her age, but until she knew where she and Peter were headed, she'd take no chances.

For now, she'd spend the next couple of hours in a warm bath and snuggled up in her favorite pajamas before Freddie and Tia came home from helping Trinity and Gabby set up the diner for the free Christmas Day feast.

Her body happily buzzed imagining Peter's lips, his tongue, his… "What the hell?"

Parking in her driveway, she slammed her car door as she shook her head. "No. No. No. No. Go home!"

Dressed impeccably in what looked like an overpriced suit, high-end overcoat, and Prada loafers, Gill turned and flashed her his perfectly polished smile. "Shelly. I'm so glad to see you. I can't get in. My key won't work."

She shoved keys in her pocket and stood at the end of the sidewalk. "It's because you don't live here. I rekeyed the locks the day I got back."

"Why would you do that, Shelly?"

She threw her head back and laughed at his arrogance. "Why, Gill? Why would I lock you out of *my* house?"

"Our house."

"No, it's my house. I paid for it. It's in my name."

He clicked his tongue as he sauntered toward her. "You're still mad at me, aren't you?"

"Consider me nuclear."

"You're funny."

"And you're a selfish piece of shit." She moved around him, but he followed her.

He grabbed her arm before she could move completely by him. "Come on, Shelly. You know you love me."

"No, no I don't." Her finger shook so she played with her keys to keep them occupied. "I haven't for a very long time."

Hearing herself say it out loud felt cathartic. "Get lost, Gill."

"I'm really sorry this time."

"This time. This time." Whipping around, she yanked her arm free. "What about next time and the time after that? Or maybe all those other times you apologized before and you said you were *really* sorry. I guess they meant nothing?"

That mischievous grin spread across his face. "Come on, Shell, you know you miss me."

"About as much as I'd miss a raging case of herpes." She was tired of taking the high road. She was tired of dealing with his lies, his betrayals, and, this time, she absolutely believed she didn't have to. "Stay away from me, Gill and stay away from Freddie."

"You can't keep me from my son."

"I can if you're not paying child support." She pulled her keys out and found the one she needed. "Plus, he'll be eighteen soon and it'll be up to him at that point if he wants anything to do with you."

"What? I'm sorry."

"Yeah, you are sorry."

His lighthearted banter began to fade as the realization set in. "You're serious."

"Why wouldn't I be? You've done this to us before and you'll do it again whether I take you back or not." She stuffed her hands in her pockets to keep from throat punching him.

The smirk turned into a snarl. "What, you upset because she can have more babies than you? Is that why you're upset?"

"Gill, there are so many reasons I'm upset with you, I don't even know where to begin." Her hands trembled with rage and her heart slammed against her ribs to the point of pain.

He threw his hands up in frustration. "Why is it *my* problem that you can't have more kids?"

His cruel comments hurt her as much as a slap across the face. She froze and stepped away from the front door. "Get. Off. My. Porch."

"Serena kicked me out. I'll be alone for Christmas."

"And you think you get to stay here?"

"Shelly, come on. It's hell with little kids. They cry and they're demanding and I can't go anywhere. They ruin my clothes."

"Yes, speaking of that. That suit. Those shoes. Where did you get the money for all that?"

"I'm working with a friend who helped me get the clothes for a new business venture."

"I like how you left all the pronouns out of that sentence. What is she, a sales girl at Macy's? Meet her on one of your last trips to Bozeman?"

"Hey, I need a job. Serena's working and I'm stuck at home, babysitting."

"It's not babysitting if they are *your* kids. It's called parenting, but it's not that you did much of that for the past decade, is it?"

"Shell."

"If you *Shell* me one more time, I will find a way to make it look like an accident." She turned to him and in the calmest voice she could find, she replied, "Go home. Go home to your little kids and their mom."

"What about my big kid and his mom?" He reached for her hand but she slapped it away.

"Don't you dare think you're going to weasel back into our lives. You crushed Freddie with what you did and I will never forgive you for that." Sticking her finger in his chest, she pushed him away. "You literally made your bed and laid in it at least three times with Serena and the nameless other women you decided to betray our family with."

The overpowering smell of cheap Hugo Boss cologne choked her. "Stay off my porch, Gill."

"Shelly." He held his hands out like some TV evangelist. "Forgive me."

"No!" She responded so loudly, she was sure they'd probably heard her all the way to Main Street Diner.

"Shelly, I made a mistake." His shoulders slumped like a child who'd been scolded, but he only did it for theatrics.

"No, you're only sorry you got caught."

"But I've loved you since our first date. Since the first

time I saw you."

"Spare me the love-at-first-site bullshit again. Love means nothing if you can't keep promises."

He shook his head as if he'd been hit with something. "There's something different about you. Something... you're really not going to let me stay here?"

"No!"

"Shelly."

"Go away."

"Shell."

"Dad. Mom said you need to leave." Freddie's deep voice echoed in the still of the afternoon.

Relief flooded Gill's face. "Freddie. Thank God you're here. Your mother. She must be on her period or something—"

"Mom said you need to leave." He held a tray of cookies in front of him, leftovers from the decorating event at the Graff.

Tia squared her shoulders and began to walk by Gill, but stopped. "Just so you know, my dad can make it look like an accident."

A nervous laugh escaped Gill, but fear flashed across his eyes as Tia talked inside.

Shelly bit her lip to keep from laughing. "Go on, Gill. We don't need you here."

Turning, Gill faced his son. "Freddie. Come on man. Tell your mother I'm supposed to be here."

Freddie's forehead creased as his shoulders fell. He slowly approached his father and stopped when they stood nose-to-nose. "Why?"

"Freddie, please. Go inside." Shelly tugged on her son's arm, but when he refused to move, she didn't encourage him further.

He needs to know what kind of man Gill is so he will know how not to be such a worthless human being.

Shelly held her breath, hoping for once in his life, Gill would say the right thing.

I swear, if you crush him, Gill, you'll never father another child.

"Why what?" Gill shrugged. "Why what? Why did I leave? Why did I screw up again? Why did I think I could do this without your mom? Why what, Freddie?"

With his jaw clenched, her son glared at his father. "Why weren't we enough?"

If Shelly hadn't seen it for herself, she wouldn't have believed it.

For the first time in his life, Gill Westbrook had no immediate response.

No canned answer.

No flippant comeback.

No excuse.

In fact, if Shelly didn't know any better, a hint of guilt might have flickered across his face, but Gill never took responsibility for anything.

Guilt didn't exist in his dictionary.

But the pride she had for her son overshadowed that and he would never be his father.

Freddie stood tall and defiant, half a head taller than his

father. "That why, Dad. Why couldn't you have just been happy with us? The three of us."

"Where is this coming from? I didn't raise you to question me." Gill threaded his thumbs through is belt loops as he bounced his head like an overconfident rooster.

"You're right." Freddie leaned forward making Gill take a step back. "You didn't raise me. Mom did and she and I and Tia don't need you."

"Now wait a minute—"

"You need to leave." Freddie pointed toward the street. "Right now."

"You don't get to talk to me that way." He pushed Freddie backward, sending the tray of cookies all over the hardwoods of the porch.

Fury surged to the surface and Shelly lunged at her ex-husband, making him scramble backward. "Don't you ever touch him again, do you hear me? The moment you walked away from us, you gave up any rights in this house."

A sly smirk spread across Gill's face. "Come on, Shell. You don't mean—"

She stabbed him in the chest with her finger, backing him down the stairs and halfway to the sidewalk. "Don't tell me what I mean and what I don't mean. You have no say who's in my life. You vetoed that when you started cheating on me."

"It's Christmas," he whined.

Shelly faced her ex and for the first time in her life, believed she deserved so much more than what Gill would promise. "You've made your choices. You don't get to make those kinds of unilateral decisions anymore without major consequences, no matter what day of the year it is."

"Shelly, she's not you." Gill's eyes watered with crocodile tears.

"It doesn't matter. She's the mother of your children."

"I love you. I've always—"

"Go home, Dad." Freddie cut him off.

"But this is my home." Gill put his foot on the step.

Freddie let out a long breath as though he were gathering every bit of strength he had. "Not anymore."

Without another word, she and Freddie walked away and neither ever looked back.

Chapter Twenty

THE SMALL CHRISTMAS tree and presents had been brought up to Peter's room after the children had fallen asleep on Christmas Eve.

Peter stayed up until two in the morning arranging the presents and placing some of Mr. Nicolas's hand-carved ornaments on the branches along with a short string of white and red lights and garland.

Stepping back, Peter admired his work. Pride filled his chest and he understood why his parents stayed up so late every Christmas Eve to make things as perfect as they could.

He hoped to make his children's first Christmas together more than magical.

After turning off all the lights except for the ones on the tree, he fell into bed and hoped for sugar plum fairies dancing in his head dreams.

Instead, he inhaled the sheets and could still smell Shelly's lavender body wash. Every muscle in his body tingled remembering how she reacted to his touch. How she cried out his name in this very bed.

How she made him fall apart using her talented hands.

He drifted into a deep sleep with spicy dreams.

The next morning as the sun peeked over the horizon, he heard his children's excited gasps right before they both jumped on his bed.

"Dad! Dad! He came! He came!" Polly clapped her hands as she excitedly patted Peter on the shoulder. "Peter. Dad. Santa came!"

Digory gave a thumbs-up as he put on a Santa hat. "Guess you hitting him didn't put us on the naughty list, after all."

"Where did you get the hat?" Peter stretched as she joined them at the tree.

"It was right here, on the presents."

"Okay, I guess I missed that." He rubbed the sleep out of his eyes and started a cup of coffee while Digory spent the next several minutes passing out gifts.

Once everything had been distributed, the children handed him a paper bag, decorated with Christmas stickers. "We made this for you."

"Made this? When?"

Polly twirled her stuffed unicorn's tail between her fingers. "Yesterday."

"When you and Miss Shelly went to coffee."

"Yes. Coffee." Carefully, he opened the bag so he didn't rip it and pulled out two homemade picture frames made of foam. Inside, were pictures of the three of them from the Christmas tree farm. Peter's heart jumped to his throat. "Where did you get these?"

"Freddie took this one." Digory tapped the one with the three of them feeding the horses.

"And Tia took this one." Polly handed Peter the photo of them sitting in the sleigh, all smiling as if they had no cares or worries in the world.

"Wow." Tears ran down his face realizing these would be the first pictures he'd have with his children. A captured moment of bliss. A priceless gift. "I had no idea they took pictures of us."

"They're cool." Digory grabbed a present with the Christmas rodeo wrapping paper on it and ripped it open.

"Yes, yes they are. I love them. Thank you." His vision blurred from the sudden onset of tears. He unapologetically wiped them away.

"We decorated the frames." Polly explained. "I did this one with candy canes and Digory did the one with snowmen."

"I couldn't ask for a better gift."

"What?" Digory's voice went up two octaves as he held up the University of Montana gloves. "But you said I couldn't have these."

Peter laughed. "I said I wasn't going to buy them for you that day, but to put them on your Christmas list."

Without warning, Digory launched himself at Peter and wrapped his arms around his father's neck. "Thanks, Dad."

Holding his son close, Peter nodded, but words failed him. His chest swelled with pride to the point of pain before Digory gave Peter a pat on the back and returned to opening presents.

Polly gleefully held up items she'd seen at the western wear store, including a pair of small sparkling earrings.

As the children opened their gifts, he soaked in their reactions and excitement and by the time they got to the last gift, Peter didn't know who'd enjoyed their first Christmas morning the most so far. His children or himself.

Digory held up two remote control tanks. "Hey, Dad. Do we have any batteries?"

Oh, crap. In all the crazy, Peter failed to order batteries. "No, guess we'll have to get some tomorrow. Add up what we need."

They spent the rest of the morning watching the Disney Christmas parade while trying to calculate how many batteries he'd have to buy when Big Z's hardware opened the next day.

Peter heated up some of Gabby's cinnamon orange bread he'd purchased yesterday afternoon. They greedily ate it before getting ready for Christmas dinner with his family when his phone beeped and a knock at the door occurred simultaneously.

"Merry Christmas!" Tia sashayed in and twirled. She wore a bright blue pea coat, a matching beret, and dark sparkling leggings. "You like my new outfit?"

Polly gave a thumbs-up. "*C'est très chic,* Tia."

"What brings you to the Graff today?" Peter gave her a quick hug. "Merry Christmas."

"Merry Christmas. I needed a couple of helpers to help me decorate the Main Street Diner this morning."

"I thought they would be closed today."

"Well, Gabby decided yesterday afternoon to keep the diner open for anyone who didn't have someone to spend

Christmas Day with, as well as any first responders and hospital staff who are working today. She needs help decorating it this morning."

"Helping others. That's a great idea." Peter took a long swig of his coffee. "Don't you think, kids?"

"I don't know. I'm kind of busy with my new toys," Digory answered with about as much enthusiasm as a slug in snow.

"Gabby told me to tell you that anyone who helps, gets all the pie and ice cream they can eat."

"Will Freddie be there?" Digory raised an eyebrow.

"He and Trinity are already down there helping."

Immediately, the children ran into the other room and within five minutes had dressed and were struggling to put on their coats as Peter brushed his teeth.

"You guys already done? I can be ready in a few minutes—"

"Don't worry about it. Just come down to the diner in about an hour or so." Tia gave him a quick wink before she had the kids out the door. "Enjoy a few minutes to breathe. Merry Christmas."

"Thanks, Tia."

"Oh." She snapped her fingers. "I made you this."

She handed him a book with a bow on it. "Sorry it's not wrapped. I had to rush deliver."

"Thank you."

"You're welcome. Freddie, Aunt Shell, and I picked out the best ones. See you in a few." She let the door close behind her.

When he opened the first page, the sight of him and his children felt like a hard punch to the chest. He slid into a chair, his eyes laser focused on the pages of pictures.

Pages and pages of pictures of him with his children. Them smiling, laughing. At the Christmas tree farm. Walking hand-in-hand on the trail from the parking lot to Miracle Lake.

The kids making their picture frames and icing cookies. She'd even included photos of them decorating the Christmas tree at Shelly's house.

Beautiful photos of them all skating.

Well, photos of the children skating and him trying to remain upright.

Tia even had a picture of him in midfall that made him laugh so hard, it hurt all his sore muscles.

When he'd impulsively decided to come to Marietta, he'd only anticipated spending time with his siblings and getting to know his kids. Nowhere in his plans were to meet amazingly compassionate people who gave him incredible presents at the blink of an eye.

Who helped him find Christmas gifts and stealthily hide them behind the counter.

And even had their version of good old St. Nick.

Mr. Nicolas. St. Nick. Clever.

He glanced at the book again.

Marietta had surprised him in more ways than one.

Thinking of his siblings, Peter smirked. "No wonder you two love it here."

Leave. Now, *he* didn't want to leave, but he wouldn't

make that decision on his own. Not without his children and certainly not before a strong cup of coffee.

Peter had barely had time to walk to the coffee maker for a refill when someone knocked on the door. He opened it, expecting one of the kids to have forgotten something.

Instead, he got a Christmas bonus. "Shelly?"

Without a word, she put her hand to his chest and gently pushed him inside before she turned and double-locked the door.

She dropped her coat by the door, revealing a knit dress that perfectly hugged her curves. "Alone, I see."

"Did you get Tia to take my kids out?"

"Gabby really did call for help. I simply suggested the younger two might be good helpers." She leaned forward, resting her hands on his shoulders. "You smell so good. Minty."

"I had a shower. Just brushed my teeth." His arm wrapped around her waist and he pulled her flush.

"Good hygiene. You really know how to sweet talk a girl."

"Oui."

"No other languages right now. I have better ideas for your tongue." Her hands moved under his shirt and she pushed it over his head.

He wasted no time stripping her of her dress, leaving her in beautiful red matching bra and panties. Nibbling on the pulse point of her neck, Peter worked his way to her ear and whispered, "Let me show you just how good this peppermint mouthwash is."

Not giving her time to answer, he kissed down between her breasts as he unfastened her bra in record time. Kneeling in front of her, he cupped her breasts and traced around her nipple with his tongue before taking the tender flesh into his mouth.

Her knees momentarily buckled, but she caught herself. "Wow, that's intense."

"You want me to stop?"

"You better not."

He smiled against her skin before suckling her breast as his hand caressed the other one, rolling the nipple between his fingers.

She arched her back and moaned as she rocked against him. "That feels so good."

His cock strained against his fly. He worried he'd pop before too long, but he'd dreamed all night of tasting her, intimately feasting until she cried his name. "Want to move this to the couch?"

"No." Slipping her finger through his belt loop, she walked them through the door to his room.

She reached for his jeans, but he grabbed her wrists.

"I want you out of these."

"You first. This is all about you right now, Shelly."

"But I want to touch you."

"You will, but…" He laid her back, before kissing down her body. Licking the valley between her breasts. Nibbling each nipple before kissing her belly button. When he reached the top of her panties he ran his tongue along it. "Do you want me to stop?"

"No," she panted. "No, please don't."

He smirked when she expedited things by wiggling out of her underpants.

"Patience, sweetheart." Although, he didn't know how much longer he'd hold out. She'd had him twisted tight all night. "Now, where were we?"

Peter moved back up her body and kissed her. Her arms wrapped around him as he relished her naked skin next to his. Slowly, he worked down her body again, but moved past her panties.

He chuckled at the disappointed look she shot him. "Don't worry. I haven't skipped anything."

She moaned his name while he kissed the insides of her knees, her thighs, and over her panties. "Peter, you're killing me."

He stood in awe of her. How many times had he thought of her naked?

Under him.

Over him?

Even with their chemistry, he hadn't been sure it would ever happen.

Now, he marveled at his dreams come true. Her curves. Her scent. Her soft skin.

His mouth watered at the chance to taste her. With gentle brushes of his lips, he worked his way from the inside of her knee to sensitive folds.

"You're beautiful," he whispered as his thumbs kneaded her inner thighs.

Her hands rested on her stomach as she arched her back

as he increased his pace.

Inch by torturous inch, he kissed her, inhaling her sweet scent as he moved closer to the core of her sex.

Her fingers threaded through his hair as he flicked her swollen nub with his tongue, making her gasp.

"You like that?"

"Yes." She softly moaned.

Tracing the seam of her outer lips with his tongue, he heard her whimper. "You want more?"

"Yes. More."

"What about… this?" His tongue slid between her folds and he nibbled on her clit, relishing how she writhed with his touch.

She gasped. "Yes. More. Tingles. More tingles."

He took her into his mouth and tenderly sucked her sensitive nub. His hand ran along the curve of her hip and up her body until he cupped her breast. His thumb grazed over her peaked nipple as he increased the pressure of his tongue on her sensitive nub.

Her breathing increased as her hips began to rock. "That mouthwash…it tingles. It tingles so good."

"You like that?"

"Yes, eat me. Don't stop."

His tongue tickled her intimately before he nibbled and sucked. Then he'd run his tongue along the seam of her before starting over again.

She writhed under his touch. Her reaction to him inched him to the edge of his own climax.

He'd pictured getting to taste her, but hearing her tell

him what she wanted, only turned him on more. Reaching down, he popped the button and unzipped his jeans to release the pressure and give him more time with her.

Her eyes went wide with lust. She sat up. "I want to see you. All of you."

"But I'm not done with you yet."

"We'll take turns." She threaded her fingers through his belt loops and pulled him to stand in front of her. "I've dreamed of stripping you down. Making you want more."

"That's me, the dream maker." His jeans were barely to the floor when her full lips circled his cock.

A moan escaped him as she tenderly sucked and slowly moved up and down his shaft. Her hand at the base of him, moving in tempo with her mouth. "Shelly. Feels good."

Her fingers gently brushed his inner thigh before grazing over his balls.

She let him slide out of her mouth before taking him back in and sucking again. With perfect precision, her tongue traced along the rim of his head before she slid him between her lips again.

"Damn, Shelly."

"Damn is a *naughty* word." She stroked him as the other hand cupped his butt.

"What you're doing is pretty damned naughty."

The torturously slow tempo she kept on his cock, erased any rational thoughts that might have existed in his brain.

She'd bring him to the edge and dangle him dangerously close to climax before pulling away.

When he couldn't hold back any longer, he cupped her

chin and moved away.

"Did I hurt you?"

"Not at all." He scanned her from the top of her head to her toes before leaning down and taking a nipple into her mouth. She relaxed back on the bed and arched her back. His hands wandered down the sides of her perfect curves until he moved lower.

"Yes!" She gasped as he applied a bit more suction before sliding a finger inside her.

Kissing her down her stomach, he didn't hesitate this time when he reached her sensitive nub. With his finger moving in and out of her, he nibbled and suckled her.

"Oh, yes. Yes! Just like that." Her ragged breathing increased as her fingers threaded through his hair.

Kissing her inner thigh, he growled, "You're so tight. So close."

"Yes. Please, Peter. Don't stop."

He slid another finger inside her and placed his thumb on her clit, wiggling it before nibbling her inner thigh, again.

She came unglued, grabbing the bedspread and rocking her hips as he continued to slide his fingers in and out of her.

Before he could think of anything to say, she reached up and stroked him.

"Now it's your turn." With a wicked tongue and talented hands, Shelly worked his body as artfully as he'd played hers.

By the time he'd reached climax, exhaustion and elation surged through him. He hadn't felt this alive in far too long.

He pulled her close and they basked in the afterglow for a short while before noticing the time.

"They'll be expecting us, you know," Shelly whispered as she reluctantly moved away from him and walked into the bathroom.

As soon as the door clicked closed, Peter rolled onto his back and knew he had to make a decision about staying or going sooner rather than later.

When they reached the diner, they were fresh-faced and beyond famished.

Not only were the children there, but Lucy, Thomas, Edmund, and Jade as well as Sue and Louis Westbrook, Trinity, Kyle Cavasos, and multiple first responders who had decided to take Gabby up on her offer for a free meal and good conversation, as well as a few townsfolk who would have been alone for the day. That included some frequent visitors, Phoebe and Joseph Stevenson, who hadn't anticipated everything would be closed for the day.

A loud roar from outside brought Mr. Nicolas who arrived on his motorized sleigh. He wore the same suit he had on when Peter ran into his sleigh and, when he walked in, he patted his stomach and said, "Merry Christmas!"

Everyone responded in kind and rounds of hugs and happy blessings were exchanged.

At the end of the day, Peter knew he'd fallen in love with the town as much as his siblings had. It had been easy to lose his heart to not only the people and the pace of life, but the woman standing across the room.

Still, even if he honestly considered staying, he had to discuss it with his children.

After their honest conversation yesterday, the last thing

he wanted to do was send their relationship backward by uprooting them and moving them across the country.

"What are you thinking?" Shelly asked as she offered him a mug of coffee.

"About why people move here. Stay here."

A round of laughter between Mr. Nicolas, Thomas, and Digory brought a smile to Peter's face.

His daughter and Phoebe held court with a few of the first responders and Trinity as they all told silly jokes.

Lucy, Edmund, Jade, along with Joseph Stevenson sat at the end of the long table, all drinking coffee.

Warmth filled his heart. He hadn't felt this happily content in years.

A decade to be exact and part of it was because of who stood beside him right now and his children in the room.

Polly and Digory had given him more sense of purpose than he'd ever thought possible. He looked forward to getting to know who they were and them growing their relationship together.

"You're awfully quiet." Shelly stood a bit closer to him.

"Just thinking."

"About?"

"It's hard not to fall in love here."

Her eyes went wide with panic. "What?"

Peter cleared his throat. "I mean, with the town. The people here."

Relief flooded her and she laughed nervously. "Oh, for a minute I thought you meant... I don't know what I thought."

"It's fine. It's just a great town." His heart raced as he berated himself for letting his emotions get away from him.

"Miss Shelly, can you come here for a moment?" Polly waved her over.

"Will you excuse me?"

"Of course." He sat in one of the counter stools and watched her as she talked with his daughter.

Staring at Shelly, he memorized the shape of her curves.

The way her hair framed her face.

The beauty she radiated when she laughed.

The look of bliss on her face after he'd made her scream his name.

Right then and there, Peter realized his heart had opened enough to love someone again.

And it scared the hell out of him.

Chapter Twenty-One

"I NEED A right shoulder and arm X-rays in room six." Peter pointed to nurse's aid, Poppy Henderson.

She gave him a thumbs-up.

"Room four's IV is beeping. Dr. Davidson, did you want another bag?" Dave Fletcher called out to Peter before entering the room.

Mentally scanning his patients, Peter remembered bed four's ailment. "Yes, can you do a tilt test again, Mr. Fletcher?"

"You got it, boss."

Dr. Tom Reynolds walked into the trauma room to sew up a laceration as Edmund came around the corner with EMS who'd just arrived with Mr. Nicolas who appeared to be having breathing problems, again.

Lucy hadn't been joking when she said they'd need help. The flu season had been particularly bad this year along with stomach flu, food poisoning, and broken bones and lacerations due to falls at Miracle Lake or snowboarding.

Administration welcomed another Dr. Davidson and expedited his vetting while Peter had a quick orientation of the unit. He'd still be under the ninety-day probationary period, but Peter welcomed the work and distraction.

Especially after talking to the kids' neighbor, Karen, this morning.

She'd explained the school needed to know when or if the children would be returning since they had a waiting list. If he planned to move them, they had to know by January second. He had one week to make up his mind.

Thankfully, none of his annoyance with such a critical decision would be exacerbated by the electronic medical records system he had to use. He'd used the same program in Florida. This kept his documentation time from slowing him down and getting patients seen as fast as possible.

"Your X-rays are ordered, Dr. Davidson," Poppy said before answering the unit phone on the third ring.

"Getting the swing of it?" Tom held his hands up and away from everyone as he'd already donned sterile gloves and motioned for Peter to follow him.

Peter nodded. "I didn't think I'd work this soon after getting here, but whatever I can do to help."

"Great. I appreciate you coming in, especially with you having your kids here."

"No problem. Edmund and Jade have them today. Taking them for a snowball fight and then a movie." Even with his brother and Jade taking care of his children, Peter still worried about his kids being outside of his sight.

Damn, parenting is constantly stressing.

"I might have to take a short leave of absence in the next couple of weeks. Good to know you're here to help." He tilted his chin toward the suture tray. "Can you hold up the lidocaine? I've already gloved up before realizing no one had pulled up any."

"Sure." Peter grabbed some gloves out of the box on the counter before picking up the vial.

As soon as he saw the needle the wide-eyed panic replaced the arrogant confidence of the teen on the stretcher.

"I'm not getting a shot." The kid emphatically shook his head.

"Yes. You are." His father stood to the side, his arms locked over his chest.

"What did you cut open?" Peter asked.

He lifted his arm and between his elbow and his wrist he had a long gash.

Popping the top on the lidocaine, Peter held it upside down for Tom to insert the needle and aspirate the numbing medication. "What did you do?"

With his eyes laser focused on the syringe, the kid almost spoke in monotone. "I jumped off the couch with a plate in my hand. Landed wrong."

"You were being a dumbass," the father scoffed. "You didn't jump off the couch. You tried to do a backflip off the back of the couch with that plate in your hand."

If I had a dollar for every dumbass trick people did to end up in the ER, I wouldn't have to do this job anymore. Peter glanced at Tom who rolled his eyes.

"You're lucky you didn't slice any tendons or break your arm." Tom tapped the side of the syringe to get the bubbles out.

With eyes the size of dinner plates, the patient's voice

trembled. "Is… is that needle going in me?"

Noticing the pink color at the base, Peter knew needles that size weren't used as often for medication administration as their large size would cause far more pain and stress. "Depends. If you're still, he could probably use a smaller needle. What do you think, Dr. Reynolds?"

Tom nodded. "That could be arranged."

Immediately, the teen lay flat and held his arm out. "What size needle will this get me?"

"Smaller." Tom smirked and began working as the kid kept his word as his father didn't look up from his phone.

"You good, Tom?"

"Got it, thanks."

When Peter exited, he checked the patient in room four whose food poisoning—*don't eat grandma's potato salad that's been left out all day*—had greatly improved after two bags of IV fluids. He wrote discharge instructions for him to go home.

The moment that patient vacated the room, they cleaned it and another was immediately brought back. This time, it was a set of screaming twins, both with ear infections.

He then saw a multitude of people.

A woman with a scratched cornea after she'd been hit in the face with a microphone during a family karaoke contest. She came in second.

A man with abdominal pain whose daily diet included a bag of Fritos, a three liter of soda, and a grilled cheese sandwich. Complaint? A three-week history of no pooping.

A family of eight with pinkeye.

Two cases of strep throat, five asthmatics, and two cases of croup.

Three different patients with chest pains, two that were stomach related, one who ended up getting admitted to the ICU.

When the next round of physicians and staff hit the door, Peter was more than ready to go home, but before he left, he checked on Mr. Nicolas who looked far better than he had a few hours ago.

"I lost my inhaler in another state." He chuckled as his oxygen level stayed around ninety-five.

"You gotta be more diligent about your care, Mr. Nicolas. You're going to end up with scarring in your lungs if you keep doing this." *If you haven't already.*

Peter readjusted the monitor on the patient's finger. He hoped the man's oxygen levels would improve with a different placement.

No such luck.

"You been for a chest X-ray yet?"

"Yes! Isaiah took it. He's a wonderful young man."

"I've met him once. Lucy speaks highly of the staff here."

Coughing a few times, Mr. Nicolas nodded. "He's studying for college. Working here for awhile before deciding where to go. Nothing wrong with understanding how to put in a hard day's work before deciding on what you want to do with your life."

"Amen. I'll look forward to talking with him more."

Jade entered. "Good evening, sir. I'm taking over for Dave."

"Oh, good, Ms. Carter. I'm so happy to see y-y-you…" The jolly man's chest convulsed as he tried to catch his breath.

Peter got him a glass of ice water to help clear some of the dryness of the patient's throat. "Hey, Jade."

"Hey, Peter. The kids are back at the park with Edmund and Fred. Lucy's going to take them back to the hotel." Jade patted Mr. Nicolas's back. "We offered to take them to see a movie, but they wanted to watch the *Timeless* movie again."

"It was good. I need to watch the other seasons." Under Peter's watchful eye, Mr. Nicholas's oxygen level crept up two points.

"You won't regret it." She smiled.

"Thank you for watching them."

"Anytime." She placed the blood pressure cuff on the patient's arm. "Okay, let's see what your blood pressure is doing."

The jolly man took a sip of the water. "Thank you, Dr. Davidson. I hope you have a wonderful evening."

"You too, sir."

"Oh, and Peter."

"Yes, Mr. Nicolas?"

"Remember what you wished for?"

Stepping closer, Peter's brow furrowed. "Wished for?"

"When you ran into me. We talked in the sleigh and you said you wanted answers. A home base?"

Searching his brain, the faint memory of the conversation played. "Yes, I vaguely remember it. What about it?"

"Everything you need is in that envelope."

Peter's gut dropped to the floor. "What did you say?"

"Your answers. All you have to do is open that envelope." Immediately, Mr. Nicolas's breathing improved and his oxygen level popped up to ninety-nine percent. He exhaled a long breath. "Well, I guess the meds kicked in."

"We only gave you two breathing treatments." Jade tapped on the monitor, checking the orders.

"Guess you're miracle workers." He touched his finger beside his nose and winked at Peter.

"Yeah, I guess we are." The conversation sat heavily on the front of Peter's mind for the rest of the shift. He counted the minutes before he packed his things in his backpack and before walking across the hospital parking lot back to the Graff.

The sun had already dropped below the horizon and the chill of the night cut bone deep so he welcomed the warmth of the hotel lobby.

Before he hit the stairs, he glanced into the large ballroom they were getting ready for the New Year's celebrations only a few days away.

The chandelier sparkled as a large stage was in its early stages of construction at the far end of the room.

Huge boxes from Oriental Trading Company had been lined up against the wall and Peter could only assume they included party hats, streamers, and other New Year's Eve décor.

When he got back to the room, Lucy and the kids were in the middle of a game of Harry Potter Clue. He quickly showered and joined them.

After another hour, Digory won—Crabbe and Goyle with Sleep Drought in the Owlrey—and the kids turned in.

Lucy and Peter sat up in his room after she made them each hot chocolate.

Peter repeated what Mr. Nicolas told him as he watched the marshmallows melt in the rich chocolate liquid.

"Well, I've always thought he might be Santa." Lucy shrugged before blowing on her drink.

"Come on, Lucy. That's not what this is."

"What is this then because, honestly, this past week is the happiest I've ever seen you in years." She counted off on her fingers. "You're smiling all the time. You're having fun. You're not working sixty hours a week. You're not exhausted and not constantly talking about your shifts. It's wonderful to see."

"Leave it to you to find the ray of light in my frustrations." He gave her a wink. "I don't know how you do it, sometimes."

She shrugged with a sparkle in her eye. "Because I decided a long time ago that life was too short to fester about things I can fix. Even if I don't like the answer, it can be resolved and I can go on."

Another long drag of hot chocolate gave Peter a moment to think. "That's what Mr. Nicolas is doing? Giving me an answer?"

"He's not wrong. The answers you want are in there. You're just going to have to rip the Band-Aid and get it over with."

"That's what Shelly said."

"She's a smart woman."

"She's incredible. Smart. Beautiful. Sexy." *Dammit. Why did I say that?*

Lucy's eyes went wide with excitement. "Are you in love with Shelly?"

He stood and paced. "I've spent some time with her."

"You are. You're in love with Shelly and it's barely been a week."

"Yeah, so?" he snapped. "You fell in love with Thomas in a month."

She shushed him. "And Jade and Edmund fell in love in two days."

"What the hell is in the water in Marietta? Love potion?" He put his mug down, almost afraid to drink more. "I can't hurt her. Her kids. My kids."

"What makes you think you will? Because of Simone? Because of what happened a decade ago?"

His stomach twisted uncomfortably tight, exactly like it did when Simone turned him down. He slouched in the chair across from Lucy. "Simone felt strong enough to never tell me we had children. Why didn't she tell me?"

"Maybe it has nothing to do with you. Maybe this was something *she* struggled with."

That idea made him sit straight up. "Like what?"

She shrugged. "I don't know. Don't you think it's weird that her family isn't involved at all?"

"Yes. That's damned strange. She and her brother were like we are."

"Tight. Supportive. And now she doesn't want him to

have her children? Why?" Lucy hugged her knees to her chest. "Something happened. Something she couldn't come to you about. Something she couldn't rely on her brother about."

"Damn, I didn't think about it that way." He ran his fingers through his hair, his mind trying to untangle the questions that rolled around his brain. "If that's the case, I have no idea what happened."

Reaching out, Lucy patted him on the knee. "Why haven't you opened that letter since you've been here?"

"I planned to."

She raised an eyebrow. "Really?"

"I did." He rested his forearms on his legs. "Then we got here and I ran into Santa Claus. I forgot about it for a couple of days and then we got busy. Snowball fights. Tree decorating. Christmas shopping. Me getting my ass kicked on Miracle Lake. You needing me at the ER."

His body still ached, but had moved to second-day sore.

"Are those the only reasons?"

"No." He answered quicker than he intended. Letting out a long breath, shook his head. "I met Shelly. Her kids. The people here. Thomas. Jade. Sue. The paramedics at the scene. The kids and I all started to have such a great time. I didn't think I needed to know anymore. That *we* didn't needed to know."

"What changed?" Lucy took a long drink.

"Their neighbor called this morning. Said the school has to know whether to hold their places or call the next two on the waiting list."

Her eyebrows furrowed and she placed her mug on the table. "What are you going to do?"

Peter ground his teeth at the inevitable. "I'm gonna have to read that letter. Find out why."

"What if it says something terrible?"

"You're not helping."

"No, I'm asking. Will it change anything about how you feel about your children?"

"No."

"Will it make the decision for you on whether to stay here or for you to stay in Maine?"

"Not sure. I don't think so." But it might answer some questions.

"Then why read it?" Lucy tried to grab his hand but he shook his head.

"Because I need to understand why she stole nine years of their lives from me." He choked back a sob. "Our father lost years of his life with us because of someone else's selfish decision. I swore I would do everything in my power to make sure that never happened with any kids. I didn't get the chance to be there for them and I want to understand it so when they ask me where the hell I've been all these years, I can tell them."

A look of concern spread across her face. "You sure you want to go down that road? You sure you want to tell them why their mother kept you away?"

"Yes," he snapped, then sadness punched him in the heart. "No. Hell... I want answers. Something that makes sense of all this."

"Be sure, whatever you say, it comes from a place of compassion. As the kids get older, they will want more information, but for now, this may be something only you need to understand."

He nodded, but said nothing more.

"Did you want Edmund or me here when you do?"

"No." He let out a long breath before shaking his head. "No, this is my fight. My problem."

"You know we're here for you, right? No matter what's in there. No matter what she said."

Peter's lips thinned. "Yeah, I do and I appreciate that."

"Anytime." She gave him a quick kiss and hug good night before leaving.

As he settled back in the chair, his sister's encouraging words replayed in his head. Even her positivity couldn't fight the fear of the unknown.

That Band-Aid would have to be ripped off sooner rather than later.

Chapter Twenty-Two

T HE WEEK BETWEEN Christmas and New Years Eve had raced by.

Shelly took the kids on their biannual book trip and spent far more money than she'd planned, but less than it cost for her to go on the honeymoon and a subsequent divorce attorney.

Peter and she saw each other at work as he'd come in a few times to help out during the busiest part of the day and evening.

Local weather had kept so many people inside coughing and sneezing on each other Shelly often wondered if people only came to the ER to not only get rid of their colds, flus, and allergies, but cabin fever.

Like his siblings, he worked effectively and efficiently with every member of the staff and made patients feel comfortable and cared about.

They hadn't been alone together since Christmas Day, but Shelly understood why. Being a visitor in town, Peter couldn't ask his family to watch his kids every time his libido kicked in.

Shelly more than understood single-parent struggles.

They talked regularly at work and exchanged several naughty texts. By the time the last few days of the year rolled around, she realized she'd fallen in love with the man and it made absolutely no sense.

It's been a week. Long-lasting love doesn't happen in a week.

But no matter how she tried to convince herself otherwise, Shelly's heart wouldn't listen.

It's lust. It's all it is, lust. It's been too long since I'd been with someone.

He'd made no promises to stay here. He hadn't indicated he felt emotionally the same. As far as she understood it, his children's lives were in Maine and being the fantastic father he was, he'd do what was right for his children.

Still, she wished there could be a way they'd all remain in Marietta. She'd get that happily ever after with four kids, the handsome prince, and her cat.

Instead of trying to decipher it all, she mentally threw caution to the wind and decided she wouldn't expect anything. She would bask in his constant appreciation of her body and repair her ego.

If they got more alone time, she'd soak up every moment, but she wouldn't pine for him when he left.

Sure, she'd shed a few tears, but he'd always put his children first. And he should.

That's one of the things I love about him.

Love?

Ugh, Shelly. Why do you do this to yourself?

By the time she got to New Year's Eve day, Shelly needed a break from work and reality. She'd not had much downtime since returning from Vegas so she turned down any plans to work for the next couple of days before starting back to her normal schedule.

Since Peter hadn't invited her out for a New Year's celebration evening, she decided after a long, luxurious bath with some of the strawberry bath bombs she'd purchased in Bozeman, she'd curl up in her favorite chair, drink a great glass of wine, and start working on her to-be-read pile of books.

With both children out of the house, Freddie at Trinity's and Tia at a babysitting gig, Shelly had the house all to herself.

Smelling like strawberries and wearing her favorite flannel pajamas, she settled in to the first chapter of the book when she heard a knock at the front door.

When she answered it, she couldn't believe her eyes.

There stood Peter, with champagne and what looked like dinner.

"What are you doing?" She grabbed him by the coat and yanked him inside.

He shivered as soon as the door closed behind him. "Bringing you dinner."

"Where are the kids?"

"Tia's watching them." He furrowed his brow. "She offered to watch them tonight. She didn't tell you?"

"No." Shelly laughed at her niece's concern for her social life. "Please, come in."

Rich scents of oregano, garlic, and basil filled the space between them. "What did you bring?"

"Dinner from Rocco's. Lasagna, salad, wine, and tira-misu." He placed it on the counter and offered to open the wine.

Once he'd poured them each a glass, she noticed his hands were shaking. "You okay?"

"Yes."

"Nervous?"

"Haven't done something this impulsive in a while. Don't want to screw this up." He handed her a glass and began to toast.

She leaned in. "Peter, I don't think you could ever screw something like this up. The gesture alone is fantastic."

"You smell like strawberries." He hungrily kissed her, his tongue swept through her mouth before he came up for air. "Strawberries are one of my favorite things to eat."

"Really?"

The corner of his mouth curled up into a mischievous grin. "To new adventures."

"Adventures?" They clinked their glasses.

"Yes, new adventures." He took a long swig of his wine, his glass slightly shaking.

He's the cutest, nervous man. "I'm an adventure?"

A sly smile spread across his face. "After what we've done, I'd say adventurous."

"Really? How adventurous do you want to get? Because after a little shopping in Bozeman, I can get *a lot* more adventurous." Her body purred with him so close.

Scanning him, he'd worn a deep blue button down with pressed pants and a tie that match the gray in his eyes. He'd obviously dressed to impress.

"What are you thinking?" He placed his hands on either side of her as she leaned against the counter.

"Say something in…Italian. Something naughty."

He began to answer, but took a long drink of wine first. "*Voglio le tue mani su tutto il corpo.*"

Her nipples peaked. "What did you say?"

"I want your hands all over my body."

Shelly finished off her glass of vino. "I'm thinking I'd like to show you something."

He raised an eyebrow. "What is it?"

"Wait, right, here." She kissed him before slipping out from his embrace. "Oh, would you start a fire?"

"I think you already did, *madame.*"

"You know it." When she returned, the fire blazed and he stood in the middle of the living room, looking through her library and as dashing as ever. "Happy New Year."

When he turned, the twenty minutes she'd spent shaving all the essentials and getting ready had been worth it. She sauntered around the couch in her offthe-shoulder, body-hugging red dress, the sparkling stiletto shoes, and her sheer stockings. Although, they'd probably stay home, she'd even thrown on a bit of makeup.

Peter's jaw hit the floor. "Holy shit. You look incredible."

"Shit is a naughty word, you know." She crooked her finger as she walked to the sofa. "Join me."

Without pause, he sat next to her, his hand rested on her shoulder. The warmth of his fingers made her body buzz.

"You should wear things like this more often."

With the fire burning, she walked slowly around the room, turning all the lights off before settling next to him. "You like it? I'd planned to wear it for a night out."

"We could go to the Graff. Dance. Have some champagne. I bet they have obnoxious party favors."

It sounded tempting. A fancy night out. Endless champagne.

Music. The ball drop.

But having him here all to herself, them cozied up by the fire, and an endless supply of wine, and a feast from Rocco's, she didn't want to be anywhere else. "No, I'm good with us staying here, although I do like that we got all dressed up."

He kissed her shoulder until he reached the pulse point of her neck. "You look hot in that. *Bellissima.*"

"Thank you." Every compliment. Every reaction to her touch, without understanding it, Peter repaired years of damage done to her ego and she loved him for it.

Loved? Stop it!

"I'm gonna love taking it off you." He growled.

Yep. Loved. No, lusted! "You really know how to romance a girl."

"I'm trying to get to expert flirting level."

"I have no doubt, you'll reach that level tonight. Maybe even more than once." She giggled as his hand moved up her leg, her hip, her waist.

She anticipated his touch as he cupped her breast and nibbled her ear.

"You're beautiful. So beautiful." His tongue danced

along her collarbone, his thumb grazed over her breast, sending her over the edge of self-control.

Wanting to touch him, hear him moan her name, she slid off the couch and knelt between his knees. She ran her hands up and down his thighs before loosening his belt, then the button of his pants and zipper. "Lift your hips."

"Yes, ma'am." When he did, she pulled his pants off his hips along with his underwear. His erection sprang free and her mouth watered. Her fingers wrapped around his shaft as her thumb grazed the head making him almost jump off the couch.

"It's been too long since I've done this." Her tongue danced across the sensitive skin of his belly before tickling the head of his shaft.

He groaned and rested his hands on her shoulders. "I love it when you suck me."

"Oh, yeah? Like this." She flicked the tip of her tongue against his cock.

"Yes."

"What about this?" She kissed down his erection and up again while holding him in her hand.

"Yes."

"Take off your shirt and tie while I touch you." She stroked the length of him as he removed his tie then slowly unbuttoned his shirt. The closer he got to uncovering his chest, the faster she stroked.

Once his shirt and tie were tossed somewhere near the tree, she took him in her mouth.

"Shelly, yes. Yes." Reaching over his head, he grabbed

the back of the couch.

"That's right. I love making you feel good." Shelly's lips surround him again, taking him inch by inch, then pulling back slightly, allowing her teeth to gently graze his flesh.

He growled when she pulled back again and sat forward. "I want that dress off you. Now."

"Why?" she playfully asked.

"I want to see every naked beautiful inch of you."

Standing, he kicked off his shoes and pants before he turned her around and moving his hands up her thighs and under her dress.

She smirked when his hands stopped.

"You're not wearing any underwear."

"Happy New Year," she giggled.

"Damn, you're gorgeous." He kissed down her back as he unfastened her zipper.

As the dress fell away, his hands cupped her breasts, his thumbs grazed across her nipples.

She stood in nothing but her shimmering stockings and glittery stilettos and she felt every bit as wanton as she hoped.

"Damn, your ass is perfect." He cupped her butt before pulling her flush, his shaft pressed against her cheeks.

"Touch me more." She interlaced her fingers behind his neck as he played with her. His hands wandered her body with abandon.

"You're beautiful," he repeated, his fingers grazing her flesh, making her writhe in ecstasy. "Superior."

"Let's take this to my room." She panted, leading him back to the bedroom.

Watching his toned body, she mentally chanted, "Mine."

When they reached her bed, he turned but she playfully pushed him back on the mattress.

He scanned her, his mouth crooked in a sultry smile. "I love that you're not wearing any panties."

"Nope, panties are overrated tonight."

"But I do like this stockings and high-heels thing. You should wear only that more often."

"Whatever you want." She crawled up his body and kissed him before reaching for her bedside table and pulling out a condom package.

Before she could get near enough to put it on him, his fingers slid inside her and his mouth took her nipple. His tongue danced around the sensitive tip as his fingers slid in and out of her in a torturously slow tempo.

He moved to her other breast, licking, sucking her as his fingers danced inside her and his thumb rested on her aching clit.

"You like that?" He kissed her neck.

"Yes, yes I do. Don't stop touching me."

Peter smiled and kissed her, then laid a path of kisses from her ear to her shoulder. "I need to be in you."

"Absolutely." Once the condom was out of the package, she reached down and stroked him again before taking his cock and placing the condom on the end. She pinched the tip of the barrier before rolling it down. Standing, she moved to the end of the bed and he sat back, a puzzled look on his face.

"Patience, my dear." She straddled him and slid him inside her in one swift move.

His eyes went wide and he grabbed her hips as a moan escaped him.

Shelly's hips rocked in a slow, rhythmic tempo, her clit grinding against him with each thrust, inching her close to climax. "That's it. Move with me."

His hands cupped her butt and she ran her thumbs across her nipples.

She threw her head back as he increased their thrusts, the ache building inside her, begging for release. "Peter, you feel so good."

She'd dreamed of this, of them in her bed, her screaming her name.

He plunged deeper, each time bringing her closer to the edge. His finger brushed against her sensitive nub. "Say my name again."

He plunged deeper, each time bringing her closer to the edge, his fingers working their magic. Bruching her sensitive nub, he growled, "Say my name again."

"Peter," she purred.

"Just like that."

"Peter!" Her hips moved with his cadence and she rolled her nipples between her fingertips. Tightening her pussy, she gripped his erection in a protective hold and released.

He chuckled. "Someone's been doing their Kegel's. Squeeze again."

She did and tingles fired off in small explosions through her body. "You feel so good. So good. So close."

Leaning over, she placed her hands on either side of his

head. He took a nipple in his mouth.

When he sucked, she gasped as her orgasm overwhelmed her.

He thrust one, two, three times before letting out a guttural growl. Pushing deep inside her and she felt his release.

For a few moments, the only sounds in their room were their breathing returning to normal and the gusts of winter winds outside.

"Thank you." Peter's hands lovingly stroked her curves as he admired her.

"Always the gentleman." Shelly rested her chin on his chest. She looked behind him and made a face. "Well, it's only eight thirty. How long did Tia say she could stay?"

"A few hours."

"Good, we've got time to do that again."

They'd decided to clean up after their first round, but ended up helping each other in the shower for the second round and got quite creative only to fall asleep in each other arms until…

"Did someone just come home?" Shelly sat up when the front door slammed.

Peter jumped out of bed. "You expecting anyone?"

Shelly shook her head as she scanned the room for her pajamas. "Not until after midnight."

"Mom!" Freddie's heavy footsteps made their way to her bedroom.

"Oh, crap!" Shelly threw back the sheets, quickly trying to find her robe she'd tossed somewhere in the room.

Peter lunged for… "Where are my pants?"

Retracing their evening, she realized they'd left all their clothes in the living room. "Everything is out there!"

"What do you want me to do?"

"Go, into the bathroom. Close the door." As she quickly threw on her robe, a nervous giggle took over her as she realized the absurdity of the situation.

I'm a grown-assed woman hiding my lover from my son. Happy holidays to me.

"Mom! You here?"

"Yes, Freddie. I'll be right out."

The footsteps slowed then stopped a few feet from her doorway. "You, um, okay?"

"I'm fine honey. Why?"

Peter quietly closed the bathroom door.

"Because your clothes are all over the living room and Jingles is sleeping in some guy's pants in front of the fire."

She bit her lip to keep from laughing out loud. "I see. Jingles has moved from socks to pants."

The floorboard creaked closer to her door but he'd yet to peek his face around the doorframe. "Mom, are you, um, alone?"

After being honest with her son all these years, Shelly didn't know why she bothered to cover this up. Yet, she'd spent the night with someone other than his father and admitting it felt like a betrayal.

Even though they'd told Gill to get lost, this change in her life suddenly became more complicated.

And real.

Her heart jumped into her throat but she shook off her

angst. Squaring her shoulders, she awkwardly put her fists to her hips. "No, honey, I'm not alone."

The house became uncharacteristically silent.

Uh-oh. She expected a rebuttal, even outrage. For Freddie to demand who would do such a thing to his mother, but what her son did shocked even her.

He said nothing about it. "Want some coffee? I'm gonna brew a pot."

"S-s-sure. That would be great."

"Would…" He cleared his throat. "Peter like some coffee?"

Shelly turned to see Peter peeking around the doorway, shirtless and smiling like a kid who'd been caught doing something naughty, but didn't regret it for one second.

"Coffee would be great," he whispered.

"Yes, Freddie. He would." She came out of the bedroom to gather the clothes from the living room before returning to get dressed.

They met Freddie in the kitchen a bit later as he poured coffee into three large mugs.

Once the awkwardness of Peter walking out of her bedroom appeared to subside, the three of them sat down and drank in silence for the next few minutes.

The low moan of the winter winds played against the kitchen window.

"I'm going to ask." Freddie sat up tall and cleared his throat.

"What's that, son?"

"What are your intentions with my mother?"

Peter choked on his coffee. "My intentions?"

"Freddie!" Shelly's eyebrows hit her hairline. "I don't think that's anything you get to worry about."

Although, she'd convinced herself she'd be fine with this being a fling, every second she spent with Peter, she craved more.

She'd never been so appreciated, so respected, so worshipped by a lover. To think this could only be temporary grated her gut, yet, what else could it be?

Stay focused. Be realistic. You've known the guy a week.

"No, Mom. I want to know." Freddie moved his cup out of the way and leaned forward, his eyes laser focused on Peter. "I told *you* last week not to hurt my mom."

Grabbing a paper towel, Peter dried off his shirt. "Yes, you did and I told you that was the last thing I would do."

Relief flooded her. As frustrated as she was at her son for asking such questions, she appreciated his chivalry.

"Great. Then you're planning to stay?" Freddie sat back, locking his arms across his chest.

The shocked look on Peter's face might as well have stabbed Shelly in the heart. "I didn't say that."

"Then this is what, fun and done?"

"Freddie, please!" Shelly waved off her son, but she mentally berated herself for being upset by Peter's response. "I'm a grown woman. Even if this is a fling, it's my fling. Not yours."

It's just a fling, right?

Even telling it to herself, she wasn't convinced.

Dammit! You can't feel more for him than lust. Deep like,

but not…no, no, no!

"Mom, you've been screwed over enough. You need someone who really cares about you," Freddie encouraged.

"I do care about her!" Peter slammed his fist on the table, making coffee spill out of his mug.

"Good grief, you two." Shelly grabbed another paper towel, her hands trembling with angst. "It's like two bull elephants in a closet."

Freddie jumped to his feet. "Really? If you cared about her enough, you'd stay and not screw her over like my dad did."

Oh, man. "Freddie, honey. Please calm down."

"It's not that simple, Freddie." Peter shook his head, his jaw clenched.

"Yeah, I've heard that one before." Freddie rolled his eyes. "What, you got another family too?"

A nervous laugh escaped her, realizing how deeply Gill had wounded her son. *Gill, I swear if you ever come back here, they will never find your body.* "Freddie, he's not your father, but he does have his children to think of."

Putting his hands up in surrender, Peter stepped back from the table. "I'm sorry you've been through hell. That he dragged you through that, but I… I can't promise anything right this second. I'm still—"

"This second? What about tomorrow or next week or next year?" Freddie's voice went up an octave. "If you loved her, if you really loved her, us, you'd stay."

"I do love her!"

"What?" Shelly squeaked.

"What?" Freddie's frustration immediately evaporated.

Peter swallowed hard as the silence of complete awkwardness settled between all of them. The pulse at his neck beat in rapid tempo.

"What did you say?" Shelly hoped she'd heard him wrong.

His fists clenched at his sides. "I said... I love you."

Hearing the words out loud, twisted Shelly's stomach uncomfortably tight. Being loved again should have sent her heart into the stratosphere. Instead, crippling fear took hold. "You love me? It's only been a week."

Such a lovely thing to say when a gorgeous man tells you he loves you.

He held his hand up. "Shelly, please don't say anything."

"It's been a week. Long-lasting love doesn't happen in a week!"

"Please, Shelly, listen to me. It's okay if you don't love me back." Sliding his hand across the table, he laid his hand on hers. "It's okay."

Freddie stood silently, his eyes darting back and forth from Shelly to Peter.

She couldn't form the words. All she could do was shake her head.

"It's okay, Shelly. I'll go. I need to get back so Tia can get home before midnight." Peter turned, but Freddie stood in his way.

"Wait, wait." Freddie put his hands up. "Mom, say something. This guy's into you. I mean, he really cares about you."

"People don't fall in love in a week, Freddie." She realized she kept shaking her head and stopped. "It's just lust. Right?"

What are you doing?

"Not for me, Shelly." Peter sighed. "I don't do this casually."

"Mom!"

The pain in Peter's eyes told her she'd said the words out loud, again. She swallowed a sob. "But I do care about you, Peter. I do…" *Love you.*

Peter gave her a stressed smile. "I should go."

She let out a long breath, her heart pounding against her ribs. "I know we didn't establish this before it got this far, but if this is a fun and done situation—"

"Fun and done?" Peter cringed and ran his fingers through his hair. "Shelly, I've never done a fun and done in my life."

Shelly had no idea what she wanted to hear.

He loved her and it was ridiculous because they'd known each other for almost no time and yet, the time spent with him had been some of the most fantastic moments in her life.

Her heart hurt from fighting with her fear.

The fear of being loved and let down.

The fear of betrayal, of putting her faith on another man only to be left when he decided she wasn't good enough.

Tell him you love him. "Peter, I—"

"I love you. It's stupid because I've known you for a week and I know you don't believe in it, but I do."

Words wouldn't form. All she could feel was her bottom lip quiver and the warmth of her tears run down her face.

He wiped away her sadness with his thumbs. "Talk to me."

A voice in the back of her brain screamed, "Tell him you love him!" but her fear won out and she stepped backward.

Pushing him away now would be far easier than losing him later.

"It's late, Peter. You should get home to your kids." When he stepped closer, she put her arms up. "It's okay. Please. Go take care of your babies."

"Shelly."

"It's okay. Please go." *Please stay.*

With his shoulders slumped, he nodded and began to leave.

"Come on, Mom." Freddie threw his hands up in frustration.

"Please don't, Son. Not now." A sob caught in her chest, pinching her in the throat. "Peter?"

He immediately turned around. "Yes?"

"Please hug Polly and Digory from me. Us."

"I will."

As soon as the door clicked closed, Shelly's heart shattered and she crumbled to the floor in a sobbing heap because after loving Peter Davidson, the world would never look the same.

Chapter Twenty-Three

THE CHILDREN SLEPT soundly as the twinkle of lights reflected off the buildings lining Front Street.

The Palace Movie Theater's marquis sparkled as movie goers entered to get out of the cold.

Standing at the window, Peter watched Tia's car pull out of the parking lot of the Graff. He glanced at his watch.

Ten thirty.

Way to be an idiot, Peter. You could have been ringing in the New Year in the arms of the most beautiful woman in the world. Instead you're staring at the window without a clue.

Yes, he cared about Shelly. A lot.

Dammit, he'd fallen in love with her. He hadn't meant for it to happen. He hadn't meant for any of this to happen.

Simone leaving him.

Not knowing about his children.

Dammit!

The last thing he wanted to do was tell Shelly how he felt, knowing her history with her ex-husband. That and not know if he, they were staying or going.

He'd driven Simone away and now Shelly.

What the hell was wrong with him?

HE HAD CHILDREN to raise now.

He couldn't fall in love with just anyone.

But Shelly's not anyone.

He hung his head.

No, she's not.

Snow still traced along the edges of the buildings and sidewalk. In the large grassy areas on either side of the Graff were mounds of snow that had been pushed by their plows over the past few days.

Peter soaked in the Capraesque holiday scene, appreciating all the work his siblings had done for his children over the past week, but it had gotten close to having to make a decision.

Stay or go?

If they went, where? Florida? Maine?

After his glorious evening with Shelly ended in a total disaster, he couldn't decide which way was up.

Watching the movie marquis lights slowly dim, he wondered how differently things would be if Simone had said yes. Would they still be here with their children, spending a wonderful Christmas together while visiting his siblings?

It's time to read the letter, a voice from his past whispered.

He'd pushed it aside for almost two weeks, hiding behind snowball fights and family get-togethers, but if he wanted answers, if he wanted to move forward, he had to open that letter and accept what Simone had written.

Time to rip the Band-Aid.

Taking a long, deep breath, he nodded to no one before opening his suitcase and finding what held the answers to all his questions.

The envelope had instructions on how to get into a particular email and file.

The handwritten note made his heart clench uncomfortably as he typed in the password. The way she wrote his name, the curve of the first *S* in her name, brought heartsick emotions flooding back.

Within seconds of clicking the file, his heart had been transported back a decade.

There on the screen was Simone's beautiful face.

His pride itched to close the file. To let it all live in the past, but it would solve nothing. "Rip the damned Band-Aid."

Once more, he verified the kids were sleeping before putting in his earbuds.

With trembling fingers, he pushed play and hoped this would give him the answers he wanted to hear.

"Dearest Peter." She put her hands to her chest. Tears welled in her eyes. "I'm recording this because one day you may need it when you learn what I've done."

He paused it as the sound of her voice felt like a hard punch to the chest.

Breathing slowly, he took in the curve of her face. The color of her skin. The deep green of her eyes.

"Simone." He sadly smiled before allowing the file to continue.

The corner of her mouth twitched. "If you're seeing this,

it means I'm gone and you've discovered one of my two biggest secrets."

Two. Polly and Digory.

"I'm sure you're wondering why I never had the strength to face you, especially after I told you why I said no to your proposal.

"Why I never told you about your children." Tears flowed freely down her face. "I need you to understand, it wasn't anything you did or said. It's no reflection of who you are because you were always wonderful."

"But…" he whispered, impending dread hovered over his heart.

Her bottom lip quivered. "But during your last year of medical school, I fell in love with someone else."

He instantly slapped the computer closed. *Damn. That wasn't what I expected at all.*

He glanced at his children in the other room, hoping the slap of his computer hadn't woken them.

Silence.

She'd fallen in love with someone else?

Did she think they were other man's kids?

Did she only recently get DNA tests? Is that why she didn't call?

No, it made no sense. The kids hadn't mentioned another man in their lives and Simone would never have let something as important as paternity sit unchecked for ten years.

Finish this. He blew out a long breath and opened the computer for it to continue.

"I never planned for it to happen, but she was dynamic and unlike anyone I'd ever met before. We could talk for hours about anything and what started as a mutual friendship, grew to something more."

She?

That one simple word froze him in his chair. The only movement was the tap of his index finger on the track pad. "She? Simone fell in love... with a woman?"

He hesitated to watch more, but he hit play.

"We were in the same master's program and she'd planned to go back to Maine and work after graduation."

Pause. He searched his brain for any indication, any clue that would have tipped him off about Simone being gay, but nothing came to mind.

Damn, was she with me to hide who she was?

The idea made him sick to think she didn't want to reveal herself to him, to anyone else. He had friends who'd nervously come out of the closet in college. It had never been easy for them, but he'd always been humbled by those who trusted him with their true selves.

Even before their father died, Peter had always been the one to help, to fix, to comfort family and friends when they were in distress or simply needed a safe person to talk to.

Now he discovered he was the one person Simone couldn't confide in.

And her reason for leaving him came into perfect focus.

How long were you living in silence? He tapped the track pad to continue.

She gave a stressed smile. "I had wondered for years

about my attraction to both men and women, finding it a bit unnerving, but when I met Karen, it made sense. It felt right."

Karen? The neighbor Karen?

"It felt just as right as when I was with you, Peter." She sobbed. "And for so damned long, I thought I was a horrible, horrible person."

Damn.

Discovering her love for both sexes gave Peter a hint of understanding, but his heart weighed heavily listening to her talk once again.

The cadence of her voice.

The pain in her words.

The way she'd pronounced his name.

Holding her hands up in surrender, she adamantly shook her head. "Nothing ever happened with her when I was with you. Know that. Nothing. I planned to tell you far before graduation, but there was never an ideal moment. You were exhausted from your studies. Your clinicals. And when I'd get the courage you were always so wonderful, so loving and caring."

For a few seconds, she averted her eyes and chewed on her lip. He anticipated what she'd say.

"But honestly, I couldn't do it because, I didn't want to break your heart. You'd done nothing wrong. In fact, no woman could have asked for a better friend, lover, and boyfriend." She buried her face in her hands as her shoulders bobbed up and down.

For the first time in ten years, the weight of guilt and

uncertainty lifted off his shoulders, but his heart hurt for her. "I wish you'd told me, Simone."

"When you proposed, I knew I couldn't continue the charade. Even though I loved you and still do, I couldn't lie to myself anymore about where my heart wanted to be.

"Needed to be."

She paused and grabbed a Kleenex, drying her face. "I thought Maine would be a far better place, kinder place for me to go, considering the more socially friendly environment there."

Shaking her head, her bottom lip quivered. "I thought my family would be supportive of my choice since they had always been open-minded. Supportive of equality for all."

She pressed her fingers to her lips as the corners of her mouth turned down. "Turns out it's harder to be open-minded when the 'not norm' is your family member sitting across from you at the Thanksgiving table."

His heart sank to his feet. "Oh no."

"My parents' and my relationship was never the same after I brought Karen home. My brother erased me from his life, which is why I refused to have him as the legal guardian of Digory and Polly should anything happen to me. So if you're watching this, it has." She weakly shrugged.

That's why she had no one.

"After our amazing night, I realized I was pregnant, but because of the rejection by my family combined with the pain I'd dragged you through, I simply couldn't bring myself to contact you.

"Karen and I stayed together for a few years, but she decided she didn't want the responsibility of being a full-time mom. She moved out when the children were three, but we remained friends and she did help me. She's the one who gave you all the information."

And that's why Karen called to know about the kids' school. She cares about them.

"I told my parents I'd gotten IVF, a sperm donor so they wouldn't contact you. That was met with as much disdain as my honesty for whom I loved.

"It was unfair. Wrong and cruel to leave you out of our lives, but my biggest fear was if you discovered why I'd left you, you'd reject our children and they had done nothing to deserve that."

Peter glanced toward their room and shook his head. "No, they didn't."

"They would have been lost in the world with no one to guide them.

"Pushing me away for hurting you is understandable. Pushing our children away would be detrimental to them.

"I couldn't put them in that environment, but now it appears I have no choice.

"I hope you love our children as much as I know you can.

"Please forgive me, Peter, for never telling you the truth." She dabbed her eyes with a wadded Kleenex. "Hearing me say it all out loud… I need to call you anyway. Tell you before you get sideswiped by this news, but if I don't, please care for our children with the heart I know you have. It's beautiful and loving. Kind and fair.

"In this same email, I have a list of files. I have written everything down about them I can think of. Recorded just about so many wonderful moments of their lives. They were documented so if one day, we did find each other again, whether I was alive or not, those moments were not lost forever."

"She was always organized." Peter gave a sad chuckle.

"And know this, Peter. Your siblings were always so kind to me. I have no doubt you would probably rather live near them than in Maine.

"You'll need help. You'll need guidance so I understand if you want to move the children somewhere else. All I ask is you please love them with all your heart and don't blame them for my choice.

"I'm sorry I never told you.

"I love you."

By the time Peter finished the recording, his face was soaked with purged angst from the past. He wiped his face with the backs of his hands.

Out of the corner of his eye, he noticed movement. "Digory. What are you doing up?"

"Are you... crying?" Digory's brows sharply creased. "At Mommy?"

Peter pointed to the computer. "You saw her?"

"Yes."

He didn't try to hide his reaction to Simone's confession. Why should he? He loved their mother and to hear her struggle, her rejection by her family, brutally stung.

Why didn't she trust me?

"Why are you crying?"

"Because she was an incredible woman, Digory."

He inched forward. "Why didn't you know about us?"

"It's complicated, but your mom loved you. Please remember that."

Leaning against the desk, his son cocked his head. "Complicated? Okay, but are you mad because I'd be mad if I didn't know about someone?"

Peter let out a long breath and shook his head. "Mad isn't the right word, but no. Not anymore."

"Then you didn't leave us." Now, Digory had moved within arm's length.

"No, Son. I never would have done that. No matter what your mother and I had or didn't have, I would have never left you or your sister." Peter pulled his son into a hug and Digory hugged him back. "Never in a million years would I have done that to you or Polly or your mother."

"Bobby Cranston said dads leave easier than moms." He sniffled. "He said dads stop caring and leave all the time."

Like Freddie's dad. Peter smirked at how adamant the teen advocated for Shelly to listen when Peter told her he loved her.

"Good fathers. Strong fathers don't leave. They stick it out no matter what. I won't ever stop caring about you. Do you hear me? I don't care what Bobby Cravits said."

"Cranston, Dad."

Dad.

Who would have thought such a short, simple word would hold so much power over a full-grown man?

"Cranston, then."

"Can we stay here instead of go back to Maine?"

Sitting back, Peter looked at his son in disbelief. "You want to stay here? Live here?"

He apathetically shrugged. "Yeah, I guess. I mean the snow's cool like back home. I like Aunt Lucy and Uncle Thomas and Uncle Edmund and Aunt Jade and Ms. Shelly. I like having a lot of family around. It's fun."

"And Freddie and Tia and Trinity and Gabby," Polly added as she stood in the doorway. She held her stuffed unicorn in the crook of her arm. "We met a lot of new friends at the cookie party."

Peter motioned her to come closer. "You would have to start over with friends. With your school."

"But I've already made new friends here. To tell the truth, I was kind of getting bored with my old school." She settled in next to him.

"Why's that, Polly?"

"Because they keep serving the same thing over and over again. Tater tots and pizza. Tater tots and pizza all the time." She dramatically rolled her eyes. "Ms. Gabby has much better food."

He moved to the couch so both children could sit with him. "You okay with moving from your house? Your rooms?"

Both kids looked at each other before Polly asked, "Are we each going to have our own rooms?"

"Yes."

"Can we decorate them any way we want?"

"If we buy something, yes." His heart rate sped up at the possibilities of this. Moving to an icebox of a town because of love.

Who would have thought?

"Can Trinity, who painted the wall at the diner, can she paint something on my wall?" Digory cocked his head like a dog who'd heard a funny noise. "Please?"

"I'd guess we could arrange something like that." Peter laughed.

"Is that everything?" Polly asked.

With the children onboard to stay, what would that mean if he pursued this relationship with Shelly? Would it be too much for them to take? "What if that wasn't the only thing that didn't change?"

"What do you mean?"

Peter cleared his throat. "What if one day I wanted to marry Ms. Shelly?"

"What day will that be?" Polly grabbed her backpack and pulled out her sparkly journal. "I'll need to write it down."

"You'd be okay with that?"

"Yes." Digory nodded. "She's cool and her kids are cool."

"You're right, Digs. She is cool. She's extremely cool."

And extremely scared of being hurt again.

Just like Mr. Nicholas said, all Peter's answers were in the envelope.

No longer lost or looking for purpose.

Peter had his answers. He had his reasons for living.

Now all Peter had to do was figure out how to establish a home base… with Shelly.

Chapter Twenty-Four

SHELLY SPENT THE majority of New Year's Day in her favorite chair, trying to read some of her new books, but nothing she read gained her interest.

By page two, she'd set the book aside, her mind in a full blown emotional battle.

The pain of the past mixed with her fear of letting herself be loved again.

Glancing at her bed, her body buzzed with the memories of last night. How Peter touched her, tasted, loved and worshipped her unlike any man she'd ever known.

How his three heartfelt words changed everything in a matter of moments.

What was I thinking, pushing him away?

Her shoulders sank as she curled up in the chair, staring out the window.

Watching Peter leave cut her to the core and yet, the overwhelming terror of Gill's betrayal, his lies, his crushing blows to her ego held her solidly in the past.

Damn you, Gill.

Yet, she couldn't blame the man forever otherwise he'd steal more time from her. More happiness.

He'd already stolen so much from her already.

Don't let him steal anything else, especially not time. Or a chance to find your happily ever after.

She sat up and rested her forearms on her knees.

"Call him."

Her son's voice pulled her out of her mental struggle. "What?"

Freddie leaned against the bedroom doorway. "Call him, Mom."

"Who?"

"Peter."

"It's not that simple, sweetheart."

"It is." He held up his phone. "You just push the button."

"People don't fall in love—"

"But what if they do, Mom? What if they do fall in love in a week? In a day? In a moment?"

"What if they do?" *Oh, damn. What if they do?* Panic shoved her heart rate up and she fanned herself. "Is it hot in here?"

"Didn't Grandma say she knew she'd marry Grandpa the moment she saw him?" Freddie came in and sat on the edge of her bed.

"Yes. She did." The corner of her mouth curled up, replaying her mother telling the story of that fateful night. "I never get tired of hearing that one. It always gave me hope that your father and I would work out."

"But you did your job, he didn't." He playfully wagged a finger at her. "Am I gonna have to start quoting Angie

Thomas?"

"Keep doing right." Seeing her son attempt to give her some sort of peace with the chaotic life with his father, she'd done something right in the world. "You're saying to try anyway, even if I might get hurt."

"Yes."

"I would love for it to be, but—"

"No, Mom. It can be. Call him." When she didn't move, he hung his head. "Okay, but can I just say something?"

"Sure." She wiped away escaped tears.

"I don't ever remember you smiling like that when you were with Dad. Ever. Even when things were good, you never looked that happy." Standing, he began to leave. "Just promise me you'll think about it."

"I will." She crawled back into bed. "I'm going to take a nap."

"Okay, but you deserve a good man. Peter's a good guy."

"Yes, he is." *And I'm an idiot.*

The sheets still held the faint scent of his cologne and she buried herself in the covers and cried until her eyes wouldn't stay open.

She didn't know how long she'd drifted off, but her dreams were of happier moments, laughter and light and every frame, every scene, Peter stood right by her side.

"I love you." She heard herself. No panic. No stress, just three words that floated out of her as easily as breathing.

Peter pulled her into his arms, kissing her passionately.

With every touch, with every kiss, the clutch of fear loosened its paralyzing hold on her heart, allowed hope to seep in.

When she woke, the ache in her heart didn't hurt quite as much and her mental conflict had all but resolved.

At least until panic tried to take hold again.

She pushed it away. "No, just let me think."

"Mom." Freddie gently knocked before opening the door. "They called from the hospital. They asked if you'd come in for a couple of hours."

"Tell them no." She turned over and pulled the covers over her head.

"Mom, they said they really need your help. It's a busy morning, you know because it's New Year's morning."

"It's only going to be hydrating a bunch of drunk people. Babysitting. I've already been there more than I was supposed to be."

"Peter and the kids were in an accident," he blurted.

"What?" That sent her straight up right in bed. "What happened?"

"He left town this morning and there was some ice on the road. Something with the weather and snow. They needed your help up there because Lucy and Edmund are trying to take care of the kids."

"Oh, my gosh, yes. Okay. I'll be ready in ten minutes."

"I'll drive you."

It didn't compute that her son's offer to drive was an unusual one and when they parked in the ER parking, Shelly ran in through the ambulance entrance to an almost empty unit.

"What's going on?" She panted as she scanned the

rooms. "Where's Peter? The kids?"

Sue furrowed her brow. "What? Peter and the kids aren't here."

"Where are the patients?"

"Honey, it's New Year's Day. Everyone's sleeping in, even the patients." She tapped her watch. "We won't get busy until noon when people start crawling out of bed."

Tia peeked around the corner. "Hey, Aunt Shell."

"What? Tia. I'm confused." When she turned around, there stood Peter with a bouquet of flowers.

Polly and Digory each held a single flower. They both robotically walked forward and handed them to her.

"This is for you." Polly gave Shelly a hug.

"We swiped this from a bunch of flowers in the lobby." Digory handed her another flower.

"What?" Shelly looked at Peter, her forehead creased in confusion.

"They were clearing some place settings from their New Year's Eve celebrations and Mr. Bob was nice enough to let us bring some to you," Peter explained. "I couldn't go get any at the store. Everything's closed."

"What's going on? Were you hurt or not?"

"No, we're fine, but you've been hurt." He approached her. "And I'm sorry I scared the hell out of you."

"Daddy, hell is a—"

"I know. I know."

"Come over here, kids. I've got stickers and candy." Sue and Tia beckoned them over and the younger two quickly ran behind the desk.

"Freddie. What's going on?"

"He wanted to talk to you. He called me to ask if I'd bring you."

"And you said you would?" Tears welled in her eyes at her son's compassionate gesture. "You brought me? Why?"

"Because he makes you happy, Mom. I think you deserve that, for once." He squeezed her hand and gave Peter an approving nod. "But I'll still kick your ass if you hurt her."

"Fair enough." Peter extended his hand and Freddie responded in kind.

"Freddie! Ass is a—"

"Yeah, yeah. Save me some candy." Freddie joined the others.

Shelly pulled her coat tightly around herself. "That's a sneaky way to get to talk to me. Lying about a car accident."

Peter shook his head. "Car accident? I didn't lie about anything. I just told Freddie I wanted to meet you here."

She locked her arms across her chest. "Well, what is it you want to say?"

"The kids and I have decided to move to Marietta." Peter's stressed smile almost made her laugh.

"What? What made you make that decision?"

"We needed a change of menu." Digory held up three Snoopy stickers.

"I like being near family." Polly showed off her superhero choices.

"I love you," Peter replied.

"You. Love me."

He swallowed hard and handed her the flowers. "Yes, I

do and I know that scares you. That you don't believe in love at first sight or within a week, but I love you. I want to get to know you more. Better. Here."

No rational thought played in her mind. "You're moving *here*?"

"Gabby mentioned that her boyfriend's house will be for rent soon. I'm talking to him later today. It's going to take a bit of back and forth to get the kids' things here. My stuff. Selling the different houses, but, yes. We're moving here."

"So then what? We're supposed to do what?"

"Live happily ever after!" Polly announced.

"What did you say?" Shelly's heart filled to the point of bursting.

Gently taking her hands, Peter said, "Shelly, I know you're the most beautiful, most amazing woman in my world. I want to get to know everything about you. Romance you. Love you like you deserve to be loved."

"Oh, man. I did not expect this." Freddie put his hands up in surrender and sat at the desk.

Peter smirked. "I want to build a life with you. With us. With all of us."

Turning, she soaked in the picture of Freddie, Tia, Polly, and Digory comparing stickers and swapping sweets.

Four. Four children. "I would love that."

"And I love you."

"I love you." She grabbed him by the front of the jacket and pulled him into her arms. "I love you back."

"Yeah?" His eyebrows hit his hairline. "You sure? It's only been a week."

"Shut up." Kissing him, she nodded. "Yes, I sure do."

"Ugh, is this going to be another kissing date?" Digory stuck out his tongue in disgust.

"Better get used to it, kid. I think there are gonna be a lot of kissing dates." Freddie rolled his eyes.

Moving her around the corner, away from prying eyes, Peter pulled her flush to him and whispered, "You'd damned well better believe it."

The End

The Marietta Medical Series

Book 1: *Resisting the Doctor*

Book 2: *Challenging the Doctor*

Book 3: *Doctor for Christmas*

Available now at your favorite online retailer!

About the Author

Native Texan Patricia W. Fischer is a natural born storyteller. Ever since she listened to her great-grandmother tell stories about her upbringing the early 1900's, Patricia has been hooked on hearing of great adventures and love winning in the end.

On her way to becoming an award-winning writer, she became a percussionist, actress, singer, waitress, bartender, pre-cook, and finally a trauma nurse before she realized she needed to get her butt to a journalism class.

After earning her journalism degree from Washington University, Patricia has been writing for multiple publications on numerous subjects including women's health, foster/adoption advocacy, ovarian cancer education, and entertainment features.

These days she spends her days with her family, two dogs, and a few fish while she creates a good story with a touch of reality, a dash of laughter, and a whole lot of love.

Visit her at PatriciaWFischer.com.

Thank you for reading

Doctor for Christmas

If you enjoyed this book, you can find more from all our great authors at TulePublishing.com, or from your favorite online retailer.

TULE
PUBLISHING

Made in the USA
Columbia, SC
24 June 2024

37499667R00181